The Boy From the Woods

Jen Minkman

Mein Ruf ist dünn und leicht,
verschleiert und fast schüchtern.
Spürst du mich?
Ich berühre das Gold
der Dämmerung des Lebens.

Ich bin der Engel der dich trägt.
Du bist mein Kind, mein Stern
Meine Sonne, Meine Liebe

Ich sehe durch dich;
Spürst du mich?

(German original poem used as lyrics for the song in this book)
Jen Minkman, 2009

1.

Flashing disco lights lit up a sea of faces and clusters of bodies in motion. The air in the school hall was vibrant with the booming pulse of trance music blasting from the speakers. At eleven o'clock at night, the temperature inside the building was stifling, despite the late hour and the open windows.

Julia Kandolf stood at the edge of the dance floor, her eyes scanning the crowd writhing to the beat. She couldn't find her friends. Where had Gaby run off to? And where was Axel?

"Hey, Julia." The voice startled her. She knew who it belonged to.

Julia's heart sped up as she turned around, her gaze settling on the boy behind her. Michael. His trademark cheeky smile made her blink shyly at him.

"That's a really nice dress you're wearing," he continued when she didn't respond and just kept staring at him, mouth slightly agape. He gestured at the medieval costume she'd rented for the party.

Julia swallowed, her mouth turning dry with nerves. "Your costume is really cool, too," she finally responded, letting her gaze trail down his body. He was immaculately clad in a sexy Napoleon outfit.

"Wanna dance?" He put down his glass of beer on a table and extended his hand courteously.

"Y-yes, of course!" she stammered, her stomach giving a lurch. Together, they made their way through the throng of party-goers. From the corner of her eye, Julia finally spotted Gaby on the other side of the hall, giving her an encouraging nod and a thumbs-up before taking out her plastic vampire teeth in order to gobble down some crackers from the snack table. Julia giggled nervously and followed Michael as he pulled her onto the dance floor.

"Weird, huh? Our senior year finally ending." He looked at her pensively. "I mean, we've spent, like, an entire *era* at this school. We grew up here. And now we're here, celebrating our graduation." Julia felt his arms around her waist and his hand on her lower back as he pulled her a bit closer.

"Uhm, yeah." A blush crept up her face. "It's really great everyone passed their exams, but now we'll all go to different universities. That's sort of sad, you know. We might never see each other again."

"Well, never say never," Michael commented breezily. "Don't forget those *wonderful* reunions they always organize here."

"Yeah. I guess you're right." Julia looked up at him, biting her lip. "I wouldn't mind seeing you again sooner, though," she whispered almost inaudibly.

Oh, crap. Had she just said that out loud? Or as loud as she'd dared, anyway. She looked at him insecurely, registering the look of surprise on his face.

"Me?" he asked, clasping her hand more tightly. "Why?"

She gulped down the lump in her throat. Her heart was hammering like crazy, despite Gaby's pep talk and the three glasses of wine she'd downed earlier that night.

"I, uhm..." she started out, her voice faltering. In the dimly-lit room, she saw a smile tugging at Michael's lips. That all-too-familiar, teasing, somewhat mocking smile that had made her shy in his presence for the past two years – that had followed her in her dreams, even. He lowered his face closer to hers.

"I get what you mean. I don't want to let you out of my sight tonight, either," he mumbled, his hand trailing up her arm, caressing the sensitive skin of her neck.

Julia stopped breathing altogether when he came even closer and pressed his lips to hers seductively. His arms pulled her upper body against his chest. He leaned in and kissed her again, more deeply this time.

She couldn't believe this was for real. He was kissing her. He was *really* kissing her! This was not a daydream – Michael was holding her in his arms.

Julia melted into him. When he let go of her at last and asked her if she wanted another drink, she was shivering with sheer excitement. Sporting a jubilant smile, she stayed put at the edge of the dance floor, scanning the multitude for Gaby. Her best friend waved at her from the other side of the room and was now giving her *two* thumbs-up. Julia's face split into an even stupider grin.

By the time Michael returned with a beer in each hand, her heartbeat had slowed down to an acceptable rate again. It made her hand steady enough to quickly save her number to his contacts when he handed over his Blackberry.

2.

Sunlight and green leaves.

Those were the first things she saw when she opened her eyes and peered at the sky above through squinted eyelids.

Julia held still, acutely aware of everything around her – rustling leaves, the fat trunk of the tree against her back. The oak felt steady, reliable, and supportive, the century-old life force in the trunk like an extension of the energy running through her own spinal cord. She was part of something bigger – a dream encompassing the entire forest spreading out around her.

Every once in a while, she felt the strong urge to come here to rest – or 'meditate', as her mom playfully called it. Julia loved venturing out into the woods bordering on the small Salzburg suburb where she lived. People called her loopy for it, but so what? This spot under the ancient oak tree had become her solitary hang-out, the oak being a true friend whenever she felt down and out.

This was the place she'd come to when her grandpa had passed away. This was where she'd broken down into tears when her parents had announced their divorce and her dad had told her he was moving away to Innsbruck. But this was also the place she went to when she wanted to write poems or write lyrics or sing out loud without being disturbed – or to daydream about the boy who had stolen her heart two years ago, never giving it back.

Julia opened her eyes wider and let out a heavy sigh. This time, the peaceful atmosphere in the forest wasn't enough to calm her down. She was waiting for something.

She paused for a few more beats, then sat up and grabbed her bag. Her heart started to pound as she fumbled around in the front pocket of her messenger bag to fish out her phone.

Nothing. No new messages.

With a tortured sigh, she slumped back against the tree, her mind lingering on the boy she couldn't get out of her head. Michael Kolbe's handsome face. His radiant, green eyes. The teasing smile on his lips. His lips on her trembling mouth.

She gulped for breath when her phone abruptly came to life in her hand. 'Gaby' flashed across the display, the phone blaring out a 'Friday I'm In Love' ringtone by The Cure. The forest seemed to jolt awake too, a bird overhead flying off shrieking indignantly.

Julia couldn't help laughing, following the bird in flight with her eyes. "Hiya, Gab," she answered the phone cheerfully.

"Hey! Where are you at?" her best friend said. "I called you at home, but your mom said you weren't in."

"Oh, I'm in the forest."

"Ah! Getting all cuddly with Mr. Oak, huh?" Gaby knew her too well. Ever since they'd learned the word *treehugger* in English class last year, she'd been teasing Julia with her 'unhealthy oak fascination' – Gaby's words, not hers.

"Aren't you the psychic," Julia retorted with a grin. "And no, we haven't hugged today yet. I'd rather wait for one of Michael's hugs – if he's *ever* going to reply to my messages, that is." She cringed, recoiling from the bitter tone in her own voice.

Gaby exhaled on the other end of the line. "Why don't you come to town? You won't cheer yourself up sitting around talking to trees and feeling sorry for yourself because Asshole Kolbe hasn't been as communicative as you'd hoped for. I'll see you in a half hour at Mozartplatz, okay?"

"A half hour – are you crazy? I'll have to run like the wind to catch the next bus!"

"You aced Phys Ed this year," Gaby said relentlessly. "You'll manage. And if you get here on time, I'll buy the two of us *Sachertorte* from Tomaselli's. The carbs will brighten your day."

"All right, okay," Julia caved. "I'll see you soon." She clicked off and turned around to hug the tree behind her for a second, despite her words to Gaby. She couldn't leave without doing this. It was her ritual. "Thanks for your support," she whispered against the bark, pressing a light kiss to the gnarled skin of the oak.

Her hair was dancing in the wind as she broke out of the tree line, hitching the strap of her bag onto one shoulder and sprinting to the bus stop. The doors were just closing.

"*Grüss Gott*," Julia hiccupped breathlessly as she held the door and yanked it open again. Stepping inside, she flashed her travel card to the driver and made her way to the back seat of the bus – her usual spot. Once the suburb of Birkensiedlung had disappeared from view, she dug up her MP3 player to listen to some Enya. Maybe that would help her relax.

After a few minutes of staring out the window, Julia realized she had once again pulled her cell phone from her bag, her thumb tentatively stroking the keyboard. Of course, there was no harm in sending Michael a text message, but she'd already sent him one two days ago. And three days ago. And a week ago.

She was *such* a loser. Why couldn't she have waited more patiently? Suppose he was out of town and he'd forgotten to bring his cell phone. Maybe he'd turned it off, or maybe he'd lost his charger. If he ever got round to switching his phone on again, he'd immediately find out that she was Obsessive Stalker Girl.

She frowned and put the phone away again, leaning back in her seat. Gaby's Asshole Kolbe remark had made her restless. Of course, her best friend called everyone names constantly. She was probably just kidding, but then again... she *had* kind of made it sound like Michael was playing her.

Why was she even listening to Gaby? Her friend didn't know. And shame on her, Julia, for not having more confidence in the boy who'd stolen her heart – Michael, whose kisses tasted of passion and fire. Michael, who had whispered to her how beautiful she was, as he lay her down on his bed.

She closed her eyes and bit her lip, feeling her face flood with color. Okay... maybe she should leave out a few details when she talked to Gaby. It all felt too special to divulge everything. Too precious.

Meanwhile, the bus was driving along the river Salzach, pulling over at the bus stop near the bridge leading to the Old Town. The river was low – June had been an unusually dry month in Austria.

While 'The Memory of Trees' started to trickle through her earbuds, Julia got off the bus and crossed the river. It didn't take her long, and she got to Mozartplatz by the time she'd agreed to meet up with Gaby. Her gaze swept the square, but she didn't see her friend anywhere. However, she did spot another familiar face – her cousin Axel was just exiting the bookstore on the corner, carrying a plastic bag crammed full of books.

"Ax!" she yelled, waving at him to get his attention.

"Hey, Julia!" He sauntered toward her, his blond curls dancing in the breeze. "How's life?"

"Full of surprises, apparently. What are *you* doing here? Weren't you supposed to fly out to London last night?"

"I was," Axel replied with a long face, pushing up the glasses sliding down his nose. "But Florian has a bad case of stomach flu, so we postponed our trip. Uncle Helmut bought our tickets and took aunt Verena on a short city break."

"Poor Florian."

"And poor *me*, too. I was literally storing my bag in the overhead compartment already when he suddenly called off, the miscreant."

"Yeah, I bet he was hoping for a miraculous recovery. Our eternal optimist." She rolled her eyes.

"Ha. I'd call that naive."

Julia chuckled. "Sure. So what should we call you – an optimist with life experience?"

"Ouch, Jules. You want me to run away bawling?" Axel grinned. "Sarcasm bites, you know."

"Sorry. Why don't you drop by O'Malley's tonight? I might be easier to talk to with a drink in my hand."

Axel smiled. "I'll even buy you one. See you at ten?"

At that moment, a voice rang out from across the square. "Jules! Hi!" A disheveled Gaby was racing toward them, her dyed-black hair all tangled up and her eyeliner even more smudged than usual. She reached them and extended a purple nail-polished hand to Axel. "Hey there, Axe Effect."

"Hey yourself, Gaby Gloom," he shot back. "Been crying again? Your make-up is all over your cheeks, you know."

"Meh. That joke's getting old. But you're right this time. I've *really* been crying. I just had a hotdog with hot curry sauce and it was a bit *too* spicy for my taste."

"You went and got food?" Julia asked in dismay. "I thought you wanted to go for pastries at Tomaselli's!"

"Yeah, don't your parents feed you at home?" Axel chimed in.

"I'm having my period." Gaby glowered at him.

"Okay, I'm not here," Axel decided, backing away. "See you tonight!" he told Julia before rushing off.

"That cousin of yours is peculiar," Gaby concluded, staring at his retreating figure. "But funny." She threw Julia her widest smile. "Sorry I'm late. I'll buy you *two* pastries to make up for it."

"Thanks! I'd love that. I sort of forgot to have lunch, actually."

The two girls entered Tomaselli's and made a beeline for a table at the window. Julia dug up her cell phone and glanced at the display for the umpteenth time that day. Still nothing.

"So tell me – what happened after the graduation party?" Gaby asked, catching Julia sneaking a look at her phone. She patted her friend's hand over the table. "I want to know *everything*."

Julia bit her lip. Gaby had left for a city-trip to Paris with her parents and sister after graduation, so her best friend wasn't up-to-date with all of her woes and worries.

Everything had started at prom – the Masked Ball graduation party that she'd been agonizing over for months. She'd reserved a gorgeous medieval gown at a rental store weeks beforehand, so she could make an indelible impression on Michael with her appearance in costume. It had been the perfect opportunity to catch his eye at last, erasing her previous two years of invisibility. After summer, he would move to Graz to go to college, and she'd probably never see him again. The party had been her last chance.

It had been a huge relief when Michael showed up stag that evening. And the things that had happened between them had been on her mind ever since.

Gaby practically drooled over her cake when Julia told her all about Michael asking her to dance. "Yeah, I know, right?! I saw you two. When he started kissing you, I guessed it was time to leave you guys alone and play vampire somewhere else."

"Thanks." Julia smiled weakly, prodding her cake with a pastry fork.

"Anyway… So, once you saved your number to his contacts…" Gaby prompted her to go on. "What happened after that?"

"Well, we spent the rest of the evening together. He kissed me one last time under the stars in the school yard before I caught the bus home. The day after, he called me and invited me over for dinner and a movie."

Julia slowly turned red when Gaby looked at her inquisitively. "Hmm. Were his parents around?" her friend whispered.

Michael came from a wealthy family. His parents spent more time at work than at home. "No," she muttered back.

Gaby fell silent for a moment. "Aha." She cocked her head with a small smile, staring at her friend expectantly.

Julia bit her lip, her face flaming. "It was so wonderful when it happened," she whispered, staring at her hands. "So beautiful. It was how I'd always imagined it."

When she looked back up, tears were pooling in her eyes.

"So why are you crying?" Gaby said in shock. "Darling, what happened?"

"Nothing." Julia sniffed desolately. "That's the thing. We said goodbye the morning after, and he said we'd talk soon."

"And you didn't hear back from him *at all* after that?"

Julia shook her head.

"Well, what did you tell him that evening?"

"Just… how I felt about him. What I'd been feeling for him for the past two years. How special he was to me. How I'd wanted to tell him I was in love with him before he moved away."

"And what did he say to that?"

Julia paused for a minute, looking at Gaby with growing doubt. "He said… he never noticed that I liked him so much. That I should have told him before – I had no reason to be so shy and insecure, because I was a beautiful girl," she haltingly repeated his words.

He'd caressed her everywhere, slowly undressing her in the dreamy candlelight of his bedroom. And yet, the same candle flames had also turned the two of them into erratic, unpredictable shadows on the wall.

It had been a dream, and now she was abruptly waking up.

Michael hadn't said a single word about his feelings for *her*. He had only told her how he'd never noticed her silent admiration. A heavy brick grew in her stomach.

"Didn't he say *anything* about your little, uhm, 'dance in the sheets'?" Gaby asked incredulously.

"He said he'd had a great night," Julia whispered.

"Well, *duh*!" Gaby viciously stabbed the cake with her fork as if she were staking someone's heart. "No surprise there. Jesus, what a total asshole. Flatters himself by listening to you professing your undying love to him, sets up a private date so he can get you in the sack, then never calls you back. If I *ever* get my hands on him…"

Julia went cold inside. She closed her eyes, clasping her hand over her mouth to stop herself from crying out, tears running down her cheeks.

She felt Gaby's arm around her shoulders in consolation. "Look, I'm sorry if I was being too blunt." Gaby wiped Julia's tears away. "I don't have a filter. But I'm just giving my honest opinion, as your best friend. If things really happened the way you described, I'm afraid he's been playing you."

Gaby sat down on the armrest of Julia's chair, hugging her with both arms now. "You wanted to let him know how you felt. If he can't respect that, it's his problem, not yours. You didn't do anything wrong." Her jet-black head against Julia's platinum blonde locks painted a sad black-and-white picture.

A waitress pushing a pastry cart shuffled toward them. "Is everything all right?" she asked a bit perplexed.

"Sure," Gaby replied. "We're not crying because of the pastries. They're wonderful."

Julia giggled despite her tears. "Ugh," she said, rubbing her face. "I'm such a gullible sucker. I was *so* in love with Michael. Why didn't I see this coming?"

Gaby shrugged. "Love is blind. That's the way it is."

"Maybe I should call him. So I can ask him why he didn't text me back? Who knows, he might have a very good reason."

"Yup. I bet his thumbs fell off," Gaby nodded solemnly, and Julia snickered. "But, seriously, just call him. The sooner you know what's up, the better."

Gaby chatted on about her short vacation in Paris. It was nice to listen to her friend's babbling and entertaining stories, but Julia couldn't entirely shake the dark cloud hovering over her head. When they left the café and Julia had to walk back to the bus stop all by herself, her feelings of misery returned full-force. Taking her cell phone from her bag and staring at the thing in doubt, she leaned against the wall next to the bus shelter. Wasn't it better to put off her phone call to Michael for one more day? She should give him a fair chance to respond to her text messages. Maybe Gaby was wrong after all. Couldn't she give him the benefit of the doubt for a little while longer?

A familiar sound in the distance interrupted Julia's musings. Her heart skipped a beat – she'd recognize the strangely rattling exhaust of Michael's vintage Honda motorbike anywhere. Whenever he'd pulled up into the school yard riding his prized possession, she'd been around to shyly watch from the sidelines. Her stomach tightened as she looked up, quickly stashing away her phone.

He approached the bus stop, turned off his engine and parked the bike against the same wall she was using for support. His brown hair had a golden gleam in the sunlight. Michael hadn't spotted her yet, but when she hesitantly edged toward him to catch his eye, an impatient frown crossed his handsome face for just a moment, and the broad smile he flashed at her the next second didn't quite meet his eyes.

"Julia," he exclaimed a little too brightly. "*Grüss Gott*. Coming back from town?"

"Yeah, Gaby invited me for tea and cakes at the pastry shop." She swallowed down the lump in her throat before continuing: "And where have you been?"

"Oh, you know – around," he answered glibly. "Stayed with my aunt and uncle in Hallein for a few days. Went clubbing with my cousins. Nothing special." He fumbled with his keys, surreptitiously looking past her at the narrow alley leading to the Old Town.

Julia blinked back tears, her last glimmer of hope gone. This all felt so vastly different from the morning they'd said their goodbyes. It was as if she was talking to a stranger she had nothing in common with – or hadn't shared anything with. "Why didn't you call me back?" she asked with quiet determination.

Michael sighed, putting a warm hand on her shoulder condescendingly. "Look, I thought you'd be happy with our night together." He sounded genuinely puzzled. "I mean – you told me how much you wanted me. How you longed to be with me before I moved to Graz. I wouldn't mind going on a date with you again sometime, but I've been busy. Am I missing something?"

She took a step back. This was horrifying – Michael made it sound like he had done her a *favor*. He'd been generous enough to meet up with her because she admired him, and he'd had a good time. That was all – he'd never been serious with her. All the street sounds faded into the background, leaving her and Michael in the middle of a silent, barren plain where she could no longer lie to herself or pretend she'd misunderstood him.

"You told me we would talk soon." She cringed when she heard how plaintive and clingy she sounded. "That was a week ago."

"I was out of town," he replied curtly. "It's summer vacation. Why would I hang around in Salzburg all the time? Aren't you going anywhere this summer?"

Julia closed her eyes, biting back tears. *Summer.* She desperately tried to chase away images of her and him – fantasies she'd had in the days after their date. A Salzburg summer with Michael, who'd visit the forest with her so she could show him the places that were special to her. Evenings full of kissing and embracing under the stars. Sweet words he'd whisper in her ear.

"No. I'm staying here," she said softly.

"Too bad," he replied flatly. "Oh well, maybe I'll bump into you somewhere later. I have to go now before the music store closes, okay?" He leaned over and gave her a meaningless kiss on the cheek.

"Okay, s-see you," she stammered at his back. He wasn't even listening anymore. One of Michael's friends emerged from the alley, enthusiastically thumping him on the back before dragging him along to the Old Town of Salzburg.

And then he was gone. Julia fell back against the wall, taking a long, steadying breath. Of course she should be relieved to finally know where she stood after a nerve-racking week, but she wasn't. Frankly, she couldn't feel anything. She got on the bus on auto-pilot, lowering herself onto her usual seat in the back.

Reality was harsh. She didn't mean *anything* to him. For two years she'd been staring herself blind at someone who was blind to her.

This time, the realization hit her in the gut. Julia closed her eyes and tried to hold back her tears, but his indifferent reaction to her words was too painful to forget. The way he'd impatiently looked past her while she was talking to him, so eager to get away. The way he'd looked past her at school all those years until she turned out to be easy prey at the party. What a bastard. Who the hell did he think he was?!

By the time the bus reached the end of the line, Julia's sadness had turned to anger. Instead of going home, she ran into the woods, trying to outrun the rage thudding against her ribs by heading straight for her meditation spot. When she finally slumped down against the old oak tree in the forest, hot tears were running down her face.

"You idiot," she sobbed. "You silly, stupid cow."

Mostly, she was angry with *herself* now. How could she have been this naive?

It was high time to get her act together. Julia resolutely wiped the tears from her eyes. Time to say goodbye to all the dreams she'd had about the two of them, because she'd obviously been dreaming in vain. Dreams didn't come true. Life was not a fairytale.

It was time to grow up.

"*There* you are," Ms. Gunther called out indignantly from the kitchen when Julia came home that night. "You're late, young lady. I had no idea if you'd be joining us for dinner. I thought maybe you'd eat at Gaby's."

"I'm sorry, Mom." Julia went into the kitchen to hug her mother. "I should have called, but stuff happened and I was distracted. What are we having?"

"Macaroni." Her mom stroked her head sweetly. "And I made some salad."

"Tuna salad," Anne piped up with disdain. "I don't like tuna."

"You change your culinary likes and dislikes every week." Julia rolled her eyes. "How on earth is Mom supposed to keep up with you?"

Anne shrugged. "I'll put up a list," she replied donnishly, trying to look as venerable as possible with all of ten years under her belt. Julia grinned impishly at her sister and suddenly Anne erupted in giggles. "Don't look at me like that! I'm just a fussy eater. Gran always says so, too."

"We'll visit Grandma this weekend, so maybe you should give me that list soon," their mom admonished her with a chuckle. "So I can let the poor woman know what food to steer clear of when she's cooking for us."

They sat down at the table. Julia loved the small household she was a part of. Even though she missed her dad sometimes, it was much better for her mom that he lived somewhere else now. The tense atmosphere that had pervaded the house in the years before their divorce was gone for good. Their mother had started a new and better life.

Julia's gran lived in Eichet, close to the suburbs of Birkensiedlung. Her mother's mother was like a second parent. Her grandpa had passed away a few years ago, leaving his wife by herself. When he had still been alive, Julia had visited her grandparents every Sunday afternoon to play songs for them. She loved their antique piano. At home, she only had a keyboard to practice on.

She used her Yamaha to write songs in her room, including the song she'd written for her finals in Music Ed – and secretly, she'd written it with Michael in mind. He had never been far from her thoughts when she composed it. Every time she added a new line of melody to it, she imagined playing it in front of an audience of students in the large auditorium at school. In her fantasies, an enraptured Michael had always been in the front row, gazing up at her in admiration.

In reality, he hadn't even been there.

Julia munched on a bite of tuna salad, trying to fend off the memory of Michael's handsome face and green eyes. She had to stop thinking about him. He wasn't handsome at all. He was a low-life bastard who used innocent girls like Kleenex, and she'd been too blind to recognize him for what he really was.

"Julia!" Her mother's voice snapped her out of her inner rant. "Are – are you *crying*, sweetie?"

Startled, she looked up, wiping away a few tears rolling down her face. Anne gaped at her from across the table in distress.

Smiling feebly, Julia rubbed her cheeks once more. "Sorry. It's just... I'm feeling a bit lost. School has ended, everyone's leaving, my life will never be the same... it all feels so final," she lied.

"Well, Gaby isn't going anywhere, right?" Ms. Gunther put a loving hand on her daughter's arm. "She'll be here for you. And what about Axel and Florian? They're going to college at Salzburg University too. Your old friends will still be around, won't they?"

Julia smiled. Her mom was sweet, and more importantly, she was right. The people who really cared about her would be here for her. Chances were, her life would be better now that she wasn't just focused on Michael. Up till now, she had never taken notice of all the *other* cool guys in her hometown.

Time to open her eyes to new possibilities and stop throwing herself a pity party.

When Julia emerged from her bedroom after donning new jeans and a T-shirt later that evening, she was fully prepared to make her life take a one-eighty spin. It was a beautiful evening and she was going to enjoy her friends' company at O'Malley's, their favorite pub.

"Julia," Anne called her from the room next door. "Will you read me a story?" Her sister tried to sound like a toddler on purpose. Nowadays, Anne claimed she was *way* too grown-up to be read to, but she also said Julia was the exception to the rule because her big sister was just too good at reading fairytales.

"I'm coming!" With a smile, Julia entered the room. She sat down on the edge of the bed, combing her fingers through Anne's hair. Her baby sister was mock-sucking her thumb, clutching a cuddly toy under one arm and batting her eyelashes at Julia while pushing her storybook about the enchanted forest toward her.

"The *Prince of Trees*," Julia intoned, opening the book at chapter four. She didn't even have to look – she knew it by heart. Her grandmother had always read her stories from this book, and when Anne was born, Gran had gifted her the book. "It's your turn to read fairytales to your little sister," she'd said.

The storybook was chock-full of Austrian legends, fairytales and traditions from ancient times. One part was even dedicated to folklore that pre-dated Christianity – pages full of descriptions of dark creatures of the Alps, living in forests and mountains. The *Krampus* was the wild spirit of the forest who taught young men to survive on their own. Only after the church had established their rule in the country of Austria had the *Krampus* been turned into an evil monster, taking naughty kids away to his lair the evening before Saint Nicholas Day.

Next to that, the book also featured modern fairytales. Chapter four about the Prince of the Forest had always been Julia's favorite, and Anne liked it just as much. In her best storyteller's voice, Julia recounted the story of the young prince who fell in love with a fairy living in the forest. The fairy princess would sit down on the branch of his favorite tree whenever she needed to take a rest from flying. Anne glanced over her shoulder to look at the beautiful illustrations in the book. When Julia had reached the end of the story, Anne crawled into her lap and flung her arms around her big sister. "You know, I don't feel like growing up that much," she confessed in a small voice.

"Why not, sweetheart?" Julia caressed Anne's dark-blonde hair. Her sister was going to a new school after summer as well. Her time at elementary school was over.

Anne shrugged her thin shoulders. "You're a grown-up now too, and you don't look as happy as you used to. Sometimes, it's like you don't believe in fairytales anymore."

Julia bit her lip to stop herself from making a tart remark. What was the point in telling Anne that fairytales didn't come true? No need to bother a little girl with her own embitterment. "You're right, I don't feel that happy right now. I've run into a few too many big, bad wolves lately."

"Oh. In the forest, you mean?" Anne asked half-jokingly, looking up at Julia with big, blue eyes.

Julia couldn't help smiling. "No, not in the forest. In the dark streets of Savage Salzburg."

Anne giggled. "Are you sure you want to go out tonight, then?"

"Sure. Axel and Gaby will defend me if we run into more wolves or *Krampus*-monsters."

"But Axel wears *glasses*," Anne objected, as though her cousin's bad eyesight ruled him out of a job as reliable defender.

"Well, Gaby doesn't."

"True." Anne nodded solemnly. She was always a bit intimidated by Gaby and her black outfits whenever

Julia's best friend came over. Apparently, being a Goth made her a good protector in Anne's books.

"So, I'm leaving." Julia got up. "See you tomorrow morning."

"Don't stay out too late," Anne said, suddenly sounding too motherly for her age.

Julia chuckled. "I won't." She bounced down the stairs, almost bounding into her mom in the hallway when she stepped out of the kitchen.

"Do you have the house key?" Ms. Gunther asked. "I'm turning in early tonight, so I'm locking the door before you come home."

"Check. And my travel card, and my wallet, and my cell phone, and my pepper spray, and my very best mood."

Julia pressed a kiss to her mother's forehead and walked out the door whistling a tune. Still humming, she strolled down her street and onto the Birkenstrasse leading to the bus stop. The bus wasn't there yet, so she sat down on the bench inside the shelter. The half moon illuminated the night sky, the trees in the forest across the bus stop whispering mysteriously in the summer breeze. For just a moment, it reminded her of the fairytale she'd just read to Anne. Almost inaudibly, she muttered: "Hello, my prince. How are you doing?"

Wouldn't it be fantastic to fly around on fairy wings, looking at the earth from above? She'd sit down in a treetop and watch the world go by, waiting until the chaos and madness of humanity's hustle and bustle faded away and the era of the nature spirits dawned on earth. She'd end up with a handsome, mysterious hermit for a lover who lived in a house deep in the forest, writing poems about the trees, the flowers and his love for her every day.

In the years past, she'd observed Michael for hours on end during the mind-numbingly dull maths and physics classes she had to sit through. She'd made the best out of them by watching Michael, seated two rows in front of her to the left. Sometimes, he'd sketch in his notebook while Mr. Brunner was pouring his soul into explaining yet another complicated quadratic equation, and she'd always wondered what it was that he was drawing. One day, Michael had accidentally left the notebook on his desk, and she'd peeked into his notes to look at his doodles. The last few pages were littered with drawings of trees and flowers, and that had made her happy.

Maybe she'd read too much into it.

In the distance, she could see the bus's headlights approach. Julia got her travel card from her bag to show to the driver. As she was boarding, her phone buzzed in her pocket.

"Hey, Axel," she answered it. "What's up?"

"Are you there yet?"

"No, I'm just getting on the bus. I'll be there in twenty."

"I'll be there in a half hour. Florian is coming too, he says he's feeling better."

"Great! I'll see you guys in a bit."

Julia clicked off and rooted around in her bag to get her MP3 player. The bus slowly began to fill up. At every stop, more teenagers got on, all of them dressed up for a night on the town. She smiled – it was a good idea to get out of her slump and hang out at the pub with her friends all night. Sooner or later, she'd inevitably bump into Michael again, but at least she wouldn't have to face him alone.

"Okay, who wants beer?" Tamara asked, sliding off her bar stool. Gaby's sister was getting the next round. She patted the leather of the seat and nudged Julia. "Here, you can have my stool. You deserve a seat."

Florian and Axel shot curious glances at Julia. They'd just walked in, missing the entire conversation between Julia, Gaby and Tamara about Julia's nasty encounter with Michael that afternoon.

"I deserve a beer," Florian added. "After surviving this terrible stomach flu that had me eating through a straw for four days, I could do with a nice drink."

"Yeah, that sounds like you're fully prepared to hold your liquor," Axel grinned. "Make sure you don't barf all over me, okay?"

Gaby joined her sister to help her with the drinks, and Florian grabbed the stool next to Julia. "So, what happened to you? Why are you getting a pity seat?"

"Oh, just – crap. With men."

"You wanna talk about it?" Axel said. "What man broke your heart?"

"Michael Kolbe," Julia mumbled, not feeling very forthcoming.

"*Kolbe*? That uber-dickhead?" Florian exclaimed.

"Hey, can you keep the volume down?" Julia shushed him uneasily. "Half the people in this pub celebrate his every move." In a soft voice, she recounted the short version of her running into Michael to the guys, outrage written on their faces when she finished.

"He only preys on the innocent," Florian said scornfully.

"Gee, thanks." Despite Florian's tactless words, Julia couldn't help cracking a smile. He was undiplomatic, but he was also right, actually.

"Maybe we should put up Michael's picture on the dart board," Axel suggested. "So we can throw darts at his stupid face all night."

"What a *splendid* idea for a game," Florian agreed. "We'll call it Kill Kolbe. Who knows, it might catch on. We could start a real O'Malley's trend here."

In the meantime, Gaby and Tamara had returned with a tray full of drinks, proposing a toast to the start of the summer vacation. "Here's hoping the people who hurt us in the past all drop dead," Gaby wished vindictively, shooting a wicked grin at Julia.

Julia grinned back, clinking her glass against Gaby's drink. As she expected, it felt good to be out and about. She felt stronger in the company of her friends. On the other hand, she was more than glad not to have run into Michael by the time they left the pub at eleven.

"We'll go on a shopping spree together soon," Gaby said, hugging Julia goodbye. "Or hang around in Mirabell Garden all day long to check out boys. I'll get you through this. I promise."

"Thanks." Julia hugged her friend back. This was the start of a new life full of new opportunities, and she'd make sure it would be beautiful.

3.

"I'm going to run to Gran's!" Julia called out from the hallway while putting on her running shoes. "I'll see the two of you there, okay?"

"I'll wait at the front door with a gold medal and a choir singing the national anthem," Ms. Gunther teased her daughter, popping her head around the kitchen door. "Have fun."

Julia sauntered down the road leading to the woods, speeding up once she was under the trees. It was a beautiful Saturday morning, and the forest was peaceful and still. All she could hear were the usual sounds of nature and the steady beat of her heart. That was why she loved running here – in the stillness, her worries always faded into the background. It was like meditation to her.

Julia left the main trail and went off-track for a little ways so she could pause at the foot of her oak tree. Her breathing slowed down as she leaned against the tree trunk, opening the bottle of water that was in her small rucksack. Some clean clothes were sitting next to her water bottle, so she could freshen up at her grandmother's house after her run. And last but not least, her final report card. Her gran hadn't even seen her graduation marks yet.

All her grades were good, but Julia was most pleased with her final results in Music Education. She scored the highest mark of her year for that elective because of the song she composed. If only Michael knew it was written for *him*... he'd probably laugh his head off.

Softly, she hummed the tune to herself, feeling incredibly lonely for a moment as she rested her head against the cracked bark of the tree trunk. Above her head, the leaves rustled in the wind that suddenly picked up, as if the forest was responding to her by singing back. Somewhere in the distance, a bird chirped.

After a few minutes of reminiscing, Julia decided her break was over. She jumped to her feet and stretched her legs, putting the water bottle away. The muscles in her legs felt warm and taut after stretching. Light-footed, she cut back through the trees to continue along the dirt road running through the woods, reaching the edge of the forest close to Eichet after fifteen minutes. The main road leading to the village was deserted. Julia stuck to the middle, her sneakers hitting the asphalt like a peaceful mantra. In the heat of the late June morning, she could feel the slick sweat on her skin, vigor coursing through her body. This was just what she needed. Running always revitalized her after she'd spent too much energy on everyday worries, and lately, people had been sucking up her energy far too much.

Michael telling her, *I'll see you soon.* Her father's voice mixing in with Michael's words: *I'll come and visit you girls as often as I can.* People promising her things without meaning a single word.

Her best friend Gaby was a breath of fresh air in that respect. She was always completely honest, not bothering to beat around the bush. When Julia and Gaby met in high school, Gaby had already been in the habit of wearing strange outfits, carrying around a black backpack decorated with Placebo and Nirvana patches for a school bag, despite the teachers' rebukes.

"I don't mind sitting next to you," Gaby had declared to a bashful Julia on their first day of school. She'd plunked her old, tattered backpack down on the seat next to Julia's. "You're the only real person around here."

"How – how do you know?" Julia had asked, a bit taken aback.

"Your eyes tell me you're not that fond of people. So you don't bother lying to them either. You're not a fake."

Julia had immediately felt protected by Gaby's extravagant and rebellious behavior in class. Later, Gaby had told her that she felt safe around Julia because she exuded such peace and tranquility. Gaby's parents were loud and extroverted people with a wide circle of friends, who didn't have a lot of time to spend with their two daughters. Tamara had adapted, playing the good, oldest daughter who was never a burden to her parents, and Gaby had dug her heels in and decided to dress just like the rock stars she adored and her parents abhorred. Despite that, Tamara and Gaby got along very well.

Julia turned into her gran's street and caught sight of her grandmother waiting for her in the front yard.

"Faster, Julia," she called out. "Tea's getting cold!"

Her mom and sister had come by bike and were in the living room with tea and slices of ginger cake. Julia kissed her grandma on the cheek as she barreled inside, kicking off her sneakers in the hallway.

"Just gonna freshen up," she panted, taking the stairs two steps at a time. The water from the shower heated up quickly, so it only took her ten minutes to wash up and get back down for her own share of tea and cake.

"Any plans for the summer?" Gran inquired curiously. "You have three months off, after all."

Julia shrugged. "Don't know. I could find a job, I guess."

Her mother didn't have the money to take her and Anne anywhere special. Julia had counted on spending her vacation in Salzburg, but now that summer was here, the three months ahead seemed to stretch out endlessly. Uni would only start at the beginning of October, leaving her plenty of time to get a summer job and save up, but frankly, she wasn't stoked about the idea. Last year, picking orders in a musty garment factory had driven her absolutely nuts after two weeks.

"Axel told me he was planning a trip to London," Gran said. "Didn't he go last week?"

Julia shook her head. "Florian got sick, so they postponed."

"Why don't you join them? That might cheer you up."

Julia looked down at her hands, feeling caught. Her grandma seemed to have a sixth sense for these things. If anything was ever the matter with her, Gran always knew immediately. "I'm okay, thanks," she replied, not wanting to worry Anne and her mom. She quickly dug around in her backpack to find her report card. "Here, have a look at my scores."

Gran chuckled. Julia couldn't help but smile as well. This was stupid – she sounded like she was trying to prove her life was great by showing off her grade point average.

"Julia had the highest score in Music Ed," Anne chimed in, beaming proudly at her sister. "She played one of her own songs."

"Why don't you play it for Gran later?" her mother suggested.

Great. She'd feared as much – having to play the infamous song that reminded her of that one particular person she wanted to forget about. "Yeah, I will. Let me drink my tea first," she grumbled.

When Julia fled into the back yard after finishing her tea and her reluctant musical performance, her grandmother followed her, falling into step with her on the path along the rhododendrons.

"My sweet Julia, what is the matter with you?" she asked gently.

Julia sighed deeply. "It's nothing, really. I just... have to let go of things I should have left behind a *long* time ago." She slumped down on the bench between two large bushes.

"So what's his name?" the old woman asked after a few beats of silence.

"Michael," Julia whispered, her voice catching in her throat.

"Did you write that song of yours for him?"

"Gran, you *really* are a psychic," Julia exclaimed huffily.

Her grandmother gave her a lopsided smile that bordered on a grin full of mischief, then looked serious again. "He inspired you, and that is beautiful. You will always have that. The love you felt for him is not lost – you will learn to give it to someone else, once you've left his memory behind."

"Give it to someone else? I don't know if I can. It all felt so intense that it left me drained. Even if I know now that he didn't deserve my love."

Julia fell silent, her eyes trained on the dark-green witch ball on a stick standing next to the rhododendron bush. In the convex glass of the sphere, she looked alien, a strange, distorted version of her staring back from a far-away, green-tinted world. How nice it would be to crawl away and disappear inside a dream bubble like that.

She closed her eyes and fought back new tears. This was ridiculous – she should cheer up. Gran had said such sweet and wise things to her. Still, she couldn't help but bawl when her grandmother settled on the bench too and put an arm around her shoulders. "You should allow yourself to mourn the things you lost, dear girl. But please remember to cherish the things you still have."

Gran was right – she still had all the poems she'd written in her diary while sitting under her oak tree, dreaming of Michael. She still had her song – the haunting melody she'd performed during the graduation ceremony in front of an enthralled audience. Her mother had been so emotional when she'd brought Julia a bunch of flowers on stage right after the performance. These were moments she'd keep close to her heart for a long time to come.

That afternoon, Julia's song filled the rooms of the cozy house in Eichet for the first time. In her mind, she had always called this *Michael's Song*, but no longer. She'd made up her mind: it was time to push away all the dreams she'd had of him and her, and make room for new things.

"Come on Jules, it's going to be *awesome*," Gaby's tinny voice piped up on speakerphone.

The weekend was over. Julia was busy trawling job ads in the local newspaper. She reckoned that having a summer job might be a good idea after all – she'd be able to save up some money to go on vacation with Gaby. So far, she was feeling sort of *blah* about the classifieds page, though. All the jobs advertized in the *Salzburger Fenster* were lame – the highlight of today's sorry selection being a modeling agency looking for size-zero girls with blonde hair. With a frustrated grunt, Julia crossed out the ad with her red marker.

"So, how much are the tickets?" she asked, trying to sound more eager than she felt. Gaby was suddenly convinced they all needed to go see a *Siouxsie and the*

Banshees cover band playing at the Shamrock pub that night.

"Nothing, you silly," Gaby blared through the phone. "It's a cover band. And they're doing a Monday night show. Need I say more? Who in his right mind would pay for that?"

Julia snickered. "Okay. Stupid question, I guess. But I thought you wanted to go out for dinner with the gang tonight?"

"Still do. We can do both. The band won't start until ten. So you can't say no."

"I'm beginning to get that, yes. Are Axel and Florian coming too?"

"Oh, I'll convince them to join us when I see them this afternoon." They'd agreed to meet at Florian's place. He lived in a mansion along the river Salzach, and his roof terrace was almost as big as his spacious second-floor bedroom. In summer, their circle of friends often sat outside on the terrace, playing old records, drinking beer and sneaking in a joint every now and then. Florian always put a ladder against the façade of the house so people could climb up without going through the house and bothering his parents. This morning, Julia had bought cans of beer and bottles of herbal soda so Florian could make *Radler* drinks for all of them.

"All right, Gab, count me in. See you later!"

As she was putting her phone in her handbag, her eye fell on a small ad for the bookstore in the city center. Höllrigl was looking for sales assistants. That sounded like something she might enjoy. Who knows – she might even be entitled to an employee discount on books if she worked there. She was a total bookworm, just like Axel. He'd probably dance with joy if she took up a job there and sold him books at a lower price.

When Julia stepped out of her bedroom, Anne was lying on the couch in the hallway reading the all-too-familiar storybook. Obviously, her sister was turning into family bookworm number three.

"Don't you want to be outside?" she asked Anne, who started and sat up. "You can read that out in the yard too, right?"

"Oh, I'll go outside in a minute. I'm meeting Sabine so we can go to the woods. We want to build a tree house."

Julia raised a doubtful eyebrow. "Hmm. Sabine has a handy brother or something?" Anne's new neighborhood friend was only nine. Surely the two little girls couldn't build a tree house without any help?

Anne giggled. "No, he's sort of ham-handed, actually. But he's cute! Shall I introduce him to you?"

"No, never mind, you little matchmaker." Julia whipped around and hurtled down the stairs. Cute or not, she really didn't need boys in her life at the moment, even though Gaby insisted she needed the distraction.

Ten minutes later, she was on the bus with her iPod on, Loreena McKennitt playing a soothing harp song during the ride to town. Loreena was her antidote for the abundance of loud punk music she'd be subjected to later in the evening. Admittedly, she had never heard anything by Siouxsie and the Banshees before, but if Gaby's full-size posters of the band were anything to go by, she was pretty sure her eardrums would have a painful experience tonight.

After a thirty-minute ride, Julia got off the bus and walked the last bit to Flo's house. The weather was lovely, and the white castle of Salzburg on the mountain overlooking the city shone in the bright sunlight. She looked up at the fortress longingly. Maybe she should take the long walk uphill sometime again and buy herself a generous slice of cake in the castle lunchroom. She hadn't done that in a while. The last time was when Gaby had joined her – and her friend had suffered from muscle ache in her calves for days after their adventure together, the wuss.

Julia kept a brisk pace and soon reached the old, pastel-green house on the Imbergstrasse that belonged to Florian's family. The ladder was waiting for her, leaning against the façade. She could hear Bob Dylan talk-singing through old speakers on the second-floor roof terrace. A few years ago, Florian had discovered the sixties and gone on to plunder his parents' entire vinyl collection.

"Peace, man," Axel greeted her when Julia's head popped up above the roof terrace railing. He put up two fingers in a peace sign and smiled at her, his eyes partly hidden by a green pair of star-shaped shades.

"Give it a chance," Julia shouted back, walking up to the sitting area where Axel, Florian and Tamara were sprawled on the big lounge sofa, sipping drinks and singing along to Dylan's 'I Want You'. "Where's Gaby?"

"She's picking up some flyers from the pub where that cover band is performing tonight," Tamara replied. "If we hand those in, we'll each be entitled to one free drink."

"That band is beginning to sound desperate for attention." Julia chuckled and set down her bag of bottles next to Florian. "Here, look what I brought. Now you can make me a *Radler*."

"I would be honored, Lady Julia," Florian said with an ingratiating smile.

Axel scrambled up to put the next record on the turntable and allow Marc Bolan's frail, unearthly voice to flood the terrace. Julia let out a satisfied sigh, leaning back on the sofa to look up at the bright, blue sky. Not a cloud in sight. This afternoon was heaven.

"*Halli-hallo!*" Gaby shouted as she suddenly appeared at the top of the ladder, enthusiastically waving a hand full of Shamrock flyers. "Look what I got. Free pints of Guinness for everyone tonight." She plunked down on the couch next to Julia and gave her a broad smile. "How was your weekend, babe?"

"It was fine. I visited my gran in Eichet yesterday." She glanced at the flyers Gaby had spread out on the table. "I'm glad the show is at Shamrock," she added under her breath. Michael played darts with his friends in O'Malley's, the other Irish pub in town, every Monday evening.

Gaby nodded, a sympathetic smile on her lips. "So, when are you guys finally going to London?" she addressed the boys while pouring a beer for herself.

"Actually, I have no idea." Florian shrugged. "We have to book all over again. I guess it'll be more expensive this time. The tickets we had were booked months in advance."

"Oh, come on." Axel arched an eyebrow. "Ryanair flies almost for free. Hey, why don't the girls join us on our trip too?"

Gaby looked from Tamara to Julia, nodding slowly. "Yeah, why not indeed?" she repeated. "We have all the time in the world. And it won't break the bank either, if we get a cheap flight."

"We were planning on staying in a youth hostel," Florian said. "That isn't too expensive."

"Well, I think it sounds like a great idea!" Julia exclaimed. "I was just going to arrange a job interview at the bookstore so I can earn some extra cash. If that works out, I'll have enough money to go to London mid-August."

Everyone beamed at each other. "Well, that's settled then," Tamara decided. "I say we propose a toast to our travel plans!"

When Florian got up to flip the record, he came back with a small bag of pot. "It's time to relax," he announced.

"What… you're going to hit the Chinese all-you-can-eat joint *stoned*?" Tamara blurted out in shock. "Just so you know, I'm not sitting with you if you act like an idiot."

"He act like an idiot no matter what," Axel remarked, easily dodging the punch Florian aimed at him.

Axel went inside and got the leaflets and guidebooks about London that were still sitting on Florian's desk. Soon, everybody was absorbed in the information, making plans for a four-day trip to the English capital.

"It's pretty cool we're all going to London," Julia mumbled to Gaby. "And I can just focus on work in the weeks leading up to the trip. If I get the job, of course."

Gaby put her arms around her in a sweet hug. "You will. It was made for you, you bookworm. Plus, it will keep you off the streets so you won't run the risk of bumping into *some people* anymore."

Julia nodded. Today, she had felt empty when she'd passed the Old Town – a certain meaninglessness that couldn't be filled. It was as if she were walking the streets of an unfamiliar town in a blur, keeping up the same appearances but feeling hollow and cold on the inside. No longer could she hold out hopes of running into Michael. Gaby was right: she should go and hide for a while. And where to find a better hiding spot than in her personal Valhalla, the bookstore?

That evening, they all walked together through the narrow streets and alleys of Salzburg to the Rudolfskai along the river. The door to Shamrock was wide open, a rocker-style crowd gathering outside holding beers and smoking cigarettes.

"Why don't you give me the flyers," Axel told Gaby. "I'll get drinks for everyone."

"Hey, thanks," Gaby replied. "Guess I'll be the selfish Goth and smoke a cigarette just for me."

Axel laughed and tried to give her a friendly pat on the head, but she nimbly danced away.

They decided to wait outside. The band was clearly doing a sound check – every now and then, the loudspeakers sputtered some acoustic feedback when one of the band members pushed up the fader on a mixer channel too much.

Julia checked out the crowd and felt her heart skip a beat when she spotted two of Michael's friends stepping out of the front door.

Tamara nudged her. "You okay? You look like you've seen a ghost."

Gaby followed Julia's stare and rolled her eyes. "Just your luck. Oh well, for all we know those two came here without him. Michael is probably throwing darts all by his lonesome in O'Malley's. He's, like, the *last* person I would expect to show up at a concert like this."

Julia let out a shaky breath. Gaby was most likely right, but she couldn't relax. When Axel showed up with a tray of beers announcing that the band was ready to start, they all shuffled inside. The room was chock-full and dark, which was a blessing. Even *if* Michael had decided to come here, he wouldn't be able to see her anyway.

When the spotlights lit up and flooded the stage with bright, colored beams, loud music immediately exploded from the speakers. Julia flinched – she was standing close to the loudspeaker on the left.

"Holy hell," Gaby shouted in her right ear, "they're playing 'Cities in Dust'! I *love* this song."

Meanwhile, Florian was staring at the stage with glassy eyes. Julia looked over at the bass player he was clearly checking out. The guy had on a black wife-beater shirt and sporting a black-and-purple dyed Mohawk.

"Holy hell," he repeated Gaby's words. "Who is that? I think I'm in love."

Julia snickered. This was typically Florian – he said whatever he was thinking. She shambled a bit away from the speaker. Even though the music was played at earsplitting volume, it wasn't too bad. In fact, she was kind of enjoying it. She'd only wanted to humor Gaby by tagging along, but the band was better than expected. "This is pretty cool," she told Gaby when the next song turned out to be less loud.

Gaby beamed at Julia, her black-rimmed eyes filled with elation. "Yeah, you think?"

"Yeah, totally. Thanks for bringing me."

After a six-song set, the band announced their break. The lights went on, and Axel poked Florian. "Are you coming? We have to get some more drinks at the bar."

"Sure," Florian agreed before suddenly freezing up. ""No, wait!" he hissed. "That cute bass player is coming straight at us!"

Julia turned around to see the tall, mohawked boy stepping off the stage and making his way toward them.

"I'm dying of thirst," Axel whined.

"Don't worry, I know CPR. Just wait."

The bassist seemed to cut straight through the crowd, the sea of people parting for him as if they could sense he was a man on a mission. His eyes never left Florian, who was starting to look like a tomato suffering from cardiac arrest. Julia could almost *hear* him swallow when the gorgeous musician stopped right in front of him.

"Hey," the bassist said in a soft but resolute voice. "Do you come here often?"

Florian blinked. He was speechless. Axel visibly cringed at the trite first line, but came to Florian's aid by grabbing him by the shoulder and answering for him. "Yes, he does. In fact, I bet he'll be here every week from now on."

"Good to know." The bassist shot Florian a lazy smile.

"Would – would you like something to drink?" Florian managed to utter at last.

"Sure, I could do with a beer," the punker nodded, extending his hand. "I'm Moritz, by the way."

Florian shook hands with Moritz. "Florian. So uhm, I'll get you a beer," he stammered.

"*Now* you're running," Axel said indignantly as they both rushed off toward the bar, leaving Moritz with the three girls. Julia chuckled, shooting Tamara and Gaby a 'what-the-hell-is-happening' look.

"Nice band you guys have," Gaby started the conversation. "Are you going to do more gigs here?"

"I hope so. Let's see how this one goes. If you girls want us to be back, pretty please tell the owner so he'll book us again."

"Where are you from?" Julia asked curiously. Moritz spoke standard German without any Austrian accent, but she did hear a hint of something else in his voice.

"Oh, my dad is English. I lived in London when I grew up. When I was ten, we moved to Cologne for a while, and now we live here."

"London?" Tamara said. "Funny – we're going on a trip there next month. Maybe you can give us some tips."

Florian and Axel were back in no time, the former balancing two beers and a glass of soda on a tray. Julia raised her eyebrows at Axel. "Did he knock the rest of the people in line out of the way? That was freakishly quick."

"Turns out Florian can jump the queue *very* well when the need arises."

Meanwhile, Moritz was having an animated discussion about the best youth hostels in the center of London with the others. By the time Moritz had to go back on stage, Florian had managed to score his number.

"I can't believe this is happening to me," he enthused, casting another smoldering look at Moritz's muscular back as he disappeared among the audience. "I saw him, he saw me, we locked eyes and that was that!"

"Shouldn't you take it easy?" Julia tried to slow him down. "You don't even really know him yet."

"Not *yet*, but I will. Nothing's gonna stop me from buying calling credit for the next one hundred years, first thing tomorrow."

Unexpectedly, Julia felt a stab of jealousy. Why was it all so simple for Florian? Why did he have the good fortune of meeting a hot, cute guy this easily, who genuinely seemed to like him?

The rest of the concert went by in a blur. When the spectators flocked together outside after the music finished, Julia walked up to Moritz, Florian and Gaby having a cigarette outside. "I'm going home," she announced. "I'm completely knackered."

"That's all right." Gaby patted her sweetly on the head. "Did you have fun, though?"

"Yeah, I adored the music! And I'm not even just saying that because Moritz is standing next to me." She smiled at Florian's new flame. He smiled back.

"Why don't you borrow my MP3 player?" Gaby pulled the thing from her kangaroo pouch. "So you can listen to some of the songs on your way back home. But I'll be wanting yours in return."

"Sure you're not going to cry over parting ways with your sinister goth and rock tunes?" Axel asked with a playful grin.

Gaby shook her head. "Nope, I like Enya. Besides, I wouldn't want to ruin my eyeliner *again* and look like shit."

"Well, as long as you don't *smell* like shit."

"Shut *up*!" Gaby shoved Axel.

Julia said goodbye to everyone and got on the next available bus passing the pub. As she got on, the first raindrops of a sweltering summer storm started to patter on the roof of the bus.

The rain didn't let up on Tuesday or Wednesday. Long, summery showers hit the town of Salzburg but didn't do anything to alleviate the stifling heat. After the rain, the high temperatures were somehow even more oppressive. Wisps of clouds hung between the mountain peaks like mysterious fog from another world.

Julia stood in the yard, sniffing the air. She wanted to go for a run in the woods, but it was still way too hot now. Actually, she'd prefer running in the rain. Maybe she should wait for that.

"Are you staring down the clouds?" Anne asked, popping up next to her with the storybook under one arm.

"No, I'm calling out to them. I want to go running in the rain."

Anne sat down on the bench under the awning. "I worked on our tree house with Sabine. See, we want it to look like this." She pointed at a picture of the tree palace belonging to the fairies in the book.

"Wow. That's kind of ambitious. Are you sure you'll manage?"

"Wait till you see it, big sister. You'll be surprised. Thorsten said he'd come and help us too. You know, Sabine's brother."

"Oh, that guy you seem to like so much."

Anne snorted. "*I* don't like him. I thought he might be your type."

At that moment, Axel emerged from the house. He'd dropped by on his old scooter to have lunch with them and borrow some books. "I'm off. Hey, Jules, did you have that job interview at Höllrigl yet?"

"Going there tomorrow afternoon. I called them yesterday, but the manager won't be in until tomorrow."

"Well, let me know about those employee benefits, okay? I'll come round and reap them when you're manning the checkout. A bookworm is always hungry."

"So is a tapeworm," Anne supplied absently, her head in the storybook.

Axel suppressed a laugh. "Aren't you a little Wikipedian." He smiled proudly at her. "Come here, worm, want me to read you a story?" He sat down on the bench next to Anne.

While Anne listened to 'The Prince of Trees' yet again, Julia went inside to put on her running gear and get Gaby's iPod. When she got back outside, it was raining just as she had hoped. Dark storm clouds were gathering in the skies.

Axel pulled a face as he started his scooter and put on his helmet. "Hoping for the best," he said, looking up at the sky.

"This *is* the best!" Julia waved at him before sprinting off, popping in her earbuds before slowing down at the end of the street. She jogged toward the forest at a leisurely pace.

The wind-swept trees swished and showered raindrops on her head. It wasn't raining heavily yet, but the sound of the falling water hitting the tops of the trees sent an agreeable quiver through her body. She set course for her special oak and sat down for a minute against it, stretching her calves and staring up at the branches winding their way upward to the skies, reaching for the light, escaping the ever-present gravity of the earth. The canopy of the tree branches kept her from getting wet.

Julia switched off Nina Hagen on her borrowed MP3 player and closed her eyes, resting her head against the oak tree. Every now and then, she heard the rumble of thunder in the distance. Very softly, very far away.

When the rain started to come down faster, Julia got to her feet and ran back to the forest trail in the direction of Eichet. She wanted to pay her grandmother a surprise visit and have tea with her. After twenty minutes, she reached the edge of the woods and jogged down the asphalt road at a steady pace. In the meantime, the rain had soaked all her clothes, but it didn't bother her. The temperature outside was still agreeable.

Julia ran up to the front door of Gran's house and rang the doorbell with a wet, slick finger. The sound of Mozart's *A Little Night Music* jingled through the house.

Julia edged forward under the awning to find shelter from the rain and wring out her wet hair.

"Hello?" she called out through the kitchen window, which she saw was slightly ajar. "Gran? Are you home?"

Nothing. She peered through the ribbed glass of the front door, seeing the contours of an empty umbrella stand in the hallway. Apparently, Gran had ventured out in the rain as well. Maybe she'd just missed her.

Disappointed, Julia turned around and walked out of the front yard. At the end of the street, she suddenly spotted Sabine walking in her direction, flanked by a tall guy about twenty years old carrying a red umbrella. Julia waved at the two of them and waited for them to reach her.

"Hi, Julia," Sabine said cheerfully. "Didn't you bring an umbrella?"

Julia chuckled. "Yeah, while jogging? Not such a good idea." Her eyes drifted to the guy standing next to Sabine, who was observing her with a slight smile. He caught her eye and extended his hand.

"Thorsten Ebner," he introduced himself. "I'm Sabine's brother."

"Nice to meet you. I'm Julia Kandolf, Anne's sister." She smiled back. The boy had friendly, blue eyes and an eye-catching smile. His black hair curled out from underneath the hood of his rain jacket.

"Wow, you're one athletic girl to go out running in a downpour like this," he commented.

"Oh, it's not *that* bad," Julia replied as a blue lightning bolt split the sky in two and the thunder rumbled just above their heads. The next moment, the clouds seemed to burst, rain coming down like an impenetrable curtain pelting down on her drenched head.

"What the…" She glared up at the clouds. Thorsten burst out laughing, and Julia continued mock-reproachfully: "You know, this is all *your* fault. You shouldn't have used the word 'downpour'. That's where it all went wrong."

"Oh, really? You're blaming me? Not the best way to make friends. You know what, I'll just be on my merry way without using the word 'sunshine'." He grinned mischievously.

"Thor, can we please go to the bus stop?" Sabine asked plaintively, gripping her brother's sleeve in white-knuckled fists. "I'm afraid of thunderstorms."

"Of course we will," Thorsten said with a reassuring smile. He glanced back at Julia. "I don't think that second word actually helped. You joining us under the umbrella?"

Julia shook her head. "I'll run back. It'll be all right under the trees in the forest. Talk to you later!"

"Are you sure?" Thorsten looked puzzled.

"Yeah, absolutely! Don't worry." She quickly turned around and ran off in the direction of the woods, her socks making squishy sounds in her sneakers by now. She passed the bus stop, hesitated for a moment, then continued down the road. She'd rather walk. Of course she hadn't brought her bus card, and she didn't feel like borrowing money from a guy she'd just met one minute ago – not to mention sitting next to him looking all rained out and bedraggled. A hint of a smile crept onto her face when she re-entered the woods. Anne was actually right for once: Thorsten was a cute guy indeed. She'd wanted to make a good impression. Him being the boy next door really cheered her up.

Under the trees, it was hot, dark and damp. The leaves swished in the wind as rain still pattered down, bolts of lightning lighting up the woods every now and then. Julia's shoes left deep footprints in the muddy soil that made her slip and almost lose her balance twice.

Julia came to a stop, panting. Leaning against a thick chestnut tree, she spluttered a curse and rubbed her ankle. Damn – she'd almost twisted it due to the slippery mud. What a *stupid* idea it had been to go running in this dreadful weather. She should have just taken the bus. By now she could have been home sitting on the couch with dry clothes on, sipping hot cocoa from her favorite mug. Instead, here she was, soaking wet, half-shivering, and even somewhat afraid of the heavy thunderstorm. In the oppressive darkness of the storm, the trees seemed to surround her like a hostile army, their shadows towering over her. In fact, the forest looked like it was about to spit out an evil *Krampus* any moment. This would be a good time to bump into a mythical woodland creature waving a magic wand to transport her home, but alas – that wasn't going to happen.

Julia patted the pockets of her jogging pants looking for Gaby's iPod. Music would probably dispel her dark thoughts. She turned on the player and slowly jogged on in the semi-darkness as the first sullen tones of 'A Forest' by the Cure filled her ears. Not the most cheerful song imaginable, but the fact that it was the first song to start playing in shuffle mode was too much of a coincidence for her to skip it.

Julia wiped the raindrops from her cheeks and trudged doggedly on. The rhythm of the song spurred her on and made her run faster, her heart beating wildly in her chest, tapping out an indeterminate fear.

The singer droned in her ears. *I'm lost in a forest, all alone... I'm running towards nothing, again and again and again.* Her hands clenched into fists and her eyes squinted against the rain falling from the sky. Only a few more minutes and she'd be home.

And then something caught her eye. She froze. In the light of a bright lightning strike setting the forest ablaze with cold fire, she saw there was someone lying on the ground. The black stain of a person on the edge of the path. A motorcycle on its side, smack in the middle of the forest trail.

Julia came to a standstill, her breath ragged. With trembling, slippery fingers, she fumbled with the player to turn off the music. She'd ended up at her favorite oak tree, the place suddenly looking sinister in the gloom. Her throat turned dry as she peered at the unconscious figure on the forest trail. Step by step, she shuffled forward. Her eyes followed the tire tracks that the motorcycle had made in the muddy soil. Julia's heart stopped when she came even closer and recognized the Honda bike.

No – this couldn't be happening. She rushed the last few yards separating her from the boy on the ground. Julia fell down on her knees next to his lifeless body, her stomach filling with dread as she noticed the left side of his face was covered in blood. He'd hit his head on a sharp-edged rock. His head injury looked really, really bad.

"Michael?" she whispered softly, putting a trembling hand on his forehead. "Can you hear me?"

He lay very still, his lips almost blue in the macabre light of the thunderstorm flashing occasionally. If only she could see whether he was still breathing! She couldn't hear him breathe over the din of the rain and wind in the woods.

With shaking hands, she grabbed her cell phone from her jacket pocket, setting the camera to permanent flash. The bright light illuminated Michael's face, and tears welled up in her eyes. He looked so lifeless… so vulnerable. For just a moment, she forgot all about the horrible way he'd treated her. She'd wished for all kinds of nasty things to happen to him, but not this.

"Michael," she sobbed, her voice breaking. "Please, *please* wake up."

Her heart skipped a beat when he suddenly inhaled sharply. She took his hand. Very slowly he opened his eyes, green like the forest leaves he was lying under, his pupils dilated and black like the treacherous darkness that had caused him to slip and fall in this severe weather.

"Julia," he whispered in a soft, yet clear voice.

She swallowed.

Why did he sound so different? He pronounced her name with so much emotion that she could almost believe he was seeing her for the first time. She blinked disbelievingly.

"I'll get help," she managed to stutter before his eyes fell shut again, making him smile faintly.

Twenty minutes later, an ambulance with blue flashing lights trundled up on the bumpy path through the woods. Julia watched as if in a trance as the paramedics put Michael on the stretcher.

"Can you tell us where we can reach his family?" one of the EMTs asked her.

"Uhm, yes," Julia stammered, whipping her phone out again to look up the Kolbe family's home number. "Why? Is he still unconscious?"

The paramedic shook his head. "No, he can talk." He looked at the ambulance with a worried frown. "But he seems to have lost his memory."

4.

"This is un-be-lie-va-ble," Gaby said with a face that spelled complete shock. She'd listened to Julia's entire story about Michael's accident without interrupting. "And *you* of all people finding him! I mean, how bizarro is that?"

They were sitting in Julia's bedroom with the curtains drawn and New Age music playing in the background. It was still raining outside.

"He was more dead than alive," Julia mumbled, staring at the *Lord of the Rings* poster on her wall with unseeing eyes. "That head injury of his… it gave me nightmares last night."

"Do you think he'll ever fully recover? You said he had amnesia?"

"That's what the paramedic said." Julia shrugged. She was trying to sound unconcerned, but in reality, the EMT's diagnosis had kept her mind whirling since yesterday. The hospital personnel had only been able to contact Michael's parents after the accident because *she* happened to have had an obsession with their son. Normally speaking, she didn't have every single number of all her ex-classmates in her address book. Michael had lost his memory – he hadn't even been able to recall his own home number, or who his parents were, let alone his last name.

So why had he still remembered *her* name?

"Julia," he'd whispered to her in a weak voice. Had she been more important to him than he'd let on before? The look in his eyes had been one of joy and recognition. He had recognized *her* while he didn't even know himself anymore.

"You know, I'm kind of ashamed of myself for saying he could drop dead for all I cared, that night at the pub," Gaby admitted, toying with the rings on her right hand. "You remember?"

Julia nodded. "Yeah, he almost *did* drop dead. That paramedic said he was one lucky bastard to make it out of an accident like that alive. The blow to his head was devastating, hence the amnesia and all."

"Well, I'm glad. I wasn't being serious when I said that, of course."

"No, of course not! Oh well – for all we know, Michael will forget about his evil ways forever so he can start a new life," Julia said brightly, but she knew she was trying too hard. There were too many unanswered questions about the situation that bothered her.

"Would you girls like some lunch?" Julia's mother hollered upstairs. "I'm making pancakes."

"We're coming," Julia called back.

"Great." Gaby patted her stomach. "I'm starving. I haven't even had breakfast yet."

"I have to go out after lunch," Julia announced as they walked down the stairs. "I'm up for a job interview at the bookstore."

"Ooh, exciting! Keep me updated."

They barged into the kitchen and sat down at the dinner table. Anne was staring out the window with a pouty face. "Look at the lousy weather," she moped. "This way we'll never get to finish that tree house."

"Come on, a bit of rain won't scare you away, will it?" Gaby teased the little girl.

"Why don't you recruit Thorsten to do all the dirty work?" Julia added with a wink.

Anne looked sideways. "You ran into him the other day, didn't you? Sabine told me."

"Yeah, I did." Julia shoved a big bite of pancake into her mouth. Her baby sister was watching her like a hawk, and she couldn't stop herself from blushing a little.

Anne shrieked. "I *knew* it," she triumphed. "I *knew* you'd like him!"

Gaby glared at Julia from across the table. "Hey! Why am I not the first one to hear about this?" she demanded. "Who the hell is this Thorsten dude?"

"It's my best friend's brother," Anne replied instead of Julia. "Their family just moved here. And he's really cute." She glanced sideways at her big sister. "He also talked about Julia with Sabine, you know."

Julia flushed a shade deeper. "Uhm – oh," she stammered, too flustered to make it sound nonchalant. "Really?"

Anne gave her a wide grin that rivaled the Cheshire Cat's smile in enthusiasm. "Yes, *really*," she nodded, sounding self-congratulatory.

Gaby kicked Julia's shins under the table. "Don't hold out on me, girlfriend. I want more info ASAP."

"Yes, Your Highness Gabriella. I will see to it."

After lunch, Julia and Gaby were wordlessly walking to the bus stop when Julia decided to break the silence. "Something's bothering me," she mumbled gingerly.

"Spill," Gaby said.

"When I found Michael, he opened his eyes and he said my name, but apart from that, he didn't remember *anything* else. Isn't that odd, him still being able to recall my name? I mean, he has amnesia."

Gaby bit her lip. "Please, Jules. Don't go there. So he recognized you before he slipped back into unconsciousness. So what? It doesn't mean a thing."

"But..." Julia muttered.

"Look, I know what you want, okay? You want to believe he has more intense feelings for you than he was letting on before the accident. But seriously, you *don't* want to go down this road. He took your V-card and didn't even bother to call you back afterwards, and for *that* fact alone he should be on your shit list forever. Michael doesn't deserve you, and you don't deserve to get your heart crushed by him all over again." Slightly out of breath after her tirade, Gaby grabbed Julia's hand. "Just forget about him," she pleaded.

Julia sighed. "Okay. All right. You're right. I just thought it was strange."

"Strange but true. And now for our next topic: Thorsten. Who is he? What does he look like? And when will you see him again?"

Julia couldn't help but laugh. "He's Sabine's brother, and they live across the street. He has black hair and blue eyes. As for when I'll see him again – I have no clue. I only talked to him for a few minutes."

"So make sure they turn into hours next time," Gaby winked.

Julia looked up. "Oh, the bus is coming! Let's hurry."

The two girls broke into a run to catch the bus to town. Panting and giggling, they boarded and walked all the way to the back.

"Can I have my MP3 player back?" Julia asked once they were sitting down.

Stupidly enough, she hadn't felt like listening to Gaby's music ever since Michael's accident. The songs on her friend's player reminded her of that strange moment when she found Michael's lifeless body in the woods. She couldn't let it go. Gaby could argue all she wanted, but the few seconds in which Michael had stared up at her with that unusual, *intense* look in his green eyes were etched in her memory.

"I'll see you at O'Malley's tonight," Gaby said when she got up to change buses. "Looking forward to hearing about your interview! Good luck, babe."

Julia waved at her as the bus drove off again. They were all meeting at O'Malley's tonight. Florian had called her and promised he'd bring Moritz too. The jubilant tone had been evident in his voice: he was over the moon because of his new lover. Julia smiled faintly when she thought back to the evening in Shamrock. She was happy for Flo. It probably wouldn't take too long before he'd suggest taking his new boyfriend on the London trip as well. Moritz had spent his entire childhood in the English capital, after all, so he would be the perfect tour guide.

Julia was pulled from her thoughts when her phone vibrated briefly in her pocket. Probably another text message from one of the gang.

She dug up her phone but stopped breathing when she saw the notification on the screen. '1 new message. Michael.'

The words jumped out at her, making her heart rate speed up to a dangerous pace. Thank God Gaby wasn't here to witness her reaction – she'd probably have treated her to another 'you-must-forget-about-him' sermon.

With trembling fingers she clicked on the message icon.

'hey julia :) u got time 2 drop by l8er? x mick'.

Julia gawked at the X in front of his name. It probably meant nothing. Nothing at all. He just wanted to thank her because she'd saved him from an untimely death in the middle of the woods. No cause for alarm. Maybe his mom wanted to give her a fruit basket, or his dad wanted to pin a medal on her.

And yet, another voice in her head insisted differently. See? *See,* he thought she was special. He wanted to meet up with *her* after his terrible accident.

With a frustrated sigh, she looked up from the screen, pondering her options for a suitable reply to his message when she realized the bus had reached her stop. The doors were already closing again.

"Wait!" Julia called out to the front, hitching her bag on her shoulder. "I need to get off here!" She caught the irritated frown of the bus driver in the rearview mirror when she blocked the sensor with her foot, causing the doors to swing open again.

With a flushed face, she got off and sat down in the bus shelter. 'r u home @ 3?' she typed out after long consideration, leaving out her name or an X on purpose. Much better to sound aloof for now.

She was just getting up when her cell phone came to life in her hand. Oh Lord – he was *calling* her. Julia swallowed the lump in her throat. The vibration of the device seemed to buzz through her entire body. Again and again it hummed in her palm like a swarm of angry bees.

The girl sitting next to her glanced aside, a puzzled look on her face. "Aren't you going to get that?" she asked.

"No. I don't think I'm ready for it just yet."

Her neighbor laughed. "Let it go to voicemail. He might leave you a message."

Julia stifled a nervous chuckle. "Great idea." She hurriedly got up. If she didn't start walking now, she'd be too late for her job interview, and it would all be due to her mulling over Michael and his invitation. Muttering a curse, she zipped across the bridge leading to the Old Town. Why oh why couldn't she just have heeded Gaby's sound advice? She should have ignored his invitation. Why was it so hard to let go of her obsession with him? He'd treated her like garbage. Did she have no self-respect?

Still mentally bashing herself, she cut through narrow alleyways to get to the main square, crossing it at break-neck speed to end up in front of the bookstore at the strike of two. Outside, Julia saw a mustached man stuffing a book display rack with discounted paperbacks. She momentarily bent over to catch her breath, then addressed him.

"Excuse me." She cleared her throat. "I'm here about the job. Mr. Haider is expecting me at two."

The man turned around. "Julia Kandolf?" he asked, jovially extending a hand toward her. "I'm Martin Haider and I'm the manager. Let's go to my office."

Julia entered the bookstore and followed her possible future boss to an office on the second floor. She'd brought her resume, which Mr. Haider skimmed through while she was sipping the unavoidable 'job interview' cup of coffee. Every now and then he asked her a question. She liked him – he had a sense of humor and he didn't just ask her the dime-a-dozen questions she was used to.

"Who's your favorite author?" he wanted to know, handing her a second cup of coffee she didn't dare refuse.

Julia smiled. "Stefan Zweig. He can turn one small slice of life into something grandiose. He makes you think twice about common things."

Martin nodded enthusiastically, putting his signature on the form he'd been filling out as if her answer had sealed the deal for him. He extended his hand once more. "Welcome to the team! Can you start the day after tomorrow?"

"Of course!" She beamed at him. "Thank you so much."

"No problem. Happy to have you on board. One of your colleagues will do the job orientation with you." Martin slid the form across the table. "Could you fill out your details and sign here, please?"

Once Julia had left the bookstore, she dug up her phone to send Gaby a text about her successful interview. '1 new message. voicemail,' the display told her impassively. With nervously twitching fingers, she closed the notification and started to type out a message to her friend. After sending it off, she took a deep breath and called her voicemail.

"Hi Julia," Michael's deep, sexy voice melted into her ear. "Of course I'll be home around three. Come and have tea with me! See you later."

Brilliant move. Julia turned as red as a lobster. In less than twenty minutes, she'd be having tea with her high school obsession and ignoring all of Gaby's warnings. Michael would most likely be home alone, because his parents both worked full-time.

Reluctantly, she made her way off the square, wondering in despair where it had all gone wrong. She'd been sort-of-ready to move on before she became his savior in the forest. Why was she so impressed with the fact he had stammered her name when she found him? So *what*?

When Julia rang the doorbell of the big house on Giselakai at five to three, all courage had left her. She had *no* idea what she was doing here. Just to be polite, she'd listen to Michael's expressions of gratitude and get the hell out the second she could.

"*Grüss Gott*," she stammered in surprise when a woman in her fifties opened the door. She had Michael's green eyes. Julia thought she recognized the woman from the graduation ceremony at school. "Is – is Michael home?"

"He's expecting you." The woman extended her hand. "I wanted to personally thank you, Julia. Without you, things could have turned out quite differently."

"You are most welcome." She couldn't stop a hint of disappointment creeping into her voice. So this was the reason Michael had invited her over. His mother wanted to thank her, plain and simple. Julia wouldn't be here with just Michael for company, and he probably didn't count on her staying for very long.

"Why don't you go and see him upstairs?" Michael's mother made an inviting gesture. "He's in his room. And he's doing much better. His amnesia is gone."

Julia blinked at her. "He... he's got his memory back?" Then why did he want to see her? He remembered everything about his life – including the part where she had been completely insignificant to him.

The woman smiled radiantly. "Yes! Isn't it wonderful? Miraculous, even, according to the doctors."

The joy radiating from her face sadly wasn't enough to make Julia equally upbeat. She dragged herself up the stairs to the second floor with a nervously hammering heart.

The last time she'd walked these stairs, his hands had caressed her hips, his mouth trailing a warm path in her neck. Giggling and love-drunk, she'd tripped over the uppermost step, and he had caught her in his strong arms.

Her eyes got blurry. She only realized she was crying when she looked at herself in the long mirror hanging on the wall next to Michael's room. She sniffled in frustration, rooting around in her bag for a napkin to wipe away her tears. Of course, she shouldn't give a hoot what Michael thought of her, but her indifference to his opinion still didn't mean she should make a tear-stained entrance. She had more pride than that.

When she pushed open his bedroom door at last, she did her best to keep a straight face. "Hi," she said softly.

Michael was sitting on the edge of his bed, a bandage around his head. He looked up at her and her heart skipped a beat. Once again, she had the feeling he was looking at her in a new way. As if he really *saw* her.

"Julia," he replied, equally soft. He said her name with obvious joy in his voice, and she couldn't prevent a tentative smile from tugging at her lips. He got up and took a step toward her, his eyes never leaving hers. "It's so good to see you."

She quickly looked away, staring at her feet in his lush carpet in utter confusion. On the floor under his bed, she spied a copy of *Chess Novel* by Stefan Zweig. Next to it was the jewel case of Enya's album *Watermark*. Only then did she notice that her favorite music was playing. It was like walking into her own room – as if Michael could read her mind and wanted to make her feel at home.

All of sudden, she remembered watching a TV show about near-death experiences with Gran once. It featured interviews with people who'd had a brush with death but came back to life afterward, and from that point onward they were able to feel and see things that normal people couldn't. Could something like that be going on with Michael?

"It's good to be here," she replied, a half-question in her voice. Was it?

Michael put his hand on her shoulder. When she looked back up at him, she saw something in his eyes that she couldn't quite place – a kind of melancholy was hiding in his gaze; some sort of wistfulness she had never seen there before.

"This must be difficult for you," he spoke quietly, gesturing around him. "You don't have good memories of this room." His lips formed a bitter smile. "Or of me."

A stab went through her heart. Why did he think it was necessary to drag up how things had been between them? If he regretted the way he'd treated her, he could just apologize to her.

"Why did you invite me?" she blurted out, gazing at him quizzically.

A gentle look brightened Michael's eyes, a smile spreading across his face. Not a teasing smile, nor a mocking smirk – it was the most genuine smile she had ever seen on his face. He looked delighted, enraptured like a child seeing snow for the first time. "Because I wanted to see you," he said, taking a step closer and taking her hand. "I was asleep. You woke me up again."

Julia closed her eyes despondently. Of course he was grateful to her for rescuing him from eternal sleep. That was all it was: gratitude. He was probably too proud to offer a real apology. Maybe she was too eager to believe he might have changed.

"I have to go." She carefully pulled her hand from his grasp.

"Already? You just got here."

She shrugged and didn't reply.

Michael inhaled audibly. "Just stay for a little while longer," he said hoarsely.

Seriously, what was the matter with him? He sounded so different from his usual self. Full of a longing she hadn't heard in his voice before, even though she'd wanted to hear it with all her heart.

"I'm going," she doggedly maintained in spite of his plea. "Thanks."

He gazed at her mutely for a moment. "For what?" he asked, sounding puzzled.

Julia blushed. "For your thank-you." She bit her lip.

He shook his head. "You're thanking me because I thanked you?" he established, an obviously teasing undertone in his voice now.

"Uhm, yes." She chuckled despite herself, shrugging again. He bit back a laugh, a playful light in his eyes. Julia's felt her knees buckling, her determination melting away like a Popsicle in the Sahara. She *had* to get away from him right this instant. Gaby would murder her if she knew about this. She backed away toward the door, inwardly repeating 'shit list, shit list' like a mantra.

"Don't you want some tea?" Michael pointed at the teapot and two cups on the side table by his bed.

"I really have to get going," Julia replied, retreating a few more steps. "Axel is waiting for me…"

Her voice caught in her throat when Michael bridged the distance between them in two big steps and put both hands on her shoulders, his eyes boring into hers. Julia stopped breathing when he leaned into her and pressed a soft kiss on her forehead, his body so close to hers that she wanted to lean back. "I'll see you soon," he promised.

What was that?

Her limbs turned cold. Michael had said the *exact* same words to her the morning after they'd slept together. The morning after which he'd never bothered to call her back.

Stifling a sob, Julia pushed him away. She didn't want him to see her tears. How *dare* he invade her life again after callously ditching her only a few days ago?

"Bye," she choked out before storming out the door and stomping down the stairs. Without looking back, she opened the front door and ran down the Giselakai. Michael would have the noble task of explaining to his mother why she was fleeing the scene. This was the last time she'd set foot in that place. Michael was way too dangerous to hang out with – because he still had access to her heart.

As she settled on the bench in the bus shelter, Julia noticed two new messages had come in on her phone. She opened them both.

'congrats on gettin ur book job chick!! xx Gab'

'didnt mean 2 hurt u. sorry. x mick'

She stared at the second text message with red-rimmed eyes, taking note of the time he'd sent it to her. Straight after she'd run out the door. So he really seemed to care about her feelings. But why *now*?

Julia sighed, resolutely putting away her phone. If only she could put away her feelings for Michael as resolutely, her life would be a lot easier.

That night, Julia stepped into the pub wearing a new summer dress. Yesterday's bad weather was over. It was a muggy summer night and all of Salzburg's youth hitting the town seemed to have gathered at O'Malley's. Julia could almost feel carefree, if not for the fact that her visit to Michael was still bothering her.

"Hey, you guys!" she called out enthusiastically, walking over to the table where Axel, Florian and Moritz were sitting. "The girls aren't here yet?"

"We sent them away to fetch us drinks," Axel smirked.

Julia cocked an eyebrow. "I see. Chivalry is dead."

Florian rolled his eyes. "Axel is just joking around. Tam and Gab haven't gotten here yet. Shall we go get drinks?" He tugged Moritz's purple mohawk. Florian and his new boyfriend made their way to the bar holding hands and shooting each other lovey-dovey smiles.

"So, how are you?" Axel asked seriously when she took the bar stool next to him. Julia had talked to him on Facebook after the accident, telling her cousin all about her rescue operation in the woods, but they hadn't really discussed how the whole situation had affected her.

"I'm okay." She shrugged. "What can I say? Small world."

"*Strange* world," Axel added with a frown on his face. "I mean, you of all people coming to his rescue. Plus, Kolbe is acting *really* weird. In fact, it doesn't get weirder than this."

Julia blinked at him owlishly. "What... what do you mean?" she stuttered, following Axel's gaze toward the bar. The bottom dropped out of her stomach when she made out a familiar head with light-brown curls. "What? He's *here*?!"

"As you can see," Axel replied drily. "And like I said, he's acting weird. So *nice.*"

Julia clenched her jaw, gawking at Michael in consternation. Okay, this was absurd. Why couldn't Michael just disappear from her life and *stay gone*? What was he even doing here so soon after an almost fatal accident? Only yesterday, he'd lain bleeding in her lap. He should take it easy, stay indoors and go to bed straight after *Sesame Street*. She had to stop herself from marching up to him to give him some unsolicited medical advice.

"When I came in here a half hour ago, he was playing darts with two friends," Axel continued, apparently oblivious to her inner turmoil. "He said hello, then asked me if he could buy me a drink and whether I wanted to join their game. Seriously, it was like *The Twilight Zone*. I was actually chatting with them until five minutes ago, when Florian and Moritz finally got here."

"Huh. I thought he only hung out with the cool dudes."

Axel smirked. "Yep, I hear you. I mean, I love myself just the way I am, but I can totally see how reading books, fixing computers and building model airplanes could be considered un-cool by His Highness Kolbe..." He jabbed a thumb toward Michael. "Until now, that is."

"Well, what did he sound like?" Julia asked in a hushed voice. "Did he say anything to you?"

Axel frowned down at the beermat he was busy crumbling to pieces in his hands. "Yeah, of course we talked. You know, this may sound strange, but I got the distinct feeling he was *different*." He looked up at his cousin. "You think that hit to the head did something to him?"

Julia sucked in her breath. So Axel noticed it too – Michael really *was* behaving strangely. What did it all mean?

At that moment, Florian and Moritz came back to their table, and to her mounting alarm, she saw Michael trailing behind them, making eye contact with her.

And then he was at their table. "Hey you," he said, leaning his arms on the wood of the bar table, his fingers brushing hers. "What's up?"

She prayed to God he wouldn't mention her visit this afternoon, because that meant she'd have a lot of explaining to do to the boys – not to mention to Gaby if she ever got wind of it.

"I'm fine," she replied, avoiding his gaze. She was afraid she'd turn red if she looked him in the eyes for too long. Michael was looking *way* too good tonight. He had that characteristic, irresistible smile on his lips, and his eyes looked gentle and friendly. When Julia finally dared glancing back up, he took her hand in his.

"You want to play a game of darts with me?" he asked.

Julia felt the skin of her hand turn warm under his fingers. "I can't play darts," she squeaked.

He smiled. "So I'll teach you."

She fervently shook her head. "No, I'm serious. I can't play. I'm a total disaster. You could be Phil Taylor himself and still fail to teach me."

"I can attest to that," Axel agreed. "Last time I played darts with Julia, one of her darts ended up in my *shoe* instead of the board."

"Since you already had a narrow escape from death this week, I wouldn't risk it," Florian added with a wink.

"Yeah, speaking of which, how is your head?" Axel inquired curiously. "Are you allowed to go out again? Is the doctor okay with that?"

Michael nodded. "Yep. The wound is almost healed. They called it a miracle in the hospital. That's why they discharged me this morning."

In the silence that followed, the entire group gaped at him in disbelief. Axel cleared his throat, sounding as though he was about to ask more, when Michael turned around and inched away toward the dartboard. "I'm going back to my game," he said, suddenly seeming in a hurry. He looked sideways at Julia. "You sure you don't want to join me?"

She shook her head. Axel, Florian and Moritz watched him make his way back to the other side of the pub, their jaws still slack.

"Almost healed?" Julia echoed. "That's *impossible*. I know what it looked like."

"What baffles me even more than his miraculously healed head injury is his good-guy act," Florian said dazedly. "Imagine my surprise when he popped up next to me at the bar and made some small-talk out of the blue? He even congratulated me on having a new boyfriend! Kolbe, our resident gay-basher!"

"Oh. Is that – does he really hate gay people that much?" Florian had never told her that. She was starting to discover all kinds of things about Michael that she didn't like one bit. Then again, he seemed to have a completely new side to him all of a sudden.

"Well, he never flat-out threatened or harassed me." Florian shrugged. "He'd just give me these contemptuous looks after it became obvious I was batting for the other side. You know, being his usual, condescending self."

"From what I've seen, he seems like a nice guy," Moritz protested. "He doesn't strike me as an arrogant person at all."

"I *know*! That's what I'm saying," Florian cried out. "He's *different*. He changed." He broodingly took a swig of beer and scooped up a handful of salted peanuts from the snack bowl they'd brought.

"What do you think happened to him?" Axel asked pensively.

"Who knows?" Julia mumbled. "He had a near-death experience. That must have done something to him."

Florian's eyes widened in sudden surprise. "Jules, that's *it*." He hit the table with a fist full of peanuts. "He's been at Heaven's Gates."

"Uh-huh. You think?" Axel snorted.

"Yes. And he met Saint Peter, or someone. And this saint told him he was only allowed to live out his life on earth if he promised to better it."

Axel smirked. "Of course, Flo. That must be it – he was blackmailed by an apostle. Gee, I can't believe *I* didn't think of that."

Julia giggled, but tried to stop when she saw the offended look on Florian's face. She shouldn't laugh at him for his theory. In fact, she'd thought something along the same lines; Axel just made it sound so funny.

"There are plenty of stories about people who came back from the dead," Moritz backed up his boyfriend. "They claim they saw dead relatives, or some sort of peaceful, bright light. Whatever it was this Michael guy encountered, it must have changed him."

Everyone was pondering his words when the door to the pub swung open and Gaby and Tamara trotted in. "Darlings!" Gaby hollered, sashaying toward them with Tamara following in her wake. "Have you guys started drinking without us? Shame on you."

Axel got up from his stool. "Let me prove chivalry is *not* dead," he said, winking at Julia. "What would you both like to drink?" he asked the two girls.

While Axel went off to the bar to get drinks, Gaby and her sister squeezed in between Florian and Julia. "I can't believe this heat!" Gaby huffed. She was wearing a purple-and-black striped tank top and a big purple pentacle dangling from a chain around her neck to match. "First we get rains heavy enough to make Noah bring out the Ark again, and now it's like Austria was relocated to the tropics overnight."

"Be glad," Florian said. "You're working at the riding school this summer, right? Nothing says 'this seasonal job sucks' like having to work outside in the rain all day."

"I appreciate the sun, of course. Just not to this extent."

"So, how are you?" Tamara turned to Moritz. "Any more gigs this week?"

Moritz's eyes started to sparkle. "Actually, I've been meaning to tell you all. Our band was invited to play a club in Camden Town in about one month."

"Which is in London," Florian explained.

"Awesome!" Gaby and Tamara blurted out at the same time.

"That's why I thought it might be a good idea to go to London during the same week," Florian continued, probing their reactions. "So we can see Moritz and the band perform?"

"Of course we should," Julia enthused, looking around the circle of faces. "He's gotta have his homefront supporters with him. And in return for our attendance, he can be our guide in London."

"We'll be there," Gaby nodded. "Goes without saying."

Moritz looked so genuinely happy, a broad grin splitting his face in two, that he resembled a cheerful toddler despite his mohawk and numerous piercings.

Axel returned holding two drinks, squeezing himself between Gaby and Tamara as he sat the beers down on the table. "Here you go, ladies."

"What do we owe you?" Gaby asked, digging around in her purse to find her wallet.

"A heart-felt kiss, darling. What else?" Axel winked lecherously.

"Sounds like a good deal to me." Gaby inched closer and pressed her lips to Axel's cheek. "By the way, we *have* to tell you about the new London plan," she quickly prattled on. "Moritz is about to make history in England. Listen to this."

As Gaby, Florian and Tamara filled Axel in on the details of Moritz's shot at fame next month, Julia observed her cousin over the rim of her beer glass. She could be mistaken, but she was fairly sure he'd turned slightly red when Gaby had kissed him just now. A hint of a smile crossed her face. Well have you ever – she never would have seen *that* coming.

"What the hell?" Gaby suddenly blared, shooting a glance in the direction of the dartboard, her eyes widening. "Do my eyes deceive me? Is that *Michael*? Shouldn't he be in the hospital?"

Julia moaned inwardly. Not again – she was full up on stories about Michael's amazing recovery. What's more, she didn't want to be subjected to Gaby's scrutinizing look once Axel and Florian told her how he'd invited her for a game of darts. If she started blushing, Gaby would have it in for her.

"I'm going to the restroom," she announced abruptly, pushing her way through the O'Malley's crowd without looking back. She kept gazing ahead, just to make sure she wouldn't catch a certain someone's eye while passing the games corner.

When Julia emerged from the restroom, Gaby was waiting for her at the door. "I'm sorry I brought him up," she apologized, sounding contrite. "Axel explained to me you already talked to Michael and how he made you kind of nervous."

"Well, nervous…" She shrugged.

"And no surprise there. I mean, seriously, what is he *doing* here? Shouldn't he be in bed with some kind of IV drip in his arm? He looks like nothing happened to him. Good call, by the way, turning him down for that game of darts. The bastard."

"Yeah, I thought it was best to avoid him." Julia felt her face turn hot. Not because Gaby had paid her a compliment, but because she was lying through her teeth. She *didn't* want to avoid Michael. She wanted to know what was up with him, what had changed him, but at the same time, her inner voice of reason agreed whole-heartedly with Gaby.

Frowning, she followed Gaby and rejoined their group. When Michael left the pub with his friends about ten minutes later, he gave her a look over his shoulder and caught her eye, smiling warmly at her. Julia bit her lip and looked away without smiling back.

"Well done," Gaby mumbled next to her. "Ignore him. He did the same thing to you."

"So, are we going to Shamrock next time?" Julia asked. That way, she'd at least be able to avoid encountering Michael with all her friends around.

Florian nodded vigorously. "Good idea – I'm telling you, that place is good for our love lives. I bet you'll meet someone to play white knight to your damsel there too, Jules."

Gaby nudged her. "Maybe you should invite Thorsten along," she suggested, waggling her eyebrows.

"Who's Thorsten?" the rest of the group asked in unison.

Julia rolled her eyes. "Gee, *thanks*," she grumbled.

Gaby shot her a wide smile. "You're quite welcome. It's time for the winds of change, sweetheart."

The following morning, Julia woke up to the sound of swooping music coming through the thin wall of her bedroom. Apparently, Anne was watching her *Lord of the Rings* DVDs for the umpteenth time at maximum volume.

She yawned, reaching out for her cell phone on the nightstand to look at the time. Half past eight. *Way* too early to be woken up on a vacation day. Her little sister was risking her life.

Still half-spinning with sleep, Julia got up and dragged herself outside to pound on the door of Anne's bedroom.

"Hey!" she shouted. "Can the hobbits tone it down a bit? Some people are trying to sleep in, you know."

She heard Anne clattering through the room. The door swung open, showing her little sister sporting the most lovable smile imaginable. "Will you watch with me?" she asked, her eyes radiant. "I got us milk and cookies downstairs."

Julia bit back a smile. "Why not. I'm awake anyway." She wanted to sound grumpy, but found she couldn't. *She* used to be the one waking up before anyone else, waiting downstairs for her sister with milk and cookies so they could watch cartoons. When their father had still been around. The fact that Anne wanted to do the same thing for her made her choke up a little.

Julia sat down on the bed and watched Anne pour her a glass of milk. She accepted the glass and the plate of cookies, scooting to the left so Anne could sit down next to her. Her sister had hit pause on the DVD. Legolas was frozen on-screen, squinting his eyes to peer at the horizon and make one of his elven Captain Obvious remarks.

"Jules," Anne mumbled next to her around a bite of cookie. "You think the prince of the trees could also have long, blond hair?"

Julia's eyes swerved from the handsome Legolas on TV to Anne's questioning eyes. "Sure. It's a fairytale, and you spin those yourself. If *your* prince has long, blond hair, the story adapts." She poked Anne in the side. "That's the fun thing about dreaming."

"Isn't it better when a dream really comes true?" Anne asked timidly.

Julia fell silent, worrying her lip. She didn't know what to say to that.

"Sometimes, I dream Daddy comes back to live with us again," Anne continued even more quietly, picking at the hem of her PJs.

Julia swallowed down a little lump. "Honey, it's better if he *doesn't* come back." She stroked Anne's dark-blonde hair. "Mommy is way happier without him. They were fighting all the time."

"Mommy is angry with him," Anne whispered. "Because he never comes round to visit the two of us anymore. I heard her talking to Grandma."

Julia pulled Anne into a hug. "She'll let go of her anger one day. She'll understand we don't need him anymore. *She* is raising us, and we love her the most."

The ghost of a smile flitted across Anne's face. "That's what Gran told her too."

Julia chuckled. "Isn't Gran a smart woman."

Anne sat up and gave the elf on TV a pondering look. "Still, I think fairytales can come true. You think the prince could also have blue eyes?"

Julia frowned at her sister's thoughtful expression. Suddenly it dawned on her. Could it be her little sister was secretly in love with Thorsten, the new, handsome neighbor with his bright, blue eyes?

"Yes, he definitely can," she played along. "Long, blond hair and blue eyes. It's your fairytale, and you hold the illustration rights." She winked.

Anne nodded, looking pleased. "The prince will never reveal his true name," she stated pedantically. "He remains a mystery to the adults around him, because they can't see him for what he truly is."

Julia smiled. "Maybe you should write a book," she suggested. Realizing she was actually serious about the idea, she continued: "Really. You should. You've got talent. You have such a wonderful way of expressing yourself, Anne."

She hugged her sister again, her hug turning into a tickle of death until Anne begged for mercy screaming and kicking. By the time their mom woke up an hour later and went downstairs to make breakfast for all of them, Julia felt a lot more energetic than she had in a long time.

"I'm going for a run to Gran's," she announced at the breakfast table, stuffing a large bite of omelet in her mouth. "Do you want me to bring her anything?"

"No, you don't need to. I'm dropping by as well tonight," Ms. Gunther replied. "I'm working the afternoon shift, so I'll visit her afterwards and cook for her. You know, a bit of mother-daughter time. I hope you can fix dinner for yourself and Anne?" Julia's mother worked as a store manager at the supermarket in Eichet.

"Sure. I'll think of something." Julia gave Anne a conspiratorial wink meaning 'pizza and ice-cream!'. Her sister shot her a huge, goofy smile.

"Can I go on a play date with Sabine this afternoon, Mommy?" Anne asked.

"Of course. In fact, you'll *have* to stay at Sabine's. Someone has to mind you, right? I arranged things with her mom."

After breakfast, Julia went on her way. It was a nice, sunny day, but strong winds were also stirring up the forest. She was shivering in the cold breeze when she decided to take a break after ten minutes, crouching down next to her oak and wiping the sheen of sweat off her brow. It wasn't just the cold that made her shiver – something felt different about the woods. The leaves above her head whispered restlessly, yet there was a certain stillness in the forest that she couldn't explain. It was almost as though the forest was holding its breath, waiting for something.

Julia leaned her head against the gigantic tree trunk, listening to the blood rushing in her ears. "Hello, Mister Oak," she said quietly, putting her hands on the roots underneath her feet.

Nothing happened. The eerie silence was now all around her as the tree leaves stopped rustling. The oak didn't answer her.

Julia couldn't help rolling her eyes at herself all of a sudden. Why was she being so ridiculous? Hadn't she decided to say goodbye to the fairytales she'd surrounded herself with in order to keep reality out? And here she was, thinking she could communicate with a tree. It was clear she was a nutcase.

With a grimace on her face Julia got up again. The woods weren't bringing her the peace she'd hoped for. This morning's energy buzz had dissipated.

She sprinted away, still feeling confused. Up till now, she had always managed to slow down and take her mind off things in this place, but today was different. The woods felt different, or maybe it was she who was different. She didn't know.

Out of breath, she arrived at her grandma's house. The old woman was in the front yard, cutting the hedge and whistling a tune. She waved at her granddaughter and walked over to meet Julia at the gate.

"You're panting," she noticed. "Out of practice?"

"I'm not," Julia puffed indignantly. "Nothing wrong with my endurance. I just … pushed myself a little too hard. I was trying to run off some stress." She plunked down on the bench outside and took off her backpack.

"So did you manage to outrun your own ghosts?" Her grandmother put down the hedge trimmers and went inside to get something to drink, leaving Julia to ponder the answer to that question by herself for a minute.

"A ghost has returned," she admitted, when Gran sat down next to her with two glasses of water. She gulped down her drink eagerly.

"That one boy," Gran said without a question mark in her voice.

Julia didn't reply.

"Your mother told me you saved a classmate of yours in the woods," Gran continued. "Is that *the* Michael?"

"Yes and no," Julia blurted out without thinking. Her grandmother looked at her curiously. "Yes, it was Michael Kolbe in the forest, and no, he is no longer *the* Michael." The more she said it, she more she felt it was the truth,

"Why do you think that?" Gran asked calmly. If she was surprised, she didn't show it.

Julia sighed deeply. "I can't explain, but I can *sense* it. I *know* it. He's changed because of that accident. And yet, I know I should be careful. Gaby's been on my case the whole time. She thinks I should stay away from him, and frankly I can't do anything but agree with her."

"Just let it flow," Gran said softly. "Stay away from him, but let him come to *you* if he really wants to. How do they say it these days? Your neighborhood, your rules."

Julia snorted. "Gran, just stop. *I* don't even know what the rules are. Believe me, I *want* to be all strong and independent, but for this guy, I'm willing to bend the rules so much they look like a pretzel. And it's pissing me off. I don't *want* him to have this effect on me anymore."

"He can only have that effect on you if you want him to," the old woman said unperturbed. Julia was close to gritting her teeth out of frustration because Gran was right. She *did* want him to. She still did.

"So… I'm going to hit the shower," she said in the ensuing silence.

She got up and slogged upstairs. As the warm water pelted down on her head, she thought about her grandmother's words. Of course Gran was right – she had to let things flow and follow her own heart. Common sense told her she should steer clear of Michael, but her heart's desire won over logic and reason. Something was up with him, and she intended to find out what it was.

After she got back downstairs, Julia played some songs on the piano while her grandmother was cleaning the kitchen. After that, they each got a pair of hedge trimmers and attacked the shrubs in the back yard. At two o'clock sharp, they set out to the supermarket. Julia was saddled with the task of rolling the 'old-ladies'-cart' down the sidewalk – that's what her grandma had nicknamed the old-fashioned tartan-patterned trolley bag she used for groceries.

"What time will your mother be coming?" Gran inquired.

"No idea. After work, she said."

"I'll ask go and ask her." The old woman walked to the back of the store, where a red door gave access to the storage area and the back office.

Julia stopped at some crates of tangerines, scanning the selection of fruit and vegetables for fresh mangoes. Absent-mindedly, she picked up three tangerines from the crate in front of her, staring at them indecisively. She didn't really want tangerines, but it looked like the mangoes were sold out.

A modest cough startled her from her musings. "Can I help you with anything?" a familiar-sounding voice asked.

Julia looked up, straight into Thorsten's blue eyes. He was standing next to her in a supermarket uniform, a cheerful smile gracing his face.

"Uhm, hey," she fumbled. "I had no idea you worked here."

"Since yesterday. Sabine told me your mother worked here, so I thought, let's ride her coattails and give it a shot."

"Well, it worked," Julia chuckled. "How are you liking it so far?"

"Just fine!" His eyes darted to the three tangerines she was still holding. "I've actually been observing you for quite some time. I was kind of hoping you'd start juggling with those." He smiled playfully, and Julia started to laugh.

"Oh, and that's what you wanted to help me with?" she asked in mock-bewilderment. "Maybe you'd better quit this job and join the circus."

Thorsten's face fell. "Please don't tease me with my red nose and floppy feet. It really hurts, you know. I expected more from you."

"No, you misunderstand. I'm not teasing you! It's good to know your strengths, right?"

"True, true." His gaze fell on the trolley bag. "Cute cart," he continued with a wink. "Do you always take that to the supermarket?"

"I'm here with my grandma, okay?" Julia retorted defensively, glaring at him.

"I know." He shot her a half-smile. "I saw the two of you come in."

Julia bit her lip, suddenly wondering just how long Thorsten had been watching her. He turned around to pick some bruised peppers out of a vegetable crate, pausing for a moment. "So, you got any plans for the weekend?" he asked, re-arranging the cucumbers for no apparent reason. He didn't look at her, and Julia realized he sounded a bit nervous. Her stomach gave a lurch and she swiveled around to put back her tangerine-juggling balls and hide her red cheeks from view.

"Yeah, I'm working. I'm starting at the bookstore tomorrow. Pretty cool." All the while, she was pondering Gaby's suggestion. She could ask Thorsten to join her and come to Shamrock tomorrow night, surely. He would fit right in with her circle of friends, but she felt a bit guilty for inviting him just to distract her from Michael. He was way too nice for that. On the other hand, what would be the harm in introducing him to new people? He had just moved here, after all.

"Have you made any friends our age in Salzburg yet?" she asked, getting her act together. Thorsten shook his head, looking at her expectantly. "Well, if you feel like it, you can come with me to the Shamrock pub tomorrow night and you can meet my friends. Hang out."

"Of course I feel like it," he responded enthusiastically. "Where's Shamrock?"

As Julia told him which bus to take to get to the pub, she saw her grandmother sidling up to them from the corner of her eye. Gran was careful not to interrupt their conversation.

"Okay, see you tomorrow then," Thorsten said after saving her number to his contacts.

"Yeah, see you! Enjoy work!" Julia waved at him as he strolled off to stock some shelves in the cereals aisle.

"Who was that?" There was Gran's inevitable and curious question.

"Thorsten. He's Sabine's brother. You know, Sabine is Anne's new best friend."

Grandma nodded thoughtfully. "I see." She glanced in the direction of the cereals aisle. "And what about him? Is he going to be *your* new best friend?"

Julia turned red. "Gee, Gran, I don't know. I just want to figure out... I can't just let Michael... I don't think I'm ready for... he's nice, though." Wow, so much for coherence. She sighed in frustration.

"Well, he certainly likes you," Gran said casually, trotting off to the checkout with her trolley bag.

"Huh? Why do you say that? Is this your sixth sense kicking in again?"

"Oh, come on now, you don't need psychic powers to see that. His eyes tell the whole story."

Julia didn't reply. His eyes? She'd thought Michael's eyes had told her a story too, but it had made her none the wiser. "Whatever."

"Now, why so surly? It's just an observation. Ignore it if you want."

Julia started laughing. "I'm sorry, Gran. Forget it."

Julia and her grandmother spent the rest of the afternoon gardening, drinking tea and playing cards.

"I'd better go home," Julia muttered, when Gran put down a joker for the third time in one game of Mau Mau.

The old woman winked. "Ha! I sent you running for your life."

Julia pouted in mock disappointment, then got up and went to the bathroom to change into her running clothes. She hugged her grandma in the hallway. "See you on Sunday. We'll be round for tea."

The breeze ruffled her hair as she jogged back at a relaxed pace. In the forest, the tree branches swept back and forth like the waves of a wild sea. Julia breathed deeply in and out. The familiar feeling of serenity had returned to the woods, as if the strange and oppressive atmosphere of early morning had been blown away by the wind that had picked up. She could sense it. Her mind was empty when she left the forest trail and cut through the brush to get to the oak tree. Maybe she'd be able to relax at 'her' spot this time around.

A frown appeared on Julia's face, though, when she rounded a patch of trees and spotted a lone figure sitting with his back against the oak. Panting softly, she came to a halt, feeling a familiar knot forming in her stomach. She recognized that figure.

What the hell was *he* doing here?

Slowly, she approached the oak tree. Michael didn't seem to notice her – he was sitting motionless with his eyes closed, resting his hands on his knees.

This guy was driving her insane, little by little. Ever since she'd decided to try and avoid Michael, she kept tripping over him at every turn. Of course it was unreasonable to blame *him* for her restlessness, but it bugged her to find Michael here. It didn't compute. This was *her* meditation spot – he shouldn't be here.

Just as she was about to turn around and silently retreat into the woods, Michael opened his eyes.

"Julia," he said, turning his head and staring straight at her, almost as if he'd sensed she was there.

"Hey," she replied curtly, a tiny shiver running through her body. How had he known?

He smiled, and the wind stirred the leaves of the tree he was leaning against.

Julia grudgingly walked toward him. She couldn't in all decency just storm off now. After all, he'd greeted her kindly enough.

"What are you doing here?" she asked a bit too tartly.

Michael got up, running a hand through his hair. "Thinking," he replied softly, then looked around him. "This is where it happened."

Julia took in his serious face, suddenly feeling ashamed for hating his presence here so much. He had every right to visit the place where he'd almost met an untimely end. It was obviously just coincidence it happened to be *her* special place, too.

"Don't you have bad memories associated with the forest?" she asked cautiously.

Michael smiled broadly and shook his head. "I feel at home here," he answered. "More than... at home."

Julia thought of his beautiful, expensive mansion, of his wealthy parents who were mostly absent. A sudden feeling of pity overwhelmed her.

"I'm sorry," she mumbled.

He shrugged. "I'm not. This is a beautiful place to feel at home." He took her hand as if it was the most normal thing in the world. "And you come here a lot," he continued, happiness showing in his eyes.

"I do." Julia stared at her hand in his. How did he know that, actually? She hadn't told Michael that much about herself in the hours she'd spent with him in private. They'd been busier making out than talking. Julia felt herself redden when she looked up and became aware of his proximity. He was closer than she'd thought. Her hand was growing hot in his palm. "I – I feel at peace here," she stuttered, shyly taking a step backward and releasing his hand. "I come here to clear my head."

"But I bet you come here for inspiration too?"

Julia nodded mutely. "Writing poems. That kind of thing," she mumbled at last.

"Composing?"

She nodded again.

"You play the piano, right?" He nonchalantly put both hands in the pockets of his jeans. "You should come over again. That grand piano is just gathering dust in the living room anyway. My mother never has time to play."

Julia looked at him in surprise. "Me? Playing that Steinway?" she stammered, perplexed.

Michael moved closer. Julia felt the oak tree against her back. She leaned back her head and looked up at him. Slowly, a crooked smile crept across his face.

"Yes," he replied calmly. "You. Playing that Steinway."

He was *way* too close for her to feel comfortable. Why did her treacherous heart still race when he was standing this close? She knew very well what kind of person he was… or had been, at the very least.

"I dunno," she hedged. "I'll think about it."

"You should. The invitation stands. That piano is gonna feel lonely until you decide to grace it with a recital."

Julia swallowed hard. "So, I should be on my way…" She pointed vaguely in the direction of the path, tiptoeing around Michael as if he would stop her. "I have cooking duty."

"What's on the menu?"

"Pizza." She shrugged. "I know how to cook properly, though. I'm just being lazy today because I have to babysit my sister." Oh, she could *kick* herself for that – apologizing for having fast food tonight. What did he care? What did *she* care?

"Hey now, mind your words. Pizza *is* proper food. Don't let the Italians hear you. My grandpa on my mom's side is an Italian. I love pizza."

"Amy's Kitchen isn't exactly Italian," Julia objected.

"No, but it sure is tasty." He shot her a playful look. "My favorite brand, in fact."

Oh my God. She was literally *this close* to inviting Michael for dinner, and it was pretty obvious he was angling for it, dropping hints the size of bricks.

"Yep, mine too. Looking forward to it already." She gingerly took a few steps back. "So, yeah, I'll see you around."

"I hope so," he said.

Julia quickly took off before she could start blushing again or – oh, horror – change her mind in a fit of insanity and invite him anyway. At break-neck speed, she crashed through the woods as if the devil were chasing her.

When she got home all sweaty and out of breath, she called Gaby to invite her over for a movie night after Anne's bedtime. By now she could use some support. Frowning deeply, she shoved two mushroom pizzas into the oven.

Anne was sitting at the kitchen table reading a Donald Duck comic. "Is something the matter?" she asked, observing the testy way Julia slammed the oven door closed.

"No."

"I'll take that as a yes."

Julia couldn't help but laugh. "It's nothing in particular, Annie. I'm just nervous because of my first day at work tomorrow."

They are their pizza and ice cream while watching Toy Story. When dusk set in, Anne went to bed and Gaby showed up at their doorstep with three big bags of popcorn and a DVD.

"Just how many movies are we watching tonight?" Julia shot a look at the intimidating amount of snacks her friend had brought. "Or have you invited some more people?"

Gaby waved the DVD case in front of her. "It's going to be quite a session, Jules. This movie lasts for *hours*, and on top of that, Axel told me we have to be focused and we're probably going to need to pause it every now and then to philosophize about it."

"Uh-oh. Axel lent you a movie for geeks."

Gaby nodded enthusiastically. "Yeah, Florian and Moritz were talking about Moritz's band's name last night, right?"

"*Waiting for the Kick?*"

"Precisely. And then Axel said Moritz and his buddies must have watched *Inception* because that expression was used in the movie. So he called me today telling me he'd burned me a copy, because I'd gotten all curious about it."

All of a sudden, Julia remembered the tiny spark flying between Gaby and her cousin. "Well, Ax should congratulate himself on turning you onto geekdom, too."

"What? Me? No way Jose. I love my dark, alternative self too much for that."

Julia studied Gaby's flustered face. Should she ask what her best friend thought of Axel? That might be too confronting. She didn't want to ruin things between Axel and Gaby before they'd even had a chance to blossom. Maybe she could trick her friend into spilling her guts by making a juicy confession of her own.

"I asked Thorsten out today," she said, flashing a sultry smile.

Gaby yelped. "You *didn't*. You did?! For real? When are you guys going on a date?"

"Just, tomorrow. So he can tag along to Shamrock."

"Way to go, diva!" Gaby slapped Julia on the shoulder. "I'm so proud of you! When did you ask him?"

"Oh, I bumped into him at the supermarket in Eichet. He works there now."

"Good, good. I'm taking it you'll be grocery-shopping for your mom all week, am I right?"

Julia smiled. Thorsten was a cute guy and he'd click well with her friends. This was the right road to take. She conveniently forgot to mention her less-than-casual encounter with Michael in the forest.

"On Sunday we're going to book the plane tickets to London." Gaby flopped down on the couch. "We'll make sure we can see Moritz play. He's leaving a few days before we do. Flo said we should all meet up at his place on Sunday night, so we can print off the boarding passes straight away."

"I'm so excited! When are we leaving?"

"Third week of August." Gaby pointed at the copyright warning appearing on the TV screen. "Axel is such a smart rat, isn't he? He even copied the warning against copying DVDs."

"Yeah, my cousin is our resident Einstein." Julia grinned. It wouldn't hurt Axel's chances if she tried to talk him up a bit. "And not to mention, a dedicated friend. He must have slaved away for you, ripping and burning that DVD at top speed so you'd have it within a day."

"Yup. He's the best," Gaby nodded, reaching for the bottle of soda on the table. "You want a drink?"

Julia chuckled. No matter how fast a talker Gaby was, she hadn't managed to hide the tiny blush creeping up on her face.

"Well, at least make yourself a sandwich to take with you!" Julia's mother yelled from the kitchen the next morning, as her daughter was running around in a panic trying to leave on time for her first day of work. "You need breakfast, don't you?"

"I don't have time! I have to leave five minutes ago." Julia quickly put on a jacket while struggling to tie her shoelaces.

Resolutely, Julia's mom snatched away one of Anne's sandwiches and packed it in a Zip-loc bag.

"Hey," Anne piped up, sounding offended. "My peanut butter sandwich!"

"I'll make you a new one," Ms. Gunther promised. "Now shush."

"Thanks, mom." Julia grabbed the on-the-go breakfast. "Sorry Anne! See you guys tonight!"

With an anxiously pounding heart, she sprinted to the bus stop. Why had she slept through her alarm clock *today* of all days? She could only hope the traffic was quiet on Saturday morning, or else the bus would definitely be late. She didn't want to make a bad impression by showing up late for work on the very first day. Epic fail, as Gaby would say.

Once she was on the bus, she calmed down somewhat. No traffic jams and all the lights were green.

Julia leaned back in her seat and popped in her ear buds while munching on her sandwich. After a twenty-minute ride, she got off and hastily crossed the bridge leading to the Old Town, ending up in front of the store at exactly half past eight. Martin was just unlocking the door when she appeared.

"Hello, Mr. Haider," Julia called out.

Martin swiveled around. "If it isn't Julia! Happy to see you. The store won't open until nine, but I wanted to give you a quick company tour and sit you down to fill in two more forms. I need to know where to transfer your generous salary to, after all," he winked.

Julia chuckled. She was beginning to really like her new boss. "Let's hope it is. I'm going on a trip to London this August."

"You are? Great choice. It's a magnificent city. How's your English? Reasonable?"

Chatting amiably, they walked to the back of the store where they climbed the stairs to the office where Julia had done her job interview. After letting her fill out her bank details, Martin accompanied her to the break room further down the hall. "This is the kitchen where all the members of staff eat between one and two, when the store closes for lunch break. We close at five today, by the way. Saturday timetable."

Another flight of stairs led up to the stockroom and the toilets. Julia's boss went into the room to get her a black T-shirt with the store logo, which she put on over her own tank top. Once they got back down to the first floor, Martin showed her which categories of books were shelved on the first and second floors of Höllrigl, after which she was more or less good to go.

"Why don't you grab some coffee?" he suggested. "The store opens in a few minutes, and I'll ask one of your colleagues to introduce you to the rest of the team and explain to you how the cash register works so you can man that position in the afternoon. Is that okay?"

"Sounds cool." Julia couldn't help but grin like an idiot as she looked around at all the books in the store. This was a dream come true – she was having a Beauty-in-the-Beast's-library moment. Martin had told her she was entitled to a pretty good discount on all in-store purchases. Axel would cry with joy when she told him the news. Whistling cheerfully, she walked up the stairs again to get some tea. When she returned, Höllrigl was open for business and she bumped into another girl in a company T-shirt going up the stairs.

"Hi," the girl said, extending her hand. "You must be the new one."

Julia shook the girl's hand. "Julia. The new one," she said ceremoniously.

"Donna," the girl replied. "The old-timer." They both laughed.

"I'm on my way to the checkout," Julia said. "I need some lessons before being thrown to the wolves. Talk to you later?"

"Absolutely!" Donna beamed at her and continued up the stairs.

Julia hummed happily to herself as she made her way to the front of the store. She was such a lucky bastard for finding this job! The work seemed easy enough, her boss was a nice guy, her colleagues were friendly and the pay wasn't bad either – not to mention the discount Martin had promised her. What else could she wish for?

"Ah, there you are." Martin popped up from behind a towering pile of bestsellers. "Please come with me."

Julia trailed behind him as she walked over to the cash register, looking left and right to catch a glimpse of her other colleagues.

"Kolbe!" her brand-new boss shouted toward the entrance. "Come and help me out, will you?"

Julia stopped dead, frozen in her tracks. Was she going deaf, or had Martin just said... Her heart hammered ridiculously fast as her eyes zoomed in on the front door.

"He'll come and help you at the register." Martin's voice sounded as though it was coming from far away. He left her standing there, rooted to the spot.

Julia tried to snap out of her paralysis and stumbled the final few steps to the counter. Her breath hitched when she saw an all-too-familiar figure walking in her direction. She swallowed. But surely it *couldn't* be. Oh God, no. No, no, no. This was *not* happening.

And then, she couldn't look anywhere else but up, straight into two eyes green as the forest.

5.

"**W**hat on earth are *you* doing here?" Julia stared at him in alarm.

"I work here," he replied unfazed, a half-smile tugging at his lips.

"Since when?" It was simply *not* possible that she, in her unfailing stalker mode, had somehow missed this: Michael holding a job at the same bookstore she'd applied to two days ago.

"Since last week."

His smug composure quickly turned her initial befuddlement into outright infuriation.

"Why?" she demanded fractiously.

He raised an eyebrow. "To earn some extra cash?" he declared in an 'isn't-that-really-obvious' tone.

"But why *here*?"

Michael started to chuckle. "Why are you giving me the third degree?"

"Are you following me or something?" she grumbled, her heart treacherously leaping in her chest for a moment as she considered the possibility.

"Well, I'm sorry to burst your bubble here, but I think it's the other way around. First, you turn up at the pub I always hang out at on weeknights, then, you decide to take a jog near the place where I almost had a fatal accident, and now you turn out to have applied for a job at the same store I've been working at for the past week. What does it look like to *you*?"

Shucks, he was right. Julia resisted the urge to stamp her foot like a little girl. "In your dreams, you arrogant bastard," she muttered. "Everybody says I should stay away from you."

In the silence that followed, she could still hear her heart beating in her throat.

"I can imagine," Michael quietly said, in such a low voice she wasn't even sure he'd actually said it until she saw the look in his eyes. It was a look of shame.

"Look, I'm sorry. I didn't mean to sound so mean." Julia's face grew hot with embarrassment. "It's not like I can't work together with you – that won't be a problem."

Michael was still watching her, his mouth set in a grim line. "I'm sorry he hurt you like that." Once again, he spoke so softly she wasn't sure she'd heard him correctly. Julia blinked in confusion. Who was he talking about – himself?

"Okay, why don't I go and do what Mr. Haider has asked me to do," Michael abruptly switched to business mode. Apparently he'd caught sight of their boss. He walked over to the cash register and beckoned for Julia to join him. "By the way, you can call him Martin. Don't feel shy about it – he insists. He says he feels like a grandpa if we call him sir."

With wobbly knees, Julia stood next to him and listened with half an ear as Michael explained to her things about ringing in customer purchases, punching in the codes for regularly-priced books, special prices, discounts, and completing sales.

Her gaze swerved to his face instead of the buttons under his hands. He looked so relaxed and at ease. So handsome. She just couldn't forget about that last kiss he had given her, the morning after. She wanted to know if he had really changed. She wished she could feel him that close once more. She wanted…

Oh, she had to stop doing this to herself! He'd never even said he was sorry. In fact, he acted like nothing had happened. And here she was – daydreaming about dragging him behind the first available pile of books to suck face with him out of sight, when she was really supposed to *pay attention*. Her lewd ways would turn her into a clumsy, incompetent mess on her first day at work. She'd sell new books to customers at a ninety percent discount by accident, and Martin would fire her on the spot.

"You think you'll be okay?" Michael interrupted her inner harangue, looking at her from aside.

"Yeah. I'll manage." Quickly, she scuttled away, determined to ask Donna for help later so as not to perish ingloriously. She didn't look back on purpose, running up the stairs to unpack the day's shipment like Martin had asked her.

'Gab... 3 guesses who works here 2 :$' she texted Gaby as soon as she entered the stockroom. She couldn't help it – she had to share this.

'thorsten??' her phone dinged one minute later.

'no... kolbe.'

'is the mofo stalking u?!' Gaby texted.

'can't b. he was here b4 me. this = NOT good 4 my rep...'

'hang in there. ttyl. X!'

With a big sigh, Julia put away her phone and tried sticking to her task. After ten minutes, Donna came in with a boy and a girl who were clearly siblings. She introduced them both to Julia. When she sat down for a cup of coffee in the break room around eleven with Marco and Silke – the twins – Michael was nowhere to be found, fortunately.

"Have you guys worked with the cash register yet?" she wanted to know.

Marco nodded. "Yeah, it's pretty simple. Didn't Michael explain it to you this morning?"

Julia shrugged. "Yup, but I wasn't paying attention. Sorry."

Silke started laughing. "He's quite a distraction, huh?"

"Why do you say that?" Julia turned red.

"Oh, come on, don't think I didn't see you ogling him, girl. The guy is glorious." She patted Julia's hand. "But don't you fret. I'm dating someone, so fair Michael is all yours."

"Pfff. As if," Julia huffed sarcastically.

Silke and Marco both eyed her curiously, causing her to grumble inwardly. Why couldn't she keep her big mouth shut for a change?

"We went on a few dates," she explained tartly. "And then he decided to grow cold and ignore my calls, and ever since, I keep bumping into him when all I want is to forget about the jerk. End of story."

"Oh, one of *those* guys." Silke cocked her head in surprise. "I wouldn't have pegged him as the type."

Her twin brother nodded his agreement. "Yeah, color me confused. He seems like a very nice guy."

Julia snorted derisively. "Well, why don't *you* ask him out then. You might be luckier than me."

Marco grinned. "Not gonna happen. First of all, I'm not into guys, and second of all, he still likes you. He stares at you, you know."

Julia swallowed, her face flooding with color. Right at that instant, the door to the break room opened and Michael entered the room together with Donna. They all grew quiet.

"Time for a drink." Michael looked at the three of them and hesitated. "Uhm... am I interrupting something?" He sounded genuinely insecure.

"No, of course not," Silke hastened to say. "We were just gossiping about Martin, so we stopped talking because we thought it was him." She winked at Julia, who purposely ignored Michael and took another cookie from the jar. She suddenly had the irrepressible urge to flee the scene.

"I'm going to the bathroom." She abruptly stood up. "Will you help me with the cash register later?" she mumbled at Silke before barreling out of the room and running up the stairs to the restrooms.

With a long-suffering sigh, Julia slammed the door shut and sat down on the toilet seat, running a hand through her hair in frustration. Okay, so Marco had also picked up on Michael's fascination with her. She couldn't deny his interest in her any longer. But why did it manifest itself *after* she'd saved him in the forest? She still didn't get it. Maybe he felt like he had to make things right between them. Was that why he wanted to be friends?

'I'm sorry he hurt you like that.' The words he'd spoken earlier that day popped into her mind. She'd probably misheard him, or maybe the knock on his head had done more damage than everybody realized. Who *talked* about himself like that? Was he suffering from disassociation?

One thing was certain – locking herself up in a bathroom stall wouldn't solve her inner turmoil. Julia left the restroom and hurried downstairs. She was happy to see Silke had already returned to man the checkout. This time, she would pay extra attention during her explanation.

Things weren't so bad, she told herself. All she had to do was get through the day. Tomorrow, the store would be closed, and tonight, she'd be able to evaluate today with Gaby and the rest of her friends. She could do this.

When lunch break arrived, Julia made sure she was chatting animatedly to Donna and Silke when Michael came in. Marco followed him, the two of them sitting down at a table near the coffee machine where Martin joined them after a few minutes.

"Any plans for tonight?" Silke asked Julia.

"Yes, we're going to Shamrock. Me and my school friends, that is. Oh, and my new neighbor is joining us. I asked him out yesterday."

"Way to go, you strong, independent woman. Is he hot?"

"Yeah, he is." Julia couldn't help cracking a goofy smile. Silke and Donna both started wolf-whistling and giggling. The three others at the next table looked sideways, and Julia felt Michael's eyes on her. She hoped he hadn't heard the cause of all the commotion. Although, of course, she shouldn't really care whether Michael knew of hot neighbor Thorsten's existence or not – in fact, it would be *good* if he realized she had moved on.

"I'll keep you girls posted," she cut the conversation short, leaving it to Donna and Silke to fill her in on their own plans for the weekend.

"If you feel like it, please come to our birthday barbecue on Sunday," Silke said. "Marco and I are turning eighteen tomorrow, but our parents won't be there to congratulate us reaching adulthood – they're still on vacation. So, to make up for their poor parenting skills, they said we could throw a big garden party. We have enough meat to feed an orphanage, so don't hesitate to bring some of your friends. Thorsten, for example." She nudged Julia conspiratorially.

Julia smiled. "Thanks for inviting me. I have no idea whether Thorsten will tag along, but I might bring some of my other friends, if that's okay with you."

"Totally. As long as they're not vegetarians. The more carnivores, the merrier!"

Silke and Julia swapped phone numbers, and after lunch Julia walked downstairs for the last few working hours of her day.

At about four o'clock, Martin asked her to bring up a few orders and unbox them in the stockroom. Feeling grateful she could leave the checkout behind for a while, Julia climbed the stairs to the third floor holding a large box of books. Once there, she put the box down to open the door. To her surprise, the light was already on, and her heart sped up when she saw Michael standing in the corner, reaching for a set of encyclopedias on the top shelf.

"Oh, hi," she mumbled. "I have to shelf some books here." She pointed at her box.

"And I have a customer downstairs who has never heard of Wikipedia." Michael held up the heavy tomes by way of explanation.

Julia cracked a smile. "Oh well, so much the better for Martin. He'll never get rid of those things otherwise."

He grinned back. "Who knows, he might put some in our Christmas hampers."

"Looking forward to that already. Actually, I think it's pretty neat, having an encyclopedia at home. It feels so nostalgic – you know, reminiscent of my mom's childhood, when Internet was only used by the CIA, not by puny mortals like us."

"For real? Was the Internet developed by the CIA?"

"Uhm, I don't really know. Axel knows a lot about that kind of stuff – you should ask him." Julia coughed shyly, suddenly wondering why she'd started this conversation with him. And *why* had she picked a topic she knew next to nothing about?

"I will." He walked past her without really looking away, then lingered at the door. She could see his hesitation. "So, how about playing my mom's grand piano sometime after the weekend?" His eyes bored into hers.

Julia averted her eyes and stared hard at the floor. "I don't know yet. I work almost every day, so I probably won't have time."

"Just consider the offer," he said quietly. "I'm going back downstairs."

She only dared to look up after he'd left. With a deep sigh of frustration, she dragged the box full of books to the shelf they belonged on and started to unpack them. When she was almost done, Donna showed up with three more parcels that Martin wanted unpacked and sorted. By the time they had finished the task, it was one minute to five.

"Freedom!" Donna shouted in a booming voice, raising one arm in the air doing an imitation of Braveheart. "Will I see you tomorrow at Silke's birthday bash?"

"I think so, yeah," Julia nodded. "Have a nice evening!" She went into the kitchen to get her bag from her locker. Everybody was gone, and when she got to the first floor, Martin was the only person there.

"Have Marco and Silke left already?" Julia asked, secretly wanting to know something else.

"Yeah, Donna and you were the last of the Mohicans."

"Okay." She tried not to feel empty because Michael had left without saying goodbye. "See you on Monday. Have a great weekend!"

On the bus home, she called Gaby to invite her over for dinner. "I really need to vent, and you can be my sounding board. All day I've been walking on eggshells. My nerves are shot. What have I ever done to deserve working at the same store as Mr. Dickwad?"

"I'll be there," Gaby promised. "I'm still stuffing my face with pastries at Tomaselli's with Tamara and Axel. What time are you guys having dinner?"

"Depends on my mother. Just come over whenever you're ready."

Julia hung up and stared out the window. Just as she was about to put the phone away, the thing beeped twice, signaling two incoming text messages.

'will i cu 2nite? ;) x mick'

'what time r we meeting up 2nite? cya, thorsten'

She chuckled nervously. Wow, wasn't she wildly popular all of a sudden. She stared at the winky face in Michael's message with a burning face. What the hell – he was *teasing* her with the fact she seemed to follow him wherever he went. He probably assumed she would show up at O'Malley's tonight, because she normally did on Saturday nights.

"No, you won't see me tonight, you tragically deluded megalomaniac," she muttered. "I won't be there, and I'm not gonna tell you where I *will* be." She texted Thorsten to tell him he was welcome to join her and Gaby at her place before they went to Shamrock. That way they could all take the bus together from Birkensiedlung.

'gr8! cu there :)' she got back after a few moments.

Only when she got off the bus did she realize that her invitation to Thorsten was mildly ill-timed if she wanted to sit down and talk to Gaby about how to deal with Michael as a colleague. Harping on and on about the guy who had brutally dumped her and yet somehow still had a hold on her would rightly give Thorsten the impression he shouldn't bother making a move. She wasn't sure what message she wanted to put across. Was she secretly hoping he'd hit on her, or was she just looking for a distraction?

With a frown on her face, she opened the front door. The smell of fried potatoes wafted into the hallway, making her mouth water. She popped her head around the kitchen door. "Hi, Mom! Do you mind if Gaby and Thorsten join us for dinner before we hit the town?"

"Fine with me. But *you'll* have to bike to the supermarket to get some extra desserts. If no one tells me I have to cater for a mighty host of friends, I can't stock up."

Julia grinned. "Will do."

"Oh, and be sure to drop by Sabine's on your way back. Anne is still at the neighbors', and I want her home for dinner."

Julia took a ten-euro note from her mom's purse and went outside to get her bike from the shed. Whistling cheerfully, she cycled to Eichet in the languid breeze of the summer evening. After doing the groceries, Julia decided to take the forest path back home.

The plastic bags dangling from the handlebars rustled due to the bumps in the road. Julia slowed down. In the orange evening light breaking through the canopy of the tree tops, she saw her spot up ahead. The oak tree stood still and silent against the backdrop of the sunset glow. She got off her bike and parked it against the tree.

"Hello, Mister Oak," Julia whispered. She pressed her cheek against its bark, hugging the trunk with both arms. Somehow it still felt something had changed about this place, and when she looked up, she spotted yellow leaves on the branches. That was very uncommon for this time of year. Could it be her Hugging Tree was sick? That would explain why she felt so different about this place lately – maybe something really *had* changed. After all, trees had to die some time, too.

She sighed morosely, letting go of the tree to get her bike and cycle home. Suddenly, she was unreasonably angry at the world for changing around her, without giving her the means to stop it.

"Anne? Sabine?" As she wheeled her bike through the gate of the neighbors' yard, Julia looked around. "Are you girls here?"

Sabine's father came out. "*Grüss Gott.* Are you here to pick up your sister? They're still in the woods, I think. Did they tell you they're building a tree house?"

Julia nodded. "Aren't they getting a bit too fanatic about it? It's close to dinner time."

"Well, Sabine's wearing a watch, but maybe they forgot about the time."

"I just cycled through the forest, actually, but I didn't see them anywhere. Where's that tree house of theirs?"

"I have no idea. I was only allowed to come and have a look at it after it's done, they said," Sabine's father explained.

Just then, Julia heard laughter on the wind. Anne and Sabine showed up, cycling down the road leading up to the house.

"Aren't you a bit late?" she snapped at her sister when Anne entered the front yard. "Mom's waiting for you."

Anne looked upset. "I'm sorry. I thought I'd make it before dinner time."

"Oh well, you're here now. Let's hurry up. Gaby and Thorsten are joining us for dinner too."

Anne's eyes lit up when she mentioned Thorsten's name. Julia bit back a chuckle. So she'd been right about her sister's puppy love for Sabine's brother. That's why she wanted to give the forest prince blue eyes in her story. Smiling, she put a hand on Anne's shoulder, taking her inside to sit her down at the kitchen table.

"Hello there!" Gaby bellowed when she stepped into the house five minutes after Julia and Anne had come back. "It's me!"

"I can hear that!" Julia shouted back, quickly getting up from the table and dragging Gaby into the living room area next to the kitchen. "Come talk with me for a minute," she hissed.

"Uhm, why? Aren't we eating yet?"

"Yes, we are. I just wanted to say I also invited Thorsten for dinner."

"Wow, you go, girl! I'm proud of you for being so straightforward."

"Yeah, thanks. The only problem is we can't really talk about Michael with him around."

"You have a point." Gaby plonked her bag down on the couch and cocked her head at Julia inquisitively. "So what's up, Jules? Something's bothering you, I can tell. Do you still have feelings for Michael? You can tell Agony Aunt Gaby, okay?" She put a hand on Julia's arm.

Julia shook her head. "There is no 'still'. I'm falling in love *again*." Her voice was so quiet Gaby had to bend forward to catch her words.

"What do you mean?"

"Well, I understand now that I never really got to know him in school. I never saw him for who he truly was – I invented my own stupid story about Michael, in which he was an awesome guy blowing magical glitter everywhere. But now… he's just so *different*."

Gaby gave her a pensive look. "You think he wants a second chance because you saved him in the woods?"

"Maybe."

"But does it mean he's truly changed? Or is he just feeling guilty?"

"I haven't got the faintest clue."

"Do you really *want* to give him a second chance?"

Julia scowled at the floor. "Okay, I know that's stupid."

Gaby worried her lip and shrugged. "I don't think you're being stupid. I get it, I do. Sorry I raised hell before when you mentioned Michael still intrigued you. All I want is for you to be careful, but what's stopping you if you want to shop around a bit? Arrange a few more dates with Thorsten, see if he isn't a better choice, and in the meantime, hang out with Michael at work to get to know *him* better. I still think he's a scumbag after the stories you told me about him, but hey, it's your life. I'm not going to be a meddling Molly."

Julia exhaled. "Thanks, Gab. That's a huge relief, actually. I was afraid to bring it up again because you went all *banzai* about it before."

"I get that." Gaby grinned wickedly. "I can be quite intimidating."

At that moment the doorbell rang, and Gaby shoved Julia playfully. "Guess that's option number two on your doorstep."

Julia giggled and walked over to the front door. When she swung it open, she looked straight into Thorsten's sparkling blue eyes. She swallowed. Man, he was hot. She was *crazy* for not focusing on him a bit more – he was gorgeous, interested, available, and he lived next door. If there was a God, He was now surely banging His head against the wall in frustration at her lack of eagerness.

"Hey, good to see you," she greeted him a bit nervously. "Gaby's already here; she's my best friend."

Gaby popped into the hallway and introduced herself. The three of them went into the kitchen and were soon chatting about school, vacation, and their majors in college.

"I'll be a sophomore in sociology here at Salzburg University," Thorsten told them. "I did the first year in Graz, but the transfer wasn't a problem, fortunately."

Julia froze for a few seconds when she heard the name of the city Michael would move to after summer. It was almost too good to be true – Michael was leaving Salzburg, but Thorsten had come here to take his place. It almost felt like the changing of the guard.

"Sociology sounds interesting," Gaby mumbled through a bite of potato. "I considered that, too. But I settled on psychology in the end."

"Just like Axel," Anne said casually. She was done eating and was coloring a picture of a unicorn with the tip of her tongue sticking out in concentration.

Julia cast Gaby a sideways glance and caught her friend getting a bit red. "Yeah, we just can't stay away from each other." Gaby put a hand over her heart in mock-infatuation. She gulped down a large swig of soda too quickly, almost choking on it. "By the way, what time are we leaving?"

Julia snickered. "Half past eight?" she suggested, shaking her head almost imperceptibly. How could she *ever* have missed what was going on between her cousin and her best friend? It was painfully clear, all of a sudden. She'd have time to interrogate Gaby later on.

After dinner, Julia and Gaby went upstairs to change and do their make-up, while Anne hijacked

Thorsten and lured him into the living room to sit him down and watch Robin Hood with her. "They're getting some new inspiration for their three house," Julia explained in front of her dressing table. "Thorsten is helping Sabine and Anne build one in the forest."

"Really? Wow, he's so awesome he deserves a cape with a giant, embroidered T. I mean, look at how he's being the sweet-big-brother type around Anne." Gaby winked at her.

"Yeah, yeah. Just knock it off, all right? You sound like a Thorsten commercial. I'm not blind, you know. I can see the guy next door is a total catch."

"Well, if *you* don't catch him, I just might swoop in and snatch him instead."

"No, you won't. You..." Julia stopped mid-sentence. Gaby was obviously interested in Axel, but of course she wasn't supposed to have picked up on that.

Gaby blinked at her like a deer trapped in headlights. "I... what?"

Julia put away her mascara. "Nothing. Forget it."

Her friend put her hands on her sides and cocked her head. "Uh-uh, not so fast. What were you going to say?"

"Just that Thorsten isn't really your type," Julia mumbled. "I hope."

"Hah! You think all that heavy mascara is obstructing my view, sister? Even a blind bat can see he's gorgeous," Gaby scoffed, sashaying toward the long mirror in the corner. Julia let out a sigh. She would have to wait until Gaby brought up the topic of Axel herself.

That evening, Julia enthused about her new job to her friends. She'd quickly skipped over the part where Michael turned out to be her co-worker – instead, she focused on the perks of the job and her nice colleagues. "I was invited to one of the girls' birthday party, actually," she smiled. "Everybody's being cool and so friendly."

"If only we felt the same vibe at the riding school," Gaby grumbled. "Me and Tamara are ready to *kill* those vapid airheads, forever rhapsodizing over horses and ponies and everything having to do with them."

Axel started laughing. "Well, don't you girls rave about horses?"

"Uhm, *no*."

"But you like all that equestrian stuff, right?"

Gaby let out a long-suffering sigh. "There is a difference, Axe Effect, a clear distinction between them and me. You can like horse-back riding as an outdoor activity, because that's cool, or you can live inside a sugar-spun dream where horses are your biggest friends, you communicate with them telepathically, you still have *My Little Pony* posters in your bedroom, and you secretly dream of a knight on a white charger galloping into your life."

Florian elbowed his friend in the ribs. "Forget about renting that white horse, man," he grinned. "She thinks it's lame."

In the silence that followed, both Gaby and Axel turned beet-red.

"*Who* wants another drink?" Tamara chirped in an effort to diffuse the palpable tension.

"Yeah, me," Thorsten replied, happily oblivious to the clanger Florian had just dropped. He got up from his chair. "Wait, I'll help you. Would you like another one?" he asked Julia.

"Yeah, sure! I'd like a small wheat beer," she quickly replied.

Once Thorsten and Tamara were out of hearing range, Florian started snickering and poked Julia mischievously. "Well, Julius Caesar, I think we have a suitable candidate. Your boy next door is *cute* and he's totally into you. Well done!"

"Done what? I haven't done anything yet."

"Well, you asked him out, didn't you?"

"Yeah, that's true." Julia slung an arm around Gaby's shoulders. "Gaby told me to take action. She's got a keen eye for candidates. We had dinner at my place too, before coming here."

Axel, Florian and Moritz babbled on as Julia felt Gaby's shoulders slowly relax a bit. She couldn't *believe* how much of a bumbling blabbermouth Florian was sometimes. Had Axel fessed up to Florian himself about liking Gaby, or had his best friend just taken a lucky guess? Either way, she hoped things wouldn't be nipped in the bud now.

Fortunately, everybody thought better of mentioning Gaby and Axel together for the rest of the evening. Axel was mostly talking to the other guys and Gaby was more or less hiding behind her sister and Julia. It was only when the pub was about to close and they were all getting up to get home that Axel approached Gaby again. He purposefully strode over to her and put a hand on her shoulder. "Shall I give you a ride home?" he asked with a half-smile.

Gaby's eyes widened. "I, uhm… I came here by bus, so…"

"I came here by scooter."

"But… I promised Tamara we'd go home together."

"Actually, I'm not going home yet," Tamara piped up next to her. "I just texted Anna and Gretchen and we're going to that new club together. I haven't seen them for a while."

Gaby gave Tamara a look that clearly spelled a desire to strangle her on the spot. "Oh. Right. Okay." She turned around to face Axel again and bit her lip nervously. "Well… okay then."

Axel didn't say anything. He just started grinning more widely and ran off to fetch his scooter.

Julia had listened in on the entire conversation with a sly smile. "Sooo," she drew out. "Will I see you tomorrow at Silke's party?"

Gaby nodded, her face still flustered. "Yes, I'll be at your place at five. So, you're going home with Thorsten?"

Now it was Julia's turn to look flustered. "I guess so. We're taking the same bus."

Just then, Axel arrived and parked his scooter on the sidewalk next to the pub. He looked at Gaby expectantly. "You ready?"

"Ready Freddy."

Julia watched Gaby getting on the back of Axel's scooter, her arms awkwardly around his waist as if she was afraid he'd break in two. She said goodbye to the others, then set off down the road toward the bus stop flanked by Thorsten.

"I had a really good time tonight," he said. "It was cool of you to invite me."

"You're welcome. I know it's hard to make new friends in the middle of summer. You'll have friends in no time once college starts in October, though."

"Oh, I don't know. I doubt I'd meet people as nice as you," her neighbor softly replied.

Julia stared at her sneakers. "Yeah, thanks." She had no idea if his 'you' was meant to be singular or plural, and she wasn't about to ask.

They sat next to each other on the bus sharing Julia's earbuds to listen to her MP3 player together.

Every now and then, Julia pointed out a landmark through the window or Thorsten asked her something about the music on her player, but apart from that, they were quiet. They kept quiet on the walk home from the bus stop to their street, too.

The silence became too pregnant for Julia's taste when they came to a stop in front of her gate and Thorsten ran a warm hand down her upper arm. She gulped when he came closer, leaning into her.

"Would you be upset if I kissed you now?" he whispered.

Julia looked up shyly. "N-no, of course not. Not upset. Just... I don't know if you should. It wouldn't be fair."

He looked at her earnestly. "You don't like me that way?"

She blushed. "I do. But something happened between me and a guy I'd had a crush on for ages, a while ago, and I haven't gotten over it yet. I'm not over *him* yet, either. It's got nothing to do with you."

Thorsten smiled gently, caressing her cheek. "Okay, duly noted. I understand. You should take your time. I can be a friendly friend too, okay?"

Julia grinned. "Thanks," she said timidly. "And sorry for giving off such mixed signals."

"No worries." He pressed a kiss to her cheek. "As long as you do, there's hope, right?"

He turned around and crossed the street. Julia let out the breath she'd been holding. As Thorsten's door fell shut, she pushed open the gate and went inside.

What a night.

6.

"**I** want juicy details," Gaby demanded when she stepped into the yard on Sunday afternoon, her eyes sparkling with excitement. Julia had just come back from a visit to her gran and was curled up on the bench next to the front door, engrossed in a *Sailor Moon* manga.

She unhurriedly put away her book as Gaby took a seat next to her. "You do, huh? Well, me too. You. My very own cousin. Last night. Spill."

Her best friend abruptly shut her mouth, staring at a pebble near her right foot like it had suddenly turned into the most fascinating object in all of Salzburg. "What do you mean?" she said shiftily. "There's nothing to tell. He just dropped me off at home on his scooter. I mean, he lives in the same neighborhood. Come on, you don't think something's going on?" She gingerly looked up, giving Julia an almost pleading look.

"Hmm."

"So what about you and Thorsten?"

Julia cleared her throat. "What do you mean? There's nothing to tell. He just dropped me off at home when we walked here from the bus stop. I mean, he lives on the same street."

Gaby moaned in frustration. "Oh, come on, don't be like that."

"Don't be like *what*?"

"Like nothing happened! Don't tell me he didn't even try." Gaby started to smile cheekily when Julia couldn't help blushing. "Hah! I knew it! So tell me."

"He asked me if... if it would upset me if he kissed me. And I confessed to him that I'm not over Michael yet and that it wouldn't feel right."

"Okay. That's pretty brave of you. But kind of a pity, too." Gaby sighed.

"Well, it's not like everything between us is ruined now or anything. He said he'd had a great night." Julia still remembered the look in Thorsten's eyes – not defeated, but filled with patience and a quiet hope.

"Sounds like not all hope is gone just yet," Gaby concluded. "So what time is this Silke expecting us?"

Julia had to stop herself from mentioning Axel again – she'd only rattle her friend by doing that. "From six o'clock onward. Shall we catch the twenty-to-six bus?"

When Julia and Gaby arrived at the gate of Silke and Marco's large country house, the entire grounds already smelled like barbecue. Julia pushed open the gate leading to the vast lawn, hesitantly stepping inside. She didn't know any of the guests who were sitting on the lawn, and was happy to discover Donna standing by the patio door sipping from a beer can. Gaby trailed behind Julia and looked around her in awe. "Wow, they have such a neat yard! Silke's mom must be an avid gardener to keep it all weed-free like this."

Just then, Silke caught up with them on the path. She was holding a bowl of potato salad in one hand and shook Julia's hand with the other. "Hey, how nice of you to come! Why don't you follow me to the patio, I'll show you the drinks and snacks table." She looked at Gaby curiously. "Hi, I'm Silke. And you're not Thorsten."

Gaby started laughing. "No, I'm sorry. Did Jules promise to bring him instead?"

Chatting, they cruched up the gravel path to the patio where the party was in full swing. A crowd had gathered around the barbecue. Silke took the present Julia brought for her with a smile and put it on the gift table.

Julia noticed the patio doors opened up into a large living room with a beautiful, white grand piano in the corner. "You play?" she asked Silke, pointing at the instrument.

"No, Marco and my dad do. If you want to play something, don't be shy!"

"Oh, cool! You don't have to tell me twice." Of course, she could have dropped by Michael's place to play *his* grand piano anytime, but that was nothing short of a bad idea. Besides, playing some songs for a group of people she hardly knew and didn't care that much about was decidedly less of a hurdle.

Julia stepped inside, sat down on the piano bench and started to play one of Enya's songs.

"Awesome," Gaby mumbled, tiptoeing up to her from behind. She always stood in holy awe of Julia's piano performances, having failed to ever play more than three notes on her recorder before chucking it out the window.

Julia's piano music floated outside and soon lured more people onto the patio. When she played the last few notes of *Watermark*, Donna started to applaud fervently and Marco smiled at Julia encouragingly. "Go on, play another one," he said. "You're really good."

Julia hesitated for a second, then started to play the song she'd written for Michael. She didn't look up at her audience again, but the silence that pervaded the patio was telling her she'd captivated her listeners. Her fingers caressed the keys, her heart beating a steady rhythm. She lost herself in the music. Once, she had poured all of her heart into writing this song, her music expressing something she'd never be able to find words for.

Suddenly, she heard Gaby gasp behind her. Absently, Julia looked up to scan the crowd for the reason of her friend's concern. Her heart stopped when she looked straight into two familiar green eyes, her hands almost tripping on the keys as she reached the chorus of her song. What was *he* doing here?

Oh, right. This was Marco's birthday party too – and he had probably invited Michael. She hadn't even thought of that. Julia quickly looked back down at the keyboard, trying to continue her recital unperturbedly, but she was fully aware of his eyes on her. In fact, she *wanted* his gaze on her. She wanted him to absorb every note she was playing. And suddenly, she found herself wishing he could somehow hear that this music had once been meant for him.

Only when the song was over did Julia risk looking up again. A stab of disappointment went through her – Michael had disappeared from the audience around the piano, who were clapping excitedly.

"Thank you," Julia said shyly, quickly getting up.

Graby grabbed her hand and unexpectedly dragged her outside even before the applause was over. "Did you *see* that?" she whispered urgently, as though she was about to tell Julia a rhino had stumbled into the fountain.

"Did I see *what*?"

"*Michael*. The way he looked at you."

Julia blinked in confusion. "What do you mean? Did he look tortured, maybe? He didn't even bother listening to the entire song."

Gaby shook her head. "I don't think he could. He... Jules, he was *staring* at you, so intensely. So focused on what you were playing. And then... look, I know this sounds ridiculous, but I swear to you, he started to cry.

He was *crying*, and that's why he walked away. He was touched to the core."

Julia gaped mutely at her friend for a second. "He *wasn't*."

"He was." Gaby opened a beer can and gulped down a few generous swigs. Julia picked up a can of beer herself, mindlessly turning it around in her hands.

"I can't believe I'm saying this, but I think you should give him another chance," Gaby continued. "That look on his face, in his eyes. There was so much emotion. Just… I don't know."

Julia bit her lip. "So where is he now?"

"No idea. He'll be back. You want to talk to him?"

"I don't know." Julia gulped down half her can of beer before anxiously looking around. Silke and Donna were just walking up to them.

"You were so cool!" Donna beamed at Julia. "Who wrote the second song?"

"I did."

"No way! Really? You should totally record that some time. I'd buy it on iTunes any day."

Silke vehemently nodded in agreement. "I'm going to make you a regular at all my parties. The audience loved your little show."

The four girls sat down on the plastic lounge chairs around the fountain. Michael was nowhere to be seen.

"What is that pendant you're wearing?" Gaby asked curiously, pointing at a small, multi-colored plastic ball dangling from the chain around Silke's neck. "Are there beads inside that ball?"

"No, they're dried rowan berries. The rowan tree is my Celtic protection tree. Everybody has a tree assigned to their date of birth, according to the Druids' thirteen-month system."

"That's one too many," Donna observed dryly.

Silke chuckled. "They use a lunar calendar, so thirteen months is just enough. That's why their astrology is different, too."

Julia's interest was piqued. "Which tree belongs to me? My birthday is at the beginning of March."

"The ash tree," Silke replied. "The sorceress tree. You are a creative dreamer with a tendency to run from the real world. And you communicate with nature."

Gaby giggled. "Those Druids have Julia down to a tee. What about me? Beginning of April?"

"The alder tree. The trailblazer, the pioneer. You don't care about other people's opinion and go your own way, even if you always surround yourself with a lot of friends."

"That's crazy," Gaby mumbled. "And eerie. I really am like that. Do you have some books I can borrow? You've made me a Druid fan."

Julia remembered Michael's birthday. "Which tree belongs to the third of July?" she blurted out without thinking. Gaby elbowed her in the ribs.

"Oh, that is a really nice one," Silke answered with a smile. "It's actually the tree that the Druids were named after – the oak tree."

Suddenly, Julia had a flashback to Michael stretched out under the oak tree in the woods, his head lying in a pool of blood. The look in his eyes when he woke up and recognized her. It made her shiver. She couldn't quite put her finger on why this was strange, but it was. It was bizarre.

"I don't see the connection between oaks and Druids," Donna said with a frown.

"The Celtic name for *oak* is *duir*. That's the word their name derives from. As it so happens, the word also means *door*, as they believed the oak was a doorway between this world and another reality. Druids would meditate under oak trees to communicate with supernatural beings," Silke chattered on, clearly on her hobby horse. "The oak is a symbol for longevity and represents the power of lightning."

Julia stared at Silke in surprise. "Lightning?" Once again, she couldn't help thinking of the thunderstorm that had raged when she'd found Michael.

"Yes. Oak trees are often struck by lightning. The oak binds the life-giving powers of the lightning bolt and the nurturing powers of the earth, opening a temporary vortex or gateway to the other side on Midsummer's Day."

"Hey, dinner's ready, High Priestess!" Marco grinned as he approached their little gathering, shoving his sister playfully. "I can hear where this conversation is going. You want me to fetch your hooded cloak and staff?"

Silke thumped him on the shoulder. "You just don't get it."

Julia didn't really get it, either, but she felt like she was onto something. All the things Silke had mentioned in correlation with Michael's horoscope... that couldn't be coincidence. As soon as she got home tonight she'd fire up her computer and Google anything and everything about the Celtic belief system and the alleged powers of the oak.

A new batch of hamburgers and buns was put on the table. "Could you make me one with lots of ketchup?" Julia asked Gaby. "I really need to use the toilet. I'll be right back."

She plunged inside, stalking past the piano into the hallway, where she fortunately found the door to the bathroom instantly. After she was done, she took out her cell phone and wrote herself a memo about what Silke had told them before she forgot important details. Tonight, the hunt for more info was on.

Lost in thought, Julia walked into the kitchen to wash her hands, but stopped dead when she saw Michael sitting at the kitchen table. His back was toward her, but he turned around when she stepped backward.

"Hey," he said softly. Julia stood glued to the spot as he stood up and closed in on her.

"Hi," she replied when she remembered how to use her voice again.

He looked so normal and relaxed. Surely this guy who was always so comfortable with himself couldn't have cried over her song? Gaby must have been seeing things.

"You played so beautifully," he said at that instant, as if he'd read her mind. "What was that song?"

"It was mine."

He nodded, a smile spreading across his handsome face. "I could hear that."

All of a sudden, something inside of her snapped. He was doing it *again* – talking to her as though he'd known her for years. Using that confidential tone of voice that suggested they had a whole history together. But they didn't, and it was *his* fault.

"I wrote it for you. Could you hear that too?" she said, viciously sneering. "I bet you're wondering how and why. How I could have been so mind-numbingly *stupid* as to write a song for you, and why I fell in love with a guy like you who crushes my heart, tramples the pieces and forgets about me the very first chance he gets?"

A silence descended in the room. Michael's face had turned pale. "Julia," he mumbled, shock evident in his eyes.

She shook her head, her hands trembling. "*Stop* it," she snarled. "Stop confusing me like this. Stop giving me all this attention you didn't think I deserved before. Why are you doing this? *Why?*"

Her breath hitched when he took another step forward, taking her in his arms without saying anything. His body felt warm and his arms were protective around her, and strangely enough all her anger subsided instantly. Her heart slowed down even despite him being so close. He exuded a calmness she had never felt from him before – in fact, she'd never felt this kind of influence from *anyone* before.

This was how she had always imagined being in his arms, but she'd never felt it. She'd felt the thrill of passion between them a few weeks ago. But now, she felt *cherished* in his arms.

"Don't be silly," she stuttered despite herself. "Let go of me, Michael. This is embarrassing." Her cheeks flushed red. His arms slipped off her and he took a step backward, a sad look crossing his face.

"I can't let go of you," he softly said. "Please, don't ask me that."

Before Julia could even respond to his puzzling remark, he turned around and dashed off into the yard. Sheepishly, she stared at his retreating figure. What in God's name was wrong with him? As a matter of fact, what was wrong with *her*? The way she'd crawled into his embrace as if Michael had comforted her like that many times before – and then, her sudden snap at him, telling him to let go of her. Julia could literally kick herself. She was turning into the Queen of Mixed Signals – first in dealing with Thorsten and now with Michael. And as icing on the big Cake of Embarrassment, she'd also blurted out that she'd written her song for *him*. Great – just great.

With an angry sigh, she whipped around and stalked outside, where Gaby was waiting for her with a big question mark on her face.

"Where the hell have you been, woman? I was about to put out an Amber Alert for you. Here you go – your cold hamburger." She shoved a plate into Julia's hands.

"Yeah, I know. Sorry about that. I bumped into Michael in the kitchen. We sort of had a fight, and then he tried to kiss and make up, also sort of."

"Oh? What were you guys fighting about?"

"Nothing in particular. I don't want to talk about it." Julia stole a glance at the other side of the lawn, where Marco and Michael were chatting to another guy she didn't know. "I went and told him I wrote that song for him," she muttered despite herself.

Gaby looked at her thoughtfully. "You know what's weird? To me it looked like he already knew that. You know, because of the way he looked at you when you were playing it. Maybe that's why he was crying – because he was touched by the way you felt about him… or still feel. I don't know."

Julia shook her head. "You're not making sense. He *couldn't* have known that. You're the only person who knows I wrote it for him."

Gaby glared at her. "I *am* making sense. Something very strange is going on with Michael. I can feel it. And yes, I know – you already tried telling me that a few days ago and I didn't want to listen to it, but I just couldn't believe it. Sorry."

"No problem. I understand."

"And by the way, did you also notice Michael's Celtic horoscope featuring a lot of elements related to his accident?" Gaby continued in a hushed tone. "You know, the lightning, the oak tree…"

"I did, and I was planning on investigating tonight. Although I don't know if I should, after that whole drama show in the kitchen."

"Of course you should. You're curious, just admit it. Shall I help you?"

"Yeah, I'd like that." Julia smiled at her friend. "Thanks."

After dinner, they quickly left the party to go to Florian's. Julia didn't want to spend one minute more than necessary around Michael – she'd have to dodge him at work tomorrow too, after all.

"I'll pay for everything in advance," Tamara said. Everybody was huddled around Florian's computer to fill out the details for their plane tickets. With a broad grin, she flashed her creditcard. "Please pay me back ASAP."

"What kind of rooms are we booking in London?" Florian asked. "Shall we just book one of those eight-bedded dorms?"

"You can't be serious," Gaby said in mock disdain. "And us having to listen to your snoring all night?"

"Yeah, or to you sleep-talking in your wet dreams," Tamara chimed in. "Oh yeah, Moritz, like that, don't stop…"

The girls started to giggle and Florian raised his chin defiantly. "Fine. Have it your way. You chicks go bunk up, the three of you. Axel and I will stick together."

"Where are Moritz and his band staying?" Axel wanted to know.

"Oh, somewhere more luxurious. Definitely outside our poor man's budget."

Florian got up and opened the double doors leading to the roof terrace, while Tamara finished up their booking and printed the boarding cards. "Are you guys staying around for a drink?" he asked.

"Sure," Axel replied. He got up and shot a quick glance at Gaby, whom he hadn't directly spoken to since her and Julia's arrival. "Can I get you something, Miss Gloom?"

Gaby looked up, startled. "Uhm, yes… I'd like a beer, please. Thanks."

Julia snickered. The fact alone that Gaby *didn't* get her panties in a strop about Axel using that nickname was evidence enough that something was going on between the two of them. "Why don't you get me one too, while you're at it," she shouted after her cousin.

Meanwhile, Gaby had installed herself at the computer. She opened Google and typed 'druids oaks' into the search bar. When Julia sat down on the armrest and looked over her shoulder, her friend had just clicked a link titled 'The Magical Tree'.

"Wow," Gaby breathed. "You see that? Oak trees can grow to be over two thousand years old! And they really attract lightning somehow. Look here – the British mythological Green Man is a forest god with a face consisting of oak leaves." She pointed at the image on the screen.

"Come outside, you nerds," Axel told them as he strolled over with their drinks. "All this staring at computer screens is gonna ruin your eyesight."

"That's rich, coming from you," Gaby shot back, getting up and taking the glass of beer Axel handed to her. "You practically *live* at your computer."

She slowly turned red when Axel slung an arm around her shoulders and replied: "Still, no reason to follow my bad example. Come on, let's go outside. I'll drag you away from this infernal device and save you."

Julia caught the look in Gaby's eyes and couldn't help but grin at her flushed face. She started when her phone vibrated in her pocket. One look on the display showed her that at least it wasn't Michael – it was her mother.

"Hey, Mom. What's up?"

"Hello, darling. What time will you be home?"

"Around nine, I guess. Why?" Somehow, her mother sounded anxious.

"Oh, it's nothing. Your father just called, and Anne was in the room with me when we got into an argument over the phone. She went outside. I think she took off to the woods, because her bike is gone."

"I'll be home shortly. Don't worry." Julia hung up, heaving a sigh. Anne didn't handle conflict very well, and it was even worse if that conflict was between their mom and their ever-absent father. She was doubtlessly upset, so she'd fled into the woods to cool off. In that respect, Anne was just like her. Mom was probably feeling really guilty right now.

"I'm leaving in a bit," she announced to her friends on the terrace. "I have to go help my mom."

"Shall I join you?" Gaby asked.

"Yeah, cool." Julia's interest was piqued by the website Gaby had discovered. She wanted to explore it some more back at her place. "Are you sleeping over?"

"Good idea! It's been a while since we had a pajama party."

In the light of the sun slowly sinking toward the horizon, Julia walked to the edge of the roof terrace and looked down at the river Salzach meandering past the house. Behind her, she heard Tamara and Florian laughing out loud and Axel animatedly telling one of his jokes. She tried to imagine Michael amidst her circle of friends, then substituted him with Thorsten. Of course, it was a pointless exercise – she knew full well Thorsten would fit in perfectly here. And yet, she somehow couldn't bring herself to make that choice just yet.

Gaby joined her at the railing. "Are we going?" she asked.

"Yeah, let's. I want to be home before dark."

"Tamara just offered to drop us off by car, so we can go to my place first and I can pack a bag of clothes for my shift at the riding school tomorrow. You know, pants I won't mind getting stained with horseshit."

"Poor you. Oh well, I wonder what's worse working with – horse manure or Michael." Julia rolled her eyes. "Speaking of which, let's see what else we can find out about the old Celts and their tree horoscopes tonight."

Gaby giggled. "Most likely, we'll discover all people with oaks in their horoscopes are arrogant assholes."

Fifteen minutes later, Tamara pulled up in front of Julia's house. When Julia got out of the car, she saw her mom standing at the gate, peering into the street in both directions.

Ms. Gunther's face lit up when she saw her eldest daughter. "Hey, sweetheart. I'm glad you're home early. Anne still isn't back, and she's not at Sabine's either."

The troubled undertone in her mother's voice wasn't lost on Julia. She exchanged a glance with Gaby. "We'll go look for her in the woods," her friend said decidedly. "Come on, let's go by bike."

They walked to the shed and got the two bicycles parked there. Julia couldn't wipe the frown off her face when she cycled down the street next to Gaby on their way to the forest edge. "I am *so* going to give Anne a talking-to," she said grimly. "She can't do this. She can't just take off and stay out for hours on end and get

Mom worried sick. My mother already feels like she's a lousy parent as it is, because she can't get my dad to show his face around here more often. She really doesn't need this on top of everything else."

When they got to the edge of the woods, the girls got off their bikes. Julia hesitantly looked at the forest path running between the trees. It wouldn't be long before the woods got completely dark. Would Anne really venture out here all by herself? She couldn't imagine it; her sister was kind of a scaredy-cat.

"Shall we call out to her?" Gaby suggested, looking a little lost.

Julia nodded. "Anne!" she shouted at the top of her lungs. "Where are you?"

"Anne!" Gaby yelled in the other direction. "Come home!"

To Julia's great relief, it didn't take more than a minute for a tiny, human figure riding a bike to appear at the bend in the road. She nudged Gaby. "There she is."

Once Anne came to a stop in front of them, Julia flung her arms around her little sister. Suddenly, she couldn't be angry anymore. All she felt was immense gratitude for Anne being there. "What happened?" she asked gently, stroking Anne's soft hair.

"They were fighting again," Anne replied in a small voice. "I didn't want to listen to it."

"Mom's sad. You shouldn't have stayed out this long."

"I know. I'm sorry. I just didn't know what to do."

"Well, we're glad you're here," Gaby said kindly, putting a hand on the little girl's shoulder.

They all got back on their bikes. "So where were you?" Julia asked curiously.

Anne remained silent for a moment. "I'm not telling," she replied resolutely, cycling away ahead of

Julia and Gaby. Julia stared at Anne's back, blinking her eyes in astonishment. That was an odd reaction – Anne could have just told her 'everywhere and nowhere' if she wanted to be vague, but she hadn't. Maybe she had a special place in the forest she didn't want anyone to know about, just like her.

Julia sighed. Her own 'special place' had lost most of its luster – Michael's accident had happened near the oak, and moreover, her hugging tree looked moribund as of late. It was probably sick, or maybe it had truly been hit by lightning in the storm, like in the Druid myth. Her thoughts turned to Silke's stories and the information Gaby had found online. It was time to do some research once they got home.

Her mother pulled Anne inside with a mixture of relief, indignation and coddling. Gaby and Julia grabbed some potato chips and soda from the pantry and disappeared upstairs to put the spare mattress in Julia's room and start up the laptop.

"Google Detectives at the ready," Gaby declared, double-clicking the Firefox icon. It didn't take her long to get back to the site they'd checked out earlier. They continued reading, captivated by the many stories the website featured. There was info about the oldest oak trees in the world, the meaning of the oak in different cultures, as well as a long paragraph about the Druids and their meditation techniques. Julia's eyes widened when she got to some familiar info. "Hey, look. This is what Silke told us." She pointed at the screen and read out loud: "The oak connects the cosmic fire of lightning with the powers of the earth. In addition, the power of this tree opens a doorway tapping into the supernatural powers of summer on Midsummer's Day."

"Midsummer," Gaby mumbled, scrolling down. "Which is – let me look for it. Oh, here it says."

Julia gaped at the screen. She couldn't utter a single word. Incredulously, she stared at the table of Celtic holidays on the screen. Midsummer was on the twenty-first of June.

The day of Michael's accident.

7.

"It's almost as if he brought something *back* with him when he regained consciousness." Julia was sitting on the bed, munching on some chips.

"Something?" Gaby prompted.

Julia stalled. She'd sound like a lunatic, but she just had to get this off her chest. "Yes. Something otherworldly. A strange kind of energy. It feels like there's some sort of supernatural force changing him from the inside. Maybe that's why he survived the accident."

Gaby looked at her pensively. "So that whole Celtic saga about the oak and the force of lightning could actually be true?"

"I have no idea." Julia stared at the screen of her laptop, which was now switched off. "I know Druids were held in high esteem in earlier times, so they can't have been completely crazy. But it sure *sounds* crazy, I'll give you that."

"Crazy with a capital C," Gaby agreed. "Something peculiar is going on with Michael, though. Even I can see that."

Julia let out a deep breath. "The stupid thing is I want him to notice me, while at the same time I can't *stand* the fact that he's sweet-talking to me, pretending we're best buddies as if nothing happened. I mean, that doesn't make sense. He hasn't even apologized." She had a flashback to their strange conversation in the bookstore. What was it Michael had said to her? 'I'm sorry he hurt you like that.' Had he been talking about his former jerk-persona? She couldn't figure him out.

That night, Julia dreamed about the bookstore. Michael kept popping up wherever she went despite her attempts to avoid him, and Thorsten was there too, wanting to buy an old encyclopedia at any cost. When the alarm clock woke her up, she felt far from rested. It was like she'd already been at work all night long.

Still half-asleep, she dragged herself to the bathroom for a quick shower and padded back to her room to wake up Gaby.

The door to Anne's room was ajar, and when she looked inside, Julia saw Anne sitting at her desk writing something in her diary. She pushed the door open to come inside and give her sister a quick hug.

Anne's head jerked up and she quickly snapped her diary shut. "Can't you knock?" she said sharply.

"Excuse me?" Julia gaped at her sister. "Why the formality all of a sudden? Should I request an audience next time?"

Anne pulled the diary toward her and clutched it to her chest as if it contained a pile of hundred-euro notes. "Sorry," she mumbled. "You just startled me. I was busy writing."

"Ooh, that sounds nice! Are you going to write a story of your own?"

Anne shrugged. "Maybe. But you're only allowed to see when it's done."

Julia chuckled. "Yeah, yeah, I know the drill. Just like your tree house, right? You're testing my patience, sweet pea."

Anne got a peculiar look in her eyes. "Yes, just like that. Sorry." She opened her desk drawer and shoved the diary inside. "Are we having breakfast yet?"

"Hmm," Julia muttered. Anne was behaving oddly as of late – or maybe it was just her having difficulty to adapt. Her little sister was growing up fast and was starting to develop a strong will of her own. She'd probably get even more pigheaded once she hit puberty.

Gaby was awake when Julia entered the bedroom. "Hey," she said. "Did you get any sleep? You were tossing and turning all night."

"Yeah, I slept all right. I did dream a lot, though."

"You said Michael's name a few times."

"Oh." Julia pulled a face. "Yeah, that sounds about right. He's such a stalker he won't even leave me alone at night."

Gaby started to snicker. "And you think that's bad?" She winked exaggeratedly.

"Of course I think that's bad! I want to know what's up with him before I can rejoice in the fact he's visiting me in my dreams."

When they got downstairs and walked into the kitchen, Julia's mother was just putting a plate of toast and a big bowl of scrambled eggs on the table. "Mom, you're amazing," Julia said gratefully. "We're famished."

Gaby and Julia started wolfing down their breakfast. Anne sat tucked into the corner of the kitchen bench seat reading an old Harry Potter paperback while munching on a banana.

"Mommy's taking me to the movies after breakfast," she announced happily. "She's working an afternoon shift."

Julia shot an inquisitive look at her mom, who pulled a 'gotta-make-amends' face. Anne was probably still upset because of yesterday's fight. Maybe she'd been writing about that in her diary this morning.

After breakfast, the two girls walked to the bus stop. They rode the same bus on the first part of the trip, but after a few stops Gaby had to change to get to the riding school. "Keep me up-to-date about developments on the work floor, okay?" She grinned mischievously. "I wonder how Michael is gonna behave toward you today."

Julia rolled her eyes. "I will. Have fun mucking out the stables."

Her stomach started to do strange flip-flops when the bus neared the Old Town. Julia got off and turned her hesitant steps to the bookstore.

On the Höllrigl doorstep, Donna, Silke and Marco were already waiting for the store to open. No sign of Michael. Julia let out a relieved sigh. She secretly hoped he wouldn't show up today. Maybe he was sick, or maybe he'd even decided to quit.

"Hey there," Julia greeted her colleagues. "Hasn't Martin opened shop yet?"

Silke shook her head. "He just called Marco to let us know he's running late. Oh well – it's not like people are breaking down the door to buy books early Monday morning, anyway."

After ten minutes, both Martin and Michael rounded the corner into the street. Julia groaned inwardly. So he *was* working today, after all.

"I'm so sorry," Martin panted. "I'm not setting a very good example here. Good to see at least *you* all are on time like you're supposed to be."

Marco coughed loudly and jerked a mock-inconspicuous thumb at Michael.

"A few aside," Martin added with a grin. He unlocked the door and everybody stepped inside one by one.

It didn't take long for Martin to give them each a task for the morning. Julia was asked to hit the stockroom with a list of titles her boss wanted to put in the bargain bin this week. It was a chore she could do alone, for which she was thankful. It looked like she'd have a quiet morning.

Humming a happy tune, Julia padded up and down the aisles, checking the shelves for the titles Martin wanted her to select. The list featured quite a few poetry collections that were to be sold at fifty percent off, so that was good news for her – she'd put some aside so she could buy them before the regular Höllrigl customers had a chance to swoop in.

Julia was just busy sorting a pile of novels when she heard a soft knock on the door. When the door swung open, Michael was standing on the threshold smiling at her. "Martin wanted to know if you need any help," he said.

She quickly shook her head. "No, I'm fine," she replied curtly.

Unperturbed, he entered the stockroom. "Well, it's sort of slow downstairs at the moment. Why don't I lend you a hand? If I read out the titles from the list, you can look them up and take them from the shelves. It'll be much quicker."

With a suppressed growl Julia scrambled to her feet. So much for a quiet morning – now she'd constantly fret over the fact he was in the same room, hoping he wouldn't bring up their awkward encounter at the party. They should have called this Mentally Taxing Monday.

Michael sat down on the stool next to the door, picking up the list from the floor in the process. "Herman Hesse, *The Song of Life*," he read out loud. Julia quickly made her way to the H section and looked up the title Michael had given her. He read out several others and she looked those up as well, without exchanging a single word with him or even looking in his direction. When she finally turned around because he'd been quiet for a while, it turned out he put the list down and was sorting through the pile of books on the floor that she'd put aside to buy herself.

"They're mine," she snapped involuntarily, as if he was trying to steal them from her. Michael Kolbe reading poetry for fun? Not very likely.

"Rainer Maria Rilke," he said, glancing in fascination at the book in his hand. "I don't know him." He handed her the poetry collection. "Here, why don't you pick one of his poems to read to me. I bet you're good at that."

Julia raised an eyebrow. "I thought you came here to help me so we'd work faster."

He raised a lopsided smile and her heart skipped a beat. "Oh, come on, live a little. A short break won't hurt."

She huffed grouchily and sat down on the floor next to the stool Michael was sitting on. Flipping through the pages, she picked a random poem and ended up reading out the twenty-fifth Sonnet to Orpheus.

"You whom I loved like an unnamed flower,
plucked too soon, I will tell them of you as I
seek your shifting image and again remember,
beautiful companion of the irrepressible cry," she read with a voice that was trailing off more with every stanza she read.

Julia felt the heat rise to her cheeks. Somehow, this poem sounded like it was about *them. She* had loved him like an unnamed flower because she'd had no idea who he had been. *She* was seeking his shifting image, trying to hold on to a memory of a romantic and mysterious guy that wasn't even real. And of course, he had almost been plucked too soon – plus the description 'beautiful companion of the irrepressible cry' seemed to fit the bill perfectly when it came to him. What twist of fate had made her read this to him out of *all* the sonnets in the damn book?

And then, he put a hand on her shoulder. She looked up like a deer trapped in headlights, her face flaming when his eyes bored into hers, gauging her thoughts.

"What is that poem about?" he said in a dark voice.

Oh, no. Michael was onto her. He could sense this poem reminded her of him. He had to know he was making her nervous, and she was no longer sure she'd be able to resist his charms.

"I… I don't know," she stammered. "I'm not some kind of Rilke expert."

He shook his head. "I mean, what this poem means to *you*?" he mumbled.

Julia swallowed when he moved closer to her and the energy in the room shifted. Staying here was way too dangerous – she had to get out right this instant.

"I, uhm, I'm not sure," Julia hedged, closing the book abruptly. "Uhm, sorry. I have to go get a drink. My throat is dry."

She hastily got up, pelting out of the door without waiting for a reply. With a trip-hammering heart, she crossed the landing and barreled into the break room without breaking stride. Michael's footsteps echoed behind her. Panting for breath, she closed the door and leaned against the kitchen counter in the right corner, her hands trembling.

But then, the door opened again. Julia shrunk away from Michael stepping into the room, coming straight at her.

"Go away," she muttered.

He came to a halt in front of her, his eyes asking her something she didn't know the answer to. Wordlessly, he raised a hand and gently traced her upper arm.

"I'm serious," Julia said hoarsely. "Leave me alone."

He came even closer and leaned into her, his body pushing her up against the counter top. Her breathing sped up when Michael used his other hand to caress her back, resting his fingers just above her tailbone.

"I can't," he replied, a desperate look in his eyes.

He had told her the exact same thing at the party yesterday, and it was still as stupid and inexplicable. "Why the *hell* not?"

Michael took a deep breath, gazing into her eyes from inches away. "Because I'm in love with you," he said with quiet determination.

This was crazy. Did he really think she would fall into the same trap twice? Blankly, Julia shook her head. "I... I don't believe you," she whispered almost inaudibly, tears welling up in her eyes. She had to tell him this because she needed to protect herself, but how she wished she *could* believe him.

Michael cupped her face with his hand, wiping a lone tear away from her cheek. "I'm sorry," he mumbled.

And then he was kissing her. Very, very softly, he pressed his lips to her mouth. It was such a tentative caress it hardly qualified as a kiss, but Julia's body begged to differ – it responded to his touch like gasoline to a spark. Her mind was trying to be sensible, but her body definitely wasn't. A pink blush graced her cheeks when she eagerly kissed him back. When she heard him moan softly it only turned her on more.

Everything about this felt perfect. *This* was the kiss she'd always imagined back in the days she had fantasized about Michael. She circled his torso with her arms and pulled him even closer. Feeling him this close was so good. As he held her tightly and met her fiery kisses with equal passion, Julia didn't have a choice but to believe he was speaking the truth.

However puzzling it all might sound, he was truly in love with her. This was *real*. She could feel it in the way her heart beat, the way his warm and gentle hands caressed her, the crackling electricity in the air between them. She had never felt this before, not even during that one particular night at his place.

Michael's breath was ragged when he finally pulled away from her. He touched her face and smiled. "I've got something for you," he said in a low voice, pulling a folded sheet of paper from his jeans pocket.

Julia accepted it with a dazed look in her eyes. "What is this?"

"I wrote it for you. Last night." Michael shyly looked at the floor. "It's a poem."

"For me?" Julia stood with mouth agape. In what kind of parallel universe did a guy like Michael write *her* a poem? This had to be a dream. She never woke up this morning, and Gaby would soon smack her on the head with a pillow to take her out of Wonderland.

"I hope you'll do me the honor of reading it. I've never written anything like this before." The insecure tremble in his voice made her heart melt. If this wasn't a dream, then it was definitely a dream come true.

"Of *course* I'll read it," she said hurriedly. "I'm just... blown away. I honestly don't know what to say." Sweet angels in Heaven – he had kissed her, apologized to her and written her a *poem*. No mortal words would suffice.

Their private talk was interrupted by Martin shouting up to Michael from the stairwell. "Kolbe! Can you come downstairs? There are customers who need your help."

Michael took a step backward and pulled the door open. "I'll be right there," he called back, all the while grinning at her mischievously.

Julia gave him a bashful smile back. "Go on," she said. "Go do your job. And thank you. I'll talk to you later."

The door slammed shut. With trembling fingers, she unfolded the sheet of paper, resisting the urge to start reading immediately. First, she walked over to the electric kettle to make herself some tea. While her bag of green tea was steeping in a mug of hot water, she glanced sideways to the poem on the table, her thoughts drifting back to the kiss they'd shared together.

Julia gently rubbed her lips and suddenly wished Michael hadn't been called downstairs. She wouldn't have minded kissing him a little longer. Even though she still had no clue what triggered his personality change, one thing was absolutely clear to her now: his feelings for her were real. She no longer doubted that.

When her tea was ready, Julia sat down at the kitchen table and took a sip before finally picking up the sheet of paper to read the poem Michael had written her.

In the background
almost timidly
in a soft and thin voice,
I call to you.
Are you aware of me?

I touch the golden break of day
in the cycle of life.

I am the angel that goes with you

My child, my star
My light, my love

You make me see
Are you aware of me?

Tears pooled in her eyes. He had written her an amazing poem. It made her feel as if he'd been with her during the countless hours she'd spent in the woods, reading her mind as she dreamed and sang and wrote her own poems. His words were so deep and mystical. She *had* to tell her best friend. Right now.

When Silke barged into the room, Julia quickly put away the poem. "Hey, what are you doing here? Having a break already?" her colleague asked in surprise.

"Uhm, yes. I was so thirsty, you know?" Julia held up her mug by way of explanation. "Anyway, I'll be on my way. I have to finish up some stuff."

"Sorry! I didn't mean to chase you away," Silke called after her as Julia headed back to the stockroom. Besides finishing her task, she also had to grab her bag from the room because her cell phone was in there. Gaby needed to hear the big news.

'HAVE 2 talk 2u. M xx-ed me & wrote me a poem!!! u got time 2nite? x'

It only took one minute for her to get a reply. 'dafuq??? F2F ASAP!! meet u after work.'

Julia put away her phone, her heart fluttering in her chest. She couldn't shake the buzz of anticipation humming through her body. Only two more hours until lunch break. Would Michael talk to her, and if so, what would he say? What would *she* say?

"Hey, you hermit!" Donna stuck her head around the door at half past twelve. "You coming? It's break time."

Julia scrambled to her feet with difficulty. Her knees were sore from crawling around on the floor, looking for a book on the lowest shelf in the R section. "Yeah, I'll be right there," she replied, despite not being particularly hungry. Her stomach was way too tense for that.

Dawdling behind Donna, she walked to the break room clutching her lunchbox. Inside, Marco, Michael and Martin turned out to have occupied the table near the coffee machine. Silke was pouring some juice at the counter and turned around when the girls came in. "What do you say we make our own table, the three of us?" she laughed. "I believe contact between men and women isn't being encouraged in this bookstore." She pointed at the 'men's table'.

Julia bit her lip. If only Silke knew how intimate things had been between some of the employees not too long ago…

"Maybe you're drawing the wrong conclusion," she commented. "Personally, I think only people starting with an M are allowed to sit at that table."

Donna started to giggle. "Girl, you've gone cuckoo in that stockroom sorting books all morning. You're alphabetizing *people,* for crying out loud!"

Laughing and chatting, the girls sat down at the other table. Julia stole a glance at Michael, who followed her with his eyes. She gave him a hesitant half-smile, which caused him to give her a high-wattage smile back. Stopping herself from grinning inanely, she quickly sat down to scarf down her cheese roll. Her appetite had suddenly returned. Donna and Silke were chatting a mile a minute, and she chimed in every now and then.

As Julia got up to get a refill of juice, Michael headed over to the fridge and stopped right next to her.

"Wanna join me outside?" he mumbled, holding up a pack of smokes.

Julia looked at him nervously. "Uhm, yes, sure," she stuttered. Admittedly, she wasn't a real smoker, but she'd gladly make an exception today for having the chance to have him all to herself for a few minutes.

She put her glass in the sink and followed Michael out the door, ignoring Donna and Silke both eyeing her inquisitively. With wobbly knees, she walked down the stairs and to the back of the store. Michael pushed open the back door leading to the small quadrangle that was used for loading and unloading.

Julia hesitated when he held out the pack of cigarettes to her. "I don't actually really smoke," she was embarrassed to admit. "I mean, I know I *did* smoke that night I was at your place, but I wasn't actually… you know…" She paused, looking for words. "I wasn't being myself," she spoke at last. Now that she said it out loud, she realized it was true. She'd pretended to be someone else that night, just to be able to meet his expectations.

Michael put away the cigarettes in his breast pocket. "To be honest, I'm not too fond of smoking myself anymore," he shrugged. "Ever since the accident." He looped an arm around her waist. "I just wanted to talk to you."

Julia rested herself against his shoulder, closing her eyes and enjoying the moment. "I loved your poem," she mumbled. "Thank you so much."

He lifted her chin and looked at her searchingly. "You really mean it? Are you being… yourself now?"

Julia turned red. Looking back, the way she had desperately tried so hard to please him was cringe-worthy. "Yes, I really mean it," she whispered.

He gave her a sweet smile. "I'm happy to hear that," he mumbled, lowering his head to kiss her warmly. Julia clasped her arms around his neck and kissed him back, her heart beating wildly when his hands roamed over her body before landing on her waist and pulling her into him. When he touched her, it was like her body was at peace and at the mercy of a raging storm at the same time. He calmed and comforted her, but he also made her hot for him. She almost felt like pleading and begging for a few kisses more when he disentangled himself from their embrace and stepped backward. "I think we need to go upstairs again," he observed, slightly out of breath.

"Too bad." Julia pouted.

Michael took her hand in his. "I'm only working the morning shift tomorrow," he said, hope evident in his voice. "What about you? Maybe we can go out in the afternoon. Like, hang around in the park or something. It's such nice weather outside."

Julia mentally sorted through her work schedule. "I'll ask Martin to swap my Thursday afternoon off for tomorrow," she replied, beaming at him. She could swear her heart almost burst with joy and love. He'd asked her out! And this time, he actually wanted to *go* somewhere – not just hang around in his room to see how far he could take things with her.

Michael smiled back happily. "I hope he'll say yes," he said with such a genuine sparkle in his eyes that it seemed like he was asking her out for the first time.

The fact that he'd brushed her off after their first date seemed like a distant memory, but it wasn't completely erased from her mind – a small stab of insecurity went through Julia's heart. She still had no idea what had changed him so much, but it wasn't a very good idea to bring up the question straight away. She'd ask him later, after they had spent more time together. Or maybe she shouldn't. It was also entirely possible he wasn't even aware of his character change after that knock to the head, in which case she should keep her mouth shut forever. She'd rather get to know the new Michael than bother with his old alter ego.

When the clock struck five, Julia left the bookstore in high spirits. Everything had turned out the way she wanted: Martin had agreed to her taking the afternoon off tomorrow, plus she'd managed to buy all the discounted poetry books she'd wanted. Her boss had even given her sixty percent off instead of fifty. Now she'd be able to read Michael more poems when they went to the park together. She wasn't shy about it anymore.

Donna was waiting at the bus stop and shot Julia a wicked grin when her colleague took a seat next to her. "So. Time to come clean. Where did you and Michael go during lunch break?"

Julia blushed. "Outside. Cigarette break."

"Sure you were. I'm not buying it. I bet things got *smoking* hot between you, though." Donna elbowed her in the side.

Julia let out a nervous laugh. "Fine, you're right. Something's going on between us. Again."

"Sounds good. Is that why you begged Martin to swap free afternoons?"

"Yeah. We're going to the park tomorrow." She smiled blissfully. "I still can't quite believe it."

Donna rolled her eyes. "I'll be in for X-rated material around every corner, won't I? Romance on the work floor – Mamma Mia. Don't make me avert my eyes every time I walk into the stockroom and you guys are there, *smoking*."

"We'll keep it family-friendly, I promise." At that moment, Julia's bus crawled up to the bus stop. She waved at Donna before getting on. Her MP3 player had died, so she entertained herself by reading Michael's poem so many times she knew it by heart when she got off at Birkensiedlung.

It was nice and quiet in her neighborhood after the bustle of the city and her day at work. Birds were singing in the trees lining the road Julia had to walk down to get to her house.

As she turned onto her street, Julia slowed down – acoustic guitar music was coming from the Ebner family's yard. Curiously, she stuck her head around the corner of the hedge lining their lawn and spotted Thorsten sitting on the grass. He was playing a beautiful melody on a classical guitar. Julia listened to him breathlessly and regretted stepping too close when his head shot up and he stopped playing immediately.

"Sorry to interrupt," she said guiltily.

Thorsten smiled. "You're not interrupting. I'm just not used to having an audience." He shrugged self-consciously.

"I'll just leave, okay?" Julia mumbled, but he shook his head.

"No, not okay. I shouldn't be silly. Come, sit next to me. Maybe you can sing something. I have no lyrics to accompany my song yet." He beckoned her to sit down.

Julia gingerly pushed open the gate. Did she understand correctly that Thorsten had written the melody himself? That was amazing. She kept bumping into creative, handsome guys who seemed to like her, lately.

"I don't really write lyrics to my own music, to be honest," Julia admitted when she sat down. "I usually just play instrumental piano music."

When Thorsten started playing his song again, however, she felt inspiration bubbling up despite her words. Michael's poem was still stuck in her head, and without thinking, she started to sing it out loud, incorporating the words into Thorsten's melody. All the feelings she had for Michael seeped into the song and it sounded astounding, combined with Thorsten's delicate picking of the strings.

Julia gave him a surreptitious look full of surprise. She hadn't thought making music together would be this simple. When she had sung the last stanza and the music faded away, she caught his gaze. Thorsten stared at her intently.

"That was really beautiful," he said, his voice cracking. He put down his guitar and leaned into her. "*You* are really beautiful," he softly mumbled.

For a beat or two, they both sat completely still. Julia's heart leaped up in her throat when Thorsten's hand landed in her neck and he inched even closer. Something in her stomach fluttered. She knew what he was about to do, but she couldn't move, couldn't speak to tell him no.

Or was it a question of not *wanting* to?

She had no time to ponder that question. Thorsten's warm lips crushed hers. Julia involuntarily closed her eyes and felt the heat radiating off his skin from up close. His breath blew softly between her slightly opened lips and his fingers tangled into her hair, caressing her neck. He kissed her again, softly, then more passionately, leaving his taste in her mouth. And then, he slowly let go of her and gazed into her eyes just inches away from her face.

"I couldn't resist," he whispered. "You were singing so beautifully, and you looked so innocent and sweet. You were angelic."

Julia met his eyes, her face burning with shame. She had sounded innocent and sweet because she'd been singing Michael's words. Because she was in love with him. And yet, she'd let Thorsten kiss her without any objection. She'd done nothing to stop him. What on earth was she thinking?!

The silence was becoming painful. She had to say something to him. "I'm... I don't mind," she stuttered, flinching instantly. "No, that's not true. I *do* mind. I mean..."

A playful smile tugged at the corner of his mouth. "Well? What do you mean?"

She bit her lip. "I should have stopped you."

"Yeah. Okay. That didn't work out so well." Thorsten grinned mischievously.

Julia blushed even harder and swallowed the lump in her throat. "Did I kiss you back?" she whispered almost inaudibly.

His blue eyes stared at her, and in the silence that ensued, she could hear the blood rushing in her ears and feel his hands still holding hers.

"It felt like that to me," he replied quietly and earnestly.

"I'm so sorry," she choked out. "I shouldn't have. I didn't mean it like that."

"Are you still in love with him?" Thorsten asked with a dull pain in his voice.

Julia awkwardly stared at her hands in his. "I'm going out with him tomorrow. Sorry. I honestly don't know what my deal is. Well, I'm sending out mixed signals. And I shouldn't be doing that. I..."

She stopped talking when Thorsten cupped her cheek with one hand. "It's okay. I kind of caught you off guard, I guess. Just let me be your friend, okay?" He pressed a kiss to her forehead and struggled to his feet. "Have fun tomorrow."

Thorsten picked up his guitar and hurried inside. Julia cursed inwardly – she was being such a bitch! It was obvious she'd hurt his feelings, even if he said he still wanted to be friends. It might be better to avoid him for a while now that she was dating Michael again. But how was she supposed to do that with him living across the street?

Feeling really fed up with herself, she got up and slogged out of the yard. Of course, Gaby would be here any minute now to hear all about Michael. She wasn't sure she should include this episode in the summary of her eventful day, even though Gaby had recommended hanging out with both guys to decide who she liked better.

"I'm home," she called into the direction of the kitchen when she stepped inside. No reply. Her mom was still at work, and Anne was most likely at her grandmother's or with Sabine. Julia went upstairs to clear away the spare mattress from her room and write in her diary.

After putting the mattress back in the hallway closet, she sat down at her desk, opened her drawer and took out the photo album she used as a scrapbook, poetry book and diary all at once. She wanted to stick Michael's poem in there. The song she'd written with Thorsten was playing in her head.

Julia's gaze wandered outside and landed on the house across the street. Thorsten was just stepping out of the shed with a pile of wooden planks in his arms, which he put down on a bike trailer as directed by Sabine. She smiled. So he was helping them with their construction project in the woods again. Maybe she should ask *him* for inside information about the tree house so she'd have an idea when Anne would be finished.

While Sabine was busy hooking up the trailer to her bicycle, Thorsten looked up at her bedroom window. It was as if he had felt her eyes on him. He waved at her with a friendly smile. Julia feebly waved back. His clear, blue eyes didn't look at her reproachfully, and yet she felt bad.

From the corner of her eye she could see Gaby rounding the corner of her street. Quickly, she stepped away from the window and rushed downstairs so she could drag her friend inside before Gaby would strike up a lengthy conversation with Thorsten. As she walked to the front door, she could hear Gaby shouting something to Thorsten, who was still helping his little sister. In a rush, she opened the door and grabbed Gaby's upper arm. "Hey, Gab. Come inside."

Gaby chuckled. "Eager to share your big news, are you?" She stepped inside and hugged her friend. "Let's go to the kitchen, Aphrodite, so you can make us tea, open a pack of cookies and tell me *everything* from A to Z about what happened today."

With a flushed face, Julia told her best friend everything that had transpired at the bookstore. Afterwards, she declaimed Michael's poem by heart.

"That is so beautiful," Gaby whispered. "So you're going on a date tomorrow? Wow, Jules, it sounds like a dream."

"Yes, it does. Sometimes, it's like I *am* dreaming. It all still feels pretty surreal." She stared at the teacup in her hands, clearing her throat before she continued. "Also, I sang a song today. Together with Thorsten."

Gaby cocked an eyebrow. "Why? Is it someone's birthday?"

Julia coughed nervously. "No, he was playing a song on his guitar when I walked past his house, and since he was actually composing the song, he asked if I wanted to join him and help him with lyrics. And at the end, he was so touched by my singing that he kissed me."

Her friend went bug-eyed. "Say *what*? For real? And what did you do?"

"I... I think I kissed him back," Julia stuttered with a red face. "I didn't mean to, but the whole gesture was just so... so *genuine*."

A grin split Gaby's face in two as she grabbed another chocolate chip cookie from the plate. "No way! I was right in nicknaming you Aphrodite. Seriously, Jules, kissing two guys in *one* day?"

"Look, I'm not planning on making it a habit. I'm going out with Michael tomorrow, and I told Thorsten that, too. I don't want to put him on the wrong track."

At that moment, they heard keys in the front door. "Hello!" Julia's mother announced herself. "I'm home." She popped her head around the kitchen door. "*Servus*, Gaby. Are you staying for dinner?"

Gaby shook her head. "No, I, uhm... I'm going out to dinner with Axel tonight. He asked me whether I wanted to try out that new Mexican restaurant in town, and he doesn't really know anyone else who loves spicy food and jalapeño and that kind of stuff, so he asked me... and I didn't have anything better to do, so I thought, what the hell, you know. And besides, they've got this introduction deal going on where you get two entrees for the price of one, so that's why it made sense for him to ask me, too."

"Right." Ms. Gunther slowly nodded, looking slightly bewildered. She disappeared into the hallway, leaving the two girls behind in awkward silence.

Gaby stared down at the table top, a pink blush on her cheeks, until Julia burst out giggling. "Wow, thanks for the *very clear* explanation. What's next, you reading out the entire menu?"

Gaby's blush reddened. "Oh, come on, you get me, right? I didn't want to give you the wrong impression."

"Ah. What wrong impression might that be?"

"Well, just, you thinking it's a date or something," Gaby mumbled.

"No, because going on a date with Axel would be downright *idiotic*."

"No! I don't mean it like that. But he's your cousin, you know. And a good friend of mine." Gaby picked up another cookie from the big plate and started chewing like her life depended on it.

Julia chuckled. "Don't go and ruin your appetite now. After all, you still have an entire menu to look forward to."

Gaby glowered at her. "Stop harassing me! I'm just..."

"Nervous? Tense? Happy? Excited?"

"Never mind. I'm never telling you anything ever again."

They stared each other down for a moment, then both erupted in fits of laughter. By the time Julia's mother returned to the kitchen, the air had been cleared. Gaby had even promised Julia to text her tomorrow and let her know how The Mexican Job had worked out.

After tea, Julia walked Gaby to the front door. "Can you tell Anne to come home?" her mom called out after them. "She's probably still with the neighbors across the street."

"I don't know about that," Julia called back as she waved Gaby goodbye. "I believe Sabine and Anne are busy in the woods again. Before Gaby got here, I saw

Thorsten lugging around big piles of wood that would put The Home Depot to shame."

"Well, go find out. We're having dinner in a few minutes. Thorsten might know where the girls are."

Dragging her feet, Julia crossed the street to do what her mother had asked. Now she had to talk to Thorsten *again*. Ignoring him turned out to be an impossible task.

Much to her relief, she saw Sabine getting off her bike and unhooking the now empty trailer in the yard. "Hey, Sabine," she said. "Is Anne with you?"

The little girl shook her head. "I just dropped off some planks at the spot where we're busy building our tree house, but she was already gone. Didn't she come home?"

"No." Julia frowned in dismay. It was all very nice that Anne loved nature and solitude, but it was irresponsible of her to take off like this. She was probably just trying to get inspiration for her book, but this would surely put her mom on edge again.

Julia dug up her phone. Anne should have her cell phone on her too, so it was worth trying to give her a call. After three rings, the phone switched to voice mail, but it didn't take long for Anne to call her back.

"Hey," Anne's tinny voice sounded through the speaker. "I'm coming home now."

"Whereabouts are you?"

"Oh, nowhere in particular. I was making some sketches for my story. I'll be there soon."

After ten minutes, Anne cycled into the yard. Julia was waiting for her at the door. "I'm glad you had your phone with you," she said sternly. "You shouldn't do that again – staying out for too long without telling anyone where you are."

Anne shrugged. "I'm not supposed to tell anyone where I am."

"What the heck is that supposed to mean?"

"Never mind," her sister muttered. Anne pushed Julia aside and quickly ran down the hallway. Julia threw an angry glare after her. She couldn't believe her ears. Of course, Sabine and Anne wanted to keep the house a secret and only show it to their families once it was completely finished, but this was nonsense. From now on, she'd make sure Anne told them exactly where she was going, or her trips to the woods would be history. Mom was always bogged down with work and didn't keep enough of an eye on Anne anymore – her little sister could practically get away with everything. When *she* was little, she wouldn't have dreamed of pulling tricks like these. Of course, Dad had still been around to share responsibility. In general, the youngest child in a family was notorious for being allowed more than the older children, but still. This didn't sit well with her.

Heaving a heavy sigh, Julia went into the kitchen to start cooking. It was her turn tonight.

8.

The next morning, Julia arrived at the bookstore too early, but Michael had still managed to beat her – he was already waiting at the entrance.

"Good morning!" She gingerly raised her hand in greeting. Did he expect her to kiss him, or was that too soon? Would she make a complete fool of herself if she did? "Wow, you're early today."

Michael shrugged. "Yeah, I woke up early and couldn't go back to sleep anymore. I was restless." He smiled at her. "You kept running through my mind."

"Oh." Julia smiled back shyly. "You kept running through mine, too. All evening, actually." Lost in thought, she'd managed to burn two pans of rice while cooking before her mom had sent her away from the stove in despair.

His smile widened. "Really?"

Julia nodded. "Uh-huh. So, have you figured out what you want to do this afternoon?"

Michael shook his head. "No, not yet. I've just figured out what I want to do right now." He wrapped an arm around her shoulders and pulled her closer. "This," he added with a twinkle in his green eyes, pressing his lips to hers.

Julia closed her eyes and slipped her arms around his waist, kissing him like there was no tomorrow. Who cared if their colleagues caught them making out? She had longed for his touch since yesterday afternoon. "Can we go to the forest after work?" she mumbled against his lips between kisses. "I'd like that."

Michael took a step backward. "We could," he replied.

Julia cocked her head. He didn't sound too eager.

He saw her puzzlement and sighed. "You know, I was looking forward to experiencing the city and the park together with you. I want to … put the accident behind me. Stay away from the woods for a while."

"Of course!" Julia nodded in understanding. "So let's go to the park. Shall we have a picnic there?"

"Sounds good. Let's prepare a basket at my place. While I'm busy making our sandwiches, you can use the time to play the grand piano, because you promised you'd come and do that some day."

"I will. As it so happens, I wrote a song yesterday, using *your* poem as lyrics." Maybe she should tell Michael about Thorsten and her jam session on his lawn. Somehow, it felt like the right thing to do. Then again, it was best to leave that unexpected kiss out of her confession – there was such a thing as too *much* honesty. "The boy from across the street was playing his guitar in the yard and invited me to join him and contribute some lyrics. So I used your poem. Who knows, I might be able to figure out how to play it on the piano."

Michael beamed at her. "That would be amazing. I'm happy you liked it so much."

Just then, Martin showed up with a few rolled-up posters tucked under one arm. "Wow! Can I say early birds?" he greeted them. "Will you do me the honor of helping me by putting up the sale posters in the window?"

It didn't take long for the rest of the team to arrive at the store. Donna sidled up to the ladder on which Julia was balancing precariously, trying to affix a banner to the parapet above the checkout counter. "Hey there,

Julia," she called up. "So what are your plans this afternoon?"

"Buzz off," Julia squeaked. "If I look down, I'll get vertigo."

She heard Donna laugh out loud. "Fortunately, Michael is *not* afraid of heights. He's been looking at you doing your thing up there for a while now, you know."

In a bout of curiosity, Julia risked glancing down to see what Donna was talking about. Michael stood next to the checkout gawking up at her legs, looking caught out when she blinked and shook her head at him incredulously. Donna's mouth twitched as she cast Michael a sidelong glance.

"Why don't you all just leave me alone?" Julia cried out indignantly, holding the top rung of the ladder in a death grip. Despite her words, she still shot Michael a playful smile. She was going to spend the entire afternoon with this wonderful, gorgeous guy, who was in love with her and couldn't keep his eyes off her. It suddenly dawned on her just how lucky she was. Her legs felt like rubber when he gave her a winsome smile back.

To her happiness, Martin sent her over to the stockroom again to fetch some books – a perfect opportunity to text Gaby about their plans for today, and to check whether her friend had sent *her* anything about last night's date with Axel.

She had. 'dinner was gr8! axel = kinda sweet :$ jules, whaddya think he thinks of me?!'

Julia scoffed, shaking her head in disbelief. 'u know what axel thinks of u ;) don't ask 4 the sake of asking. mick & me r going 2 the park & will make a picnic @ his place 1st. so nervous!! x'

Of course, no one else would be at Michael's house this afternoon, but somehow, Julia was certain this wouldn't be a rinse-repeat of that other time in Michael's empty house. She still couldn't wrap her head around his bizarre personality change, but it had rocked her world.

How could she have even been in love with him before this? Maybe it hadn't been love – maybe she had just looked up to him and admired the confidence he exuded in high school. He'd been so handsome, desirable and completely out of her league, but that was all different now. He was trying really hard to get to know her better.

She started when Silke entered the stockroom. "Time to fess up," she announced bluntly. "What's going on between you and Michael? Don't think I've missed all those sly glances between the two of you."

Julia felt herself redden, and she gave a shy shrug. "He asked me out again, and I said yes."

"Well, doesn't that bother you?" Silke crossed her arms. "I mean, it wasn't pretty, the way he chucked you before."

Silke couldn't be more right, so how could she ever explain why things were different now? She didn't even fully understand it herself.

"He's – changed," she hazarded. "I mean, *really*. He's nothing like before."

Silke nodded mindfully. "Yeah. I get what you mean. When he walked into the store on his first day here, he was being kind of a show-off. He didn't fool me, though – quite frankly, I thought he was very insecure, deep down. But he's no longer wearing the Mask of Fake Self-Confidence, if you get my drift."

"Who knows, maybe it fell off because of the accident." Julia smiled.

"Yeah, you might be onto something there. Have you looked up stuff about people experiencing character changes due to head trauma?"

She hadn't, but actually, it didn't sound unlikely. Silke had just given her the perfect explanation for Michael's changed behavior. Philosophizing about Celts, Midsummer and lightning bolts was more her style, but a concussion causing behavioral change was much more logical.

"His doctor probably warned him about the short-term effects," Julia dodged the question. "I'll ask him at some point. So, shall I help you with those?" She pointed at the pile of books at Silke's feet.

The remainder of the morning shift was uneventful. Julia stayed up in the stockroom and Michael manned the checkout. When the store closed for lunch break at noon, Julia and Michael left Höllrigl and walked to Michael's house on the Giselakai.

"The weather is lovely," he said, looking around with a big smile on his face. "Perfect to bum around in the park."

"Well, we could also do some light exercise," Julia proposed. "Don't you have badminton rackets lying around at your place?"

"I think so, yeah. You really like sports, don't you?"

"Always gives me energy."

"Funny. That's what I've always found so charming about you. You can be quiet and introverted whenever you're busy writing or composing, but at the same time, you can be so full of life and energy when you do sports."

Julia felt herself lighting up like a light bulb. Michael talked about her as if she was the most fascinating person on earth. She walked closer to him and took his hand. It was only after they had crossed the bridge to his street that she wondered how he actually knew so much about her. Had he been more attentive to her at school than she'd given him credit for?

"Is there anything you absolutely hate as a sandwich topping?" Michael inquired once they were inside, dragging her to the kitchen. When he opened the fridge, Julia observed just how many different kinds of food the Kolbe family stocked. Her little family was quite simple and poor compared to this household. Would she even feel comfortable taking him home to *her* place and introducing him to her mother?

She absently picked up an avocado from the fruit bowl on the kitchen table. "I'm not a fussy eater. I like all kinds of food," she mumbled.

A smile spread across his face. "Including that?" he pointed at the avocado. "How about wheat rolls with lettuce, chicken and avocado?"

She nodded slightly. When Michael walked up to her and put his arms around her, Julia rested her head on his shoulder and sighed deeply. "I just have to get used to things in your world," she whispered. "Sorry I'm being so awkward."

He kissed her forehead. "You're not being awkward. And I have to get used to this situation, too."

Julia blinked at him in confusion. "You?"

"Yes. To being in love, I mean."

Her face turned pink with joy. He made it sound like he'd never been in love before. And for all she knew, it was true. He'd always dated *some* girl in high school, but he'd never been steady with any of them for long. This felt like it was more serious for him, and with all her heart she wanted to open the door to her life and let him in, even if she was insecure about certain parts of it.

"Would you like to come over to my place tomorrow?" she blurted out. "After work?"

He smiled warmly, his eyes looking fondly down at her. "Of course I would. I'm secretly hoping you'll make me pizza."

"*Amy's Kitchen* pizza?"

"Yes, please. You know how I feel about Amy and her pizzas."

They both started to chuckle. Julia exhaled, feeling more at ease. "Let's get on with those rolls, shall we?" she suggested.

"No, we shall not. *I* will do it. You promised you'd play the piano!" Michael shoved her out of the kitchen despite Julia's protest, escorting her to the Steinway in the corner of their gigantic living room. He opened the fall board and pulled out the bench for her. "There you go. Have fun."

Smiling shyly, Julia sat down, letting out her breath when Michael walked back to the kitchen at once. At least he didn't hover. It would give her the peace of mind to figure out Thorsten's song on the piano. Humming the tune to herself, she picked her way through a few scales on the keyboard before settling on a pitch that would suit her voice.

When Michael returned to the living room after ten minutes carrying a picnic cooler filled with drinks and food, she was singing Thorsten's melody with her – or, actually, Michael's – lyrics. He stood next to the grand piano and gazed at her completely mesmerized.

When the song had ended, Julia looked up bashfully. "I'm happy you're still here," she said timidly.

Michael gave her a quizzical look. "Why wouldn't I be here?"

"You walked away during my performance at the twin's party."

He looked ashamed. "I'm so sorry. I was..." He faltered, and in the silence that stretched between them, Julia remembered how intensely he'd been staring at her while she was playing her own song. How Gaby had insisted to her he'd had tears in his eyes. And all of a sudden, she couldn't care less why Michael had changed so much. Whether it was thanks to lightning, head trauma or supernatural powers, he was a person she could genuinely fall in love with. She got up from the bench and impulsively flung her arms around him.

"It doesn't matter," she whispered. "I was happy you were listening at the beginning."

"Of course I was listening," he replied quietly. "That was the song you wrote yourself. For the exam."

She gawked at him. So he *had* been in the school's auditorium during her Music Ed examination. Her frayed nerves had probably made her overlook him in the audience. A warm feeling flooded her when she looked up at him. She'd always felt invisible to him, but now it turned out he had noticed her after all.

"So, shall we?" she proposed, tilting her head at the picnic cooler.

Michael put an arm around her shoulders. "Let's go."

They picked a spot under a big chestnut tree and spent all afternoon lying in the grass chatting, kissing, cuddling up and reading poems from Julia's new poetry collections. Michael had packed the badminton rackets, but it was a bit too windy to play a game. Michael was the first one to throw in the towel.

"This is more strenuous than it looks!" he puffed after playing for five minutes with the wind blowing against him. "I thought this was an easy game. You know, because of the shuttlecock being so light."

"Which is why you were the one who needed to hit it really hard," Julia snickered. "Poor guy." She wiped the sweat off her forehead as she sagged down against the chestnut tree, Michael following suit. The breeze touched the leaves above their heads.

"You know, the scene of your accident in the woods has always been very special to me." She took his hand in hers. "That oak tree near the place where you slipped with your motorcycle… it used to be my refuge. I'd take shelter under the branches of that tree. Not from the rain, but from life. It was my hugging tree."

Michael squeezed her hand. "Why the past tense?" he inquired. "Do you feel different about the place now?"

Julia gave a tiny shrug. "I think my tree is sick. The leaves look kind of yellow. And besides, I don't really *want* to run off into the woods whenever I feel sad. I just…" She bit her lip and paused for a second. "I want to live a *real* life, and I don't want to lose myself in all kinds of fantasies anymore."

Michael looked at her sideways, and just for a moment, he looked wistful. "Fantasies can be a part of real life," he objected. "They make life more beautiful, don't they?"

Julia shook her head. "Of course they can. But that's not what I meant."

"So what do you mean?"

"Well, for instance, I looked at you quite differently because I was hiding away in my own daydreams."

Michael said nothing, the curious look in his eyes urging her on.

She took a deep breath. "You know what it is? For two years, I believed I was in love with you. In my mind, I cast you as the lead in some magical fairytale. But that's just it: it wasn't you I was infatuated with. You were just a character in my play." As the words tumbled out, she trembled. Was she actually telling him this? Was she brave enough to reveal her emotions like this? It would seem so. Doing this whole exposé should scare her to death, but it didn't. In fact, it felt like the right thing to do.

"I had no idea who you were," she concluded timidly. "And when I found out you were not the Prince Charming I imagined you to be, I blamed *you* for it."

Michael flushed with embarrassment. "I'm sorry," he mumbled. "I know he... I... it must have been painful for you."

She scooted closer, her hands sliding up his chest. "It's all right," she whispered. Right in that moment, the last remnants of her anger and insecurity vanished. She no longer blamed him. "This whole situation is so new for me. To be completely honest, I am in love with *you* for the first time. You make it so easy. You've become gentler, and friendlier. Because of the accident. Or, I don't know..."

She faltered. His irises were greener than ever before, his gaze filled with a zest for life that had never shown in his eyes in all the years she had known him. And all of a sudden, she was certain she wasn't talking to Michael – she was sitting here with someone else. It wasn't *him*.

But that didn't make sense. Why was she having such strange thoughts? It was bad enough she'd more or less attributed his current, pleasant personality to an accident with near-fatal consequences. If she shared this crazy idea with him, he would probably think she was nuts.

Michael interrupted her thoughts by pulling her into his embrace, kissing her softly. "You have *no* idea how much your words mean to me," he whispered against her lips.

She dazedly kissed him back. "Seriously?" she mumbled.

He nodded. "You woke me up, Julia." He closed his eyes. "From that slumber we call death."

The way he described it, he made it sound as though she hadn't just saved him from an untimely death – she'd awoken him so he could become more like himself. Who would ever have guessed Michael could be so poetic about life?

"Where do you want to meet up tomorrow?" he asked, as they walked to the exit of the park just before dinner time. Julia didn't work on Wednesdays, but Michael would be busy all day.

"Could you be at my place at six o'clock?" Julia suggested. "If you take bus five and get off at the last stop, you should give me a call so I can meet you there."

"Sounds good to me. I don't know the way to your house yet, so..." Michael gave her one final hug, whispering in her ear: "I'll miss you tonight."

"Likewise. Have fun at your aunt and uncle's." Michael was having dinner with them together with his parents. He'd invited Julia to join them, but she wasn't ready to meet his family yet, so she declined.

Once she'd lost sight of Michael, Julia sat down in the bus shelter opposite the park. The bus would show up soon. Her cell phone showed one missed call from Gaby, so she called back but it went through to voicemail. A blissful smile spread across her face when she clicked off and looked at her phone display – her new background picture was a photo of Michael. She should drop by Gran's later so she could tell her about everything that had happened in her life since their last chat.

As she got on the bus, her phone dinged: 'can you go and pick up anne in eichet? i finish at 9!' Her mom. Well, that was a lucky coincidence. She'd be able to talk to her grandmother sooner than she thought. She'd warm up some leftovers when she got home and take a bus down to the next village to pick up her sister and tell Gran all about her new boyfriend.

Just as Julia finished her reply to her mom, Gaby called her back. "Heya Jules," she trilled. "Axel invited us over to watch a movie at his place tonight. Are you free?"

Julia chuckled. "Are you sure Axel meant to invite us both?" she teased.

"Of course!" Gaby retorted with disdain. "You don't *honestly* think I'm asking you along because I'm afraid to go alone, do you?"

"I wouldn't dream of it."

"Ha-ha, very funny. So are you coming?"

"What kind of movie are we watching?"

"One of those really creepy ones, he said. You know, some re-make of an Asian horror movie."

"Ah, yes, that makes sense. He's probably hoping for you to hold his hand. Or crawl into his arms in sheer terror."

Julia alighted from the bus and patiently listened to Gaby objecting to her comments. "What time is he expecting us?" she cut in before her friend could go into another round of outraged hysterics.

"Half past eight."

"Okay, I'll be there. I don't have to work tomorrow anyway."

"Cool!" Gaby sounded unmistakably relieved. "See you there!"

Julia hung up, sporting a wide grin. She turned the corner onto her street and felt her stomach rumble when she caught a whiff of grilled sausages in the air. Someone on their street had fired up the barbecue. The trail of smoke spiraling up to the sky seemed to be coming from the neighbors' yard.

"Hey, girl next door," a familiar voice called out to her. Thorsten appeared at the gate, waving at her with a pair of barbecue tongs. "You hungry?"

Julia nodded tentatively. "A little," she admitted.

"Well, would you like to join us for dinner? Sabine went to the pool with my dad, so it's just me and my mom."

Her heart skipped a beat. She should say no – after all, she'd promised herself to keep away from Thorsten. On the other hand, what harm would it do to join him for a little while? His mom would be there as their chaperone. Plus, this would be the perfect opportunity to tell him all about her romantic afternoon with Michael so it would be clear to him where she stood. It was a bit lame to go home and microwave leftovers if she could have fresh food and a good time with the neighbors.

"I'd love to," she replied. "Hold on, I'll just dump my bag and come right back."

Julia went inside and walked up to her room to put her bag on her desk and quickly brush her hair. She looked at herself in the mirror. Wow, she looked so much in love. Her eyes sparkled and there was a glow to her cheeks.

Tomorrow, her mother would meet Michael for the first time. She'd have to play it tactically. It might be a bad idea to mention she had already been on a date with him– and an even worse idea to disclose that she'd spent the night. Her mom was still under the illusion that her daughter had crashed at Florian's place that night because they had been to some party.

Julia headed out to the hallway and saw the door to Anne's room was open. Her little sister hadn't properly closed her window. The wind had caused some of her sketches to fall off her desk. They lay scattered around the room. Julia quickly dashed inside to pick them up and put them back.

The drawings were quite amazing. Anne had made two sketches of trees in the forest, and a portrait of a boy with long, blond hair like Legolas and blue eyes like Thorsten. Anne was engrossed in her own fairytale – that much was clear. Julia forced herself not to steal a curious glance at the other sketchbooks on the desk. She put the papers on the seat of Anne's desk chair, closed the window and left the bedroom.

When she stepped into the Ebner family's front yard, Thorsten's mother was sitting on the deck, sipping from a glass of wine. "So you're Anne's sister," she said pleasantly. "Nice to meet you."

Julia picked another deck chair and gratefully took the can of Coke Mrs. Ebner handed to her. "Thanks for inviting me."

"Of course. It's nice to finally meet face to face! Thorsten has told me a lot about you, actually. Aren't you the girl who loves going for runs in torrential downpours?"

Julia laughed. "Well, I can hear I've made a nice impression on you."

Thorsten stepped onto the deck with a plate of sausages, catching her last wods. "I told my mom I admired you a lot." He grinned playfully.

Julia blushed. "You did, huh?"

Thorsten caught her gaze. "Yup," he simply replied, no longer playful.

Quickly, she looked away, almost choking on the large swig of Coke she chugged down. Why was he still able to make her nervous? Maybe this wasn't such a good idea after all.

"Anyway, I'm starving," she announced in the silence that had fallen. "I don't know why, really. I mean, I've been on a picnic with Michael in the park all afternoon, so I should be stuffed."

Thorsten smiled. "Did you have a good time?" he asked serenely.

Julia cringed a bit. Even though he didn't sound at all jealous, it was still obvious her remark had stung him. "Yes, we did," she replied. "He's coming over for dinner at my place tomorrow night."

While enjoying the food, Julia told them a bit more about her afternoon in the park and her new job at the bookstore. She actually felt comfortable around Thorsten and his mother. When she got up at seven in order to get Anne, she was almost sorry to leave.

"Thanks again for inviting me," she said when Thorsten walked her to the gate. "It was nice to meet your mother."

He looked at her and unexpectedly took her hand in his. "It was nice to see you so radiant and happy," he said earnestly. "That Michael is a really lucky guy, you know."

Before she had time to react, he bent forward and kissed her on the cheek before swiveling around and walking back to the table.

On her way to the bus stop Julia felt a dull headache setting in. It could be due to sitting in the sun all day, but then again, it could also be all of today's impressions. By the time she rang her grandmother's doorbell, the pain hadn't subsided. It had only gotten worse.

"My sweet girl, you look like you've been put through a wringer," Gran exclaimed when opening the door. "Do you need something for that headache?"

Of course, Psychic Gran knew exactly what was wrong with her the moment she set eyes on her.

"Some paracetamol would be nice," Julia moaned. "Or something else to patch me up. I'm still going out tonight."

Gran looked at her doubtfully. "Are you sure? If I were you, I'd make it an early night."

Anne appeared in the hallway, holding a half-eaten Popsicle in her hand. "Are we going soon? I still want to go to the woods when we get back."

"No, you'll stay in until mom gets home," Julia said in a strict voice.

"But..." her sister started.

"No buts. You can go tomorrow. Those trees aren't going anywhere."

Anne glowered at her and stomped away indignantly. Julia sighed, slumping against her grandmother when the old woman put a hand on her shoulder. "Don't budge, Julia. Anne is reaching puberty and she has a very strong will of her own." Gran frowned. "I can sense something is bothering her."

"Yes, that's my impression too. She's running away from upsetting things lately, fleeing into the woods all by herself, writing in her diary a lot. I think she's beginning to miss Dad more and more."

Her grandmother nodded. "Maybe we should talk about this. Why don't you come over for dinner tomorrow night? I'll make your favorite pancakes."

Julia bit her lip. "I can't. Uhm... Michael is coming over for dinner tomorrow."

"Oh, really?" Gran shot her a curious look.

"Yes. He turned out to have a job at the bookstore too. He told me… well, he's in love with me."

"How wonderful for you, sweetheart!" Gran gave her a sunny smile. "So it wasn't as complicated as you thought after all."

Actually, it *was* complicated, but she didn't have the time or energy to explain it to Gran. Julia rubbed her forehead with a pained expression on her face. Her grandmother opened the top drawer of the hallway cupboard and pulled out a strip of paracetamol. "Stay here. I'll get you some water."

Gran popped into the kitchen and soon returned with a glass of water, Anne following in her wake.

"Are you going out tonight?" Anne wanted to know.

Julia made a noncommittal sound. "I'm just going to Axel's for a few hours. But I think I'll stay in if this headache doesn't go away."

"Hmm," Anne muttered, sounding a bit disgruntled over the fact that her big sister wasn't going out. Julia frowned. Could she be planning on sneaking out to the woods with no one around to pay attention? Perhaps it was better if she stayed at home then – she wasn't about to let Anne off the hook.

"Shall I ask Ignaz to give you a ride home?" Gran asked. "That will be quicker than the bus."

"Yes, please," Julia sighed. Gran's neighbor often helped them out by playing cabbie, and she couldn't wait to get home and lie down.

A little later, Julia was slumped into the back seat of Ignaz's old Volvo. Anne was in the passenger seat chatting animatedly to their grandmother's neighbor. Her foul mood seemed to have blown over. She hadn't mentioned the woods again, but Julia was determined not to let Anne out of her sight. Besides, she really didn't want to go out anymore – so far, the paracetamol hadn't worked at all.

"Hey, look, Sabine is having a barbecue," Anne enthused when Ignaz dropped them off at their doorstep. "Shall we go and say hi?"

"Go ahead," Julia said. "I was there before picking you up. Why don't you ask them if they have any sausages left for you, and I'll call Gaby to cancel our date."

As Anne dashed into the neighboring yard, Julia shambled inside. "Hey, Gab," she said when her friend answered the phone. "I have a killer headache. I won't be able to make it tonight."

There was a pause at the other end of the line. "But..." Gaby started, her voice sounding a little strangled. "I'm already on my way!"

"Well, good. Say hi to Axel for me. I'm sure you guys will have a good time."

"But he invited us both. Please don't ditch on me. Maybe he doesn't want to see just me."

Julia snickered. "Don't be an idiot. Why wouldn't he want to see just you? He asked you out to dinner, for crying out loud. *Just* you."

"Movie night is totally different, though," Gaby persisted.

"Oh, for the love of Pete. I can't deal with this right now. My head is about to explode, and you're not helping. You're a big girl and I'm sure you'll survive this night without me just fine."

Gaby swallowed audibly. "Well. Okay then. Talk to you later."

"Call me." Julia hung up and flopped down on her bed. Maybe her headache was a blessing in disguise: this would give Axel the opportunity to have Gaby all to himself for the night. She could only hope he'd use this golden opportunity to his advantage – if her best friend and her cousin were going to be this twitchy around each other for much longer, it would drive her stark raving mad.

Julia pushed herself off the bed and looked out the window. Anne was sitting at the neighbors' yard table having a hotdog. Good – she was being taken care of. Mom would be home in less than thirty minutes, so she could hit the sack at the same time Anne went to bed. This day, wonderful as it might have been, had left her drained.

Just as she was dozing off, her sister's voice startled her from sleep. "Hey. Have you been in my room?"

Julia sat upright, blinking at Anne holding a pile of paper in one hand. Her little sister looked upset.

"Oh. Yes, I have. I picked up some of your drawings. The wind had blown them off your desk. Why?"

Anne bit her lip and gave a tiny shrug. "Nothing. I just thought you'd secretly taken a peek."

"Why would I do that?"

Anne didn't answer the question. Instead, she clutched the drawings close to her chest. "You can't look at them," she said nervously. "They're secret."

Her sister's words stung more than Julia cared to admit. Maybe the times sharing stories and fairytales with Anne about the forest so close to their house were gone – a thing of the past. Anne wanted to keep her stories to herself now.

"Well, I didn't see anything world-shattering," she replied, smiling weakly. "Just put them away properly in the future."

At that moment, Julia heard the front door slamming shut downstairs. "I'm home!" their mother called up at them.

"I'm going to say hi," Anne said, padding out of the room still clutching her drawings. Julia decided to put on her pajamas and crawl into bed. She was dead beat. By the time her mother popped in to say hello, she had almost fallen asleep again.

"Hey, Mom," she mumbled blearily. "Michael's having dinner here tomorrow."

Ms. Gunther cocked her head. "Michael Kolbe? That boy from the woods?"

"Yeah, that one. He's one of my colleagues."

"Ah." Her mother looked at her expectantly, a smile tugging at her lips. Slowly, Julia's face flooded with color.

"We… we went out today," she floundered. "To the park. And it was fun. And so I thought it'd be nice to invite him for dinner."

"If you're cooking." Her mom winked. "How about pizza? I'm going to pay aunt Verena a visit during the day, so I won't have time to prepare anything, but you're not working tomorrow, are you?"

Julia smiled. "Leave everything to me."

"Well, why don't you get some beauty sleep now? You have an exciting day ahead." Her mother kissed her on the forehead and walked out the door humming a happy tune.

With a faint smile still on her lips, Julia switched off her bedside light and floated off to sleep in mere seconds.

9.

She was walking in the forest. The trees around her were giants looming over her, and just for a moment, Julia felt as if she herself had shrunk in size. Somewhere, far away in the distance, music resounded in the woods.

'Have you seen him?' the trees whispered to her, their ancient voices like leaves in the breeze.

'Who?' she asked without speaking.

'The boy from the woods,' the trees replied.

'Who? Michael?'

'His heart longed to be with you.'

The music grew louder. A moan escaped from Julia's throat when she slowly woke up and realized her phone was ringing.

Groping around blearily, she found her bag under the bed and rummaged around to find her cell phone and answer it.

"Hey Flo," she muttered. "Thanks for your wake-up call."

"Oh, I'm sorry!" Florian yelped. "I thought you'd be awake by now. It's eleven o'clock, you know."

"Really?" Julia sat up a bit straighter, rubbing the sleep from her eyes. "Geez, I've slept the whole morning through. And I went to bed at nine yesterday! Strange."

"Well, I bet you feel very rested then. Would you like to join me this afternoon when I go to Moritz's band practice? I'm going to be his Yoko for the very first time."

"Sounds great! What time are you going?"

"Around four."

"Oh, uhm, no. That's inconvenient for me, really. Michael's coming over for dinner tonight."

Florian started to chuckle. "Ah, yes! Axel told me. You went on a date with him yesterday, right?"

"Yeah, and it was awesome."

"I'm really happy for you," Florian said warmly. "Apparently, that blow to the head did wonders for his social skills."

"Yeah, it did. And don't ask me why, because I'm not asking any more questions myself. I'm just so sickeningly happy that I don't care."

"Well, enjoy the rest of your day, Julius. I'm going to call the others. Axel might join me. Do you know whether Gaby and Tamara are working today?"

"Haven't got a clue. Let's all meet up together some evening this week, okay? Say hi to Moritz from me."

Julia rung off. The dream images were still lingering in her mind. The trees talking to her, telling her that Michael had longed for her... was it possible the forest sprites had really known what he felt for her? Was this their way of telling her? She couldn't escape the feeling that the dream had been a message. It had felt so life-like, despite the fact that it contained very strange elements.

At that moment, her mom pushed open the bedroom door. "Hey, sleepy head! Finally back in the land of the living? There are some fresh breadrolls downstairs if you want."

"Great, Mom, thanks!"

"You're welcome. I have to go now, but I'll be back around five. Anne is going on a playdate with Sabine, so you'll have the house to yourself. Why don't you take your time to lay the table with our velvet tablecloth and take out the candlesticks, honey?"

"You're so funny, ha-ha," Julia grumbled, but still got up to give her mother a quick hug. "I'll take things easy today. Have fun at Aunt Verena's."

After her mom left, Julia rooted around in her wardrobe to dig up a light summer dress and flip-flops. Still in her PJs, she made her way to the bathroom to take a fresh shower. Anne was in her room, loudly playing the Lord of the Rings soundtrack. She was probably drawing or writing again.

Just as Julia stepped out of the shower cabin with a towel around her body, she heard Anne's phone ring in the room next door. Her sister turned off the music and answered her cell phone in a hushed voice. Strange.

"Was that Mom calling you?" she asked when she bumped into Anne in the hallway.

"No, one of my classmates. She asked if I wanted to come along to the pool."

"I thought you had a playdate with Sabine today?"

Anne stared at the floor. "I don't know if I'm going to the pool yet."

"Oh well, you don't have to choose, do you? You can also go to the pool with Sabine *and* the other girl."

"I don't know," Anne repeated, looking subdued.

Julia impulsively flung an arm around her sister's slender shoulders. "What's up, Annie? You feeling down?"

Anne shrugged. "Yes and no."

Again with the evasiveness. Julia sighed. "You know, why don't we have breakfast together? Maybe you'll want to talk about it over a nice, big plate of breadrolls. Okay?"

"All right."

In silence, they walked down the stairs. It wasn't until Julia put down two plates of food on the kitchen table that Anne opened her mouth again.

"Who's that boy who's coming over for dinner tonight?" she asked softly.

"Michael? He's a colleague of mine."

Anne looked at her attentively. "Are you in love with him?"

Julia blushed. "Busted," she joked. "Yeah, I really like him."

"How do you know when you're in love with someone? Or when someone is in love with you?" Anne continued.

Julia thought over her answer. "When you're in love with someone, you think about that person all day. You long to spend every last minute of the day with him or her. And when someone is in love with you, they often try and be around you as much as possible. And they'll say nice, sweet things to you, of course," she replied with a smile.

Her sister bit her lip. "That's the reason I like going to the forest so much, lately," she mumbled quietly.

"You're in love?"

"When I go into the woods... to that place I don't want to tell you about... the Prince of the Forest is there, too."

Julia smiled indulgently. "You mean the prince who's helping you build your tree house?" Just Thorsten's luck – the *wrong* neighbor girl had fallen for him.

Anne shook her head. "I help *him*, he doesn't help me. And it's not really a tree house, but an entrance to his palace."

"Uhm... like a gate of sorts?" Julia frowned. This story was getting stranger by the minute, Anne apparently using elements of her fairytale to talk about everyday life.

Suddenly, this all felt wrong – it didn't sound like innocent make-believe anymore. Grandma was right: something serious was going on if Anne felt the need to escape into fairytales like this.

Anne shook her head once more. "No, not a gate. A tunnel. But I can't tell you where it is." Her voice dropped. "No one is supposed to know where it is."

They both kept quiet for a moment, a shiver running down Julia's spine as she held her sister's gaze. There was something profoundly wrong with the look in Anne's eyes – she didn't look as if she was enjoying the mystery of her story. Anne was deeply *afraid*. It hit her like a punch to the stomach.

"Why can't you?" Julia continued carefully. She didn't want Anne to clamp up again, so that meant taking it easy and not firing off all the questions going through her mind at once.

"Because… it's a mystery. Just like the prince remains a mystery to the adults in the real world. They don't see him for what he truly is."

"And you do?"

Anne turned red. "Yes, but he told me I wasn't supposed to talk about him. Or about that place where he's building stuff. He'd get mad."

Julia's stomach turned. She had no idea what was going on, but every nerve in her body told her something was seriously wrong with Anne. It was almost as though she couldn't separate truth from fiction anymore. How was she supposed to handle this? She couldn't do this alone. It was best to call her mom straight away.

She pushed her chair back and stood up. "Anne, I would really like to discuss this with Mom. You look scared and I want to help you, but I don't know how. Why don't you wait here while I give her a call?"

Julia rushed out of the kitchen and ran up the stairs to get her phone and call her mom.

Fortunately, her mom answered on the second ring. "Hey, honey. What's up?"

"Mom." Hearing her mom's voice suddenly made her eyes water up. "Something weird is going on with Anne."

"What do you mean?" her mom cried out in alarm. "Is she sick?"

"No, it's not that. At least, I don't think so. It's just that she's telling all kinds of absurd stories about what she's been doing in the woods lately. You know she's building a tree house with Sabine, right? And she didn't want to tell us where they were building it? I know she's also working on a fairytale of her own. It's her version of the Prince of the Forest, and now she's telling me the *prince* told her to keep her mouth shut about the location of the tree house. She's suffering from a case of puppy love for Thorsten and she probably cast him in the role of heroic prince in her mind, but this is seriously giving me the creeps. It's so bizarre – I don't know what to think."

"Well, didn't she simply make up a story to entertain you? You girls tell each other fairytales all the time, don't you?"

"No, Mom." Julia swallowed hard. "She's afraid. Like, really scared. I could see it in her eyes. She said something terrible would happen if she talked about it. She said the prince would be angry with her if she did."

Her mother stayed quiet on the other end of the line. "I know Anne for her flights of fancy, but you're right: this doesn't make sense," she admitted at last. "If I didn't know any better, I'd say she's used drugs, triggering some kind of psychosis."

Julia laughed nervously. "I think she's a bit too young for that."

"Well, it's just a shot in the dark." Her mom paused for a few seconds. "How well do you know this Thorsten guy?"

"Not that well, but he seems nice enough."

"Do you know whether he smokes pot?"

Julia's mouth turned dry. She had no idea, but it wasn't completely unlikely. Closing her eyes, she tried to imagine Thorsten holding a joint while playing guitar at some deserted spot in the forest, watching the two girls at work.

"Are you implying Thorsten offered a joint to my little sister while they were building their hut in the woods?" she asked, her head spinning.

"I'm just thinking out loud," Ms. Gunther replied. "Maybe he has no idea what kind of effect that stuff has on young brains. And who knows, he might have actually told Anne and Sabine to keep the location a secret for now. If Anne is drugged up on something, those words may have morphed into a threat in *her* mind."

On shaky legs, Julia stumbled backward, sagging down in the easy chair in the corner of her bedroom. "I can't believe it. I can't *conceive* of it. What the hell was he thinking?" Her mom was right: this had to be what was going on. Thorsten had unwittingly scared her sister by saying the tree house should be a secret, and he might even have let her take a puff of his cannabis while they'd been at work in the woods. He probably hadn't meant any harm, but sadly he had harmed Anne nonetheless.

"Do you want me to come home?" her mom asked.

"No, I don't think that's necessary. Anne is probably going to the pool with Sabine in a minute, so she'll be fine. But rest assured I'll talk to Thorsten today. He's in *big* trouble."

Julia ended the call and stomped out of her room with a grim face. No matter how sweet and nice the boy next door was, he had managed to really piss her off now. He should have stayed away from her little sister.

"Anne?" She popped her head round the kitchen door. "I'm cycling down to Eichet to run some errands. Are you going to the neighbors?"

Anne got up and flung both arms around Julia's waist. "What did Mommy say?" she whispered.

"She said you don't have to be scared. The prince can't harm you," Julia said soothingly, deciding to play along for now. "And if you really think he's scary, you should tell him you don't want to see him anymore when you run into him again."

"Okay." Anne pressed her cheek against Julia's shoulder. "I will."

A few minutes later, Julia rolled her bike out of the yard and dropped Anne off at the neighbors' door across the street. Sabine and her mother were home and welcomed Anne with beaming faces, so her sister would undoubtedly have a good time today.

Meanwhile, Thorsten would have a *hard* time today if it were up to her. Julia was hell-bent on talking to him, and if that meant she had to disturb the peace in the local supermarket, she wouldn't shy away from it. So what if he was working and he had no time for her? She was simmering with anger, and her frantic bike trip to Eichet didn't make it any better. When she finally propped up her bike against the wall and ran into the store, she almost knocked over a cart partially blocking the entrance. Her face flushed red with fury, she cornered the first store assistant she encountered, demanding to know where Thorsten was.

"Oh, he just went to the back to get something from the warehouse," the girl replied.

"Thanks." Julia stalked toward the double doors leading to the warehouse. Fortunately, she knew her way around the supermarket because her mom worked here too. It didn't take long for her to spot Thorsten. Without breaking stride, she approached him and stopped right in front of him, her arms crossed. "I need to speak to you," she said coolly.

He shot her a puzzled look. "Uhm, sure," he said, putting down the box he was carrying. "What's up?"

"You have to stop saying weird things to Anne," Julia exploded. "You can't say things like you'll get angry if she reveals the spot where you guys are building that tree hut. She's really scared, okay? And my mom and I wouldn't be surprised to learn you were smoking dope in the woods out there while working on the damn thing. Anne is dishing up the most unbelievable, *psychotic* stories about it."

Thorsten's eyes widened, a look of deep incomprehension crossing his face. "I'm sorry, but *what* the hell are you talking about?"

"I'm talking about Anne."

"Yeah, I got that. I just don't get the rest. To be honest, I think *you* sound psychotic."

Julia drew breath and peered at Thorsten. He seemed to be genuinely perplexed. He probably couldn't have fathomed he'd have such a big impact on Anne and her wild imagination.

"Okay. I can see how my story sounds cluttered, but what I mean to say is that my sister has a very soft spot for you and whatever you say to her influences her more than you realize."

Thorsten heaved a sigh, shaking his head. "Look, I think you're barking up the wrong tree here. I didn't help Anne and Sabine in the woods at all. Well, I made a few sketches for them so they'd have blueprints and I helped them haul some timber, but that's about it. How am I supposed to help those kids every day? I'm working, right? I've been putting in shifts here four days a week."

In the silence that ensued, Julia took a few hesitant steps backward as Thorsten's words slowly sunk in.

He hadn't helped the girls. He hadn't even joined them on their trips to the woods. So how on *earth* had Anne come up with that uncanny story of hers?

"Are you sure you've never used drugs in Anne's presence?" she pressed on, but she could hear her voice falter.

"Okay, that's it," Thorsten snapped. "What kind of a person do you think I am, huh? I don't use drugs, and even if I did, surely it would never occur to me to smoke pot right in front of my baby sister and her best friend! What gives you the right to barge in here and accuse me of all kinds of horrible things?"

"I'm sorry," Julia whispered, her face red with shame. Thorsten was absolutely right. She'd been prepared to peg him as an irresponsible pothead just so she'd have an explanation for Anne's odd story. Julia wiped at the sudden tears in her eyes, letting out a shaky breath. Now that it turned out Thorsten *wasn't* the dope-smoking loser she'd accused him of being, she had no ideas left – except the thought that Anne was losing her mind. Was her sister going crazy?

"Hey, don't cry," Thorsten said, looking startled. He put his hand on her shoulder. "I'm sorry I yelled at you; I didn't mean to upset you. What exactly is Anne afraid of, then?"

"I… I don't know," Julia stuttered in confusion. "I don't understand."

Thorsten pulled her closer, his arm encircling her waist. "I think you should go home and talk with Anne one more time," he said earnestly. "Kids at that age can have vivid imaginations. Maybe a bit *too* vivid. If you really think something is wrong with her, I bet your mom could ask a specialist to look into it."

"I will," Julia replied timidly. "I'm truly sorry."

"Apology accepted," he said softly. "You're just worried about Anne, so let's forget this ever happened." He pressed a kiss to her forehead and let go of her. "Why don't you drop by my mom and ask her if she knows what they're up to in the woods these days? She might know. Hey, I finish at three today, so I'll come round and see if you're any better this afternoon, okay?"

Julia nodded. "Thanks. I'd appreciate that."

Still feeling mystified, she found herself dazedly standing next to her bike after leaving the supermarket. When she moved at last, Julia got on and rode to her grandmother's house on automatic pilot. Her grandma was in the front yard watering the plants. She waved when she saw her granddaughter coming up the drive.

"How nice of you to come visit me today before Michael demands all your attention tonight," she said with a cheeky smile, but her face fell when she looked at Julia more closely. "What's the matter? You look worried."

When her grandma came toward her and pulled her into a hug, Julia broke down in tears. Without asking anything else, Gran took her inside and walked her to the kitchen, where she silently and calmly poured the two of them a cup of tea. She pushed the cookie jar across the table and Julia dug up a chocolate cookie, eating it without really tasting anything. Her whole body felt weak and she slurped some of her tea to get warm and fight her dizziness.

"Grandma," she started in a small voice. "Didn't you say you thought something was going on with Anne the other day?"

The old woman looked at her searchingly. "I had a certain feeling something was off, yes. Has something happened?"

Julia nodded and softly related to her grandmother what Anne had told her that morning – how she seemed to really believe in the fairytale she'd made up by herself. How scared she had been.

"Oh dear." Gran looked shocked. "You're right to worry about this. I know Anne loves fairytales, just like you, but it doesn't make sense for her to escape into a story she's actually afraid of."

"Could it be she's come up with that fairytale to *protect* herself from something she's afraid of?"

Gran fell silent for a moment. "You said she mentioned she wasn't allowed to talk about it? She said it was a secret?"

"Yes?" Julia held her breath.

"It reminds me of the peculiar behavior of a friend I used to have when I was a young girl." Gran stared at the cup of tea in her hands. "She used to love making up all kinds of fantastical stories, but I always found her to be a bit anxious and guarded in her behavior. Sometimes she would mention a secret she wasn't allowed to share with anyone. At some point, we found out her father beat her up regularly. He might have done other things to her, too. I always felt as if she was harboring a great sadness."

A shiver ran down Julia's spine. "You think Anne is being *abused* by someone close to her? Someone we know?"

"I don't know. It is a possibility."

"But who? Who could it be?" Frantically, she ran off a mental list of people Anne dealt with on a daily basis: people in their neighborhood, at school, during music lessons...

Gran put a hand on her arm. "If I were you, I'd discuss it with your mother this afternoon and involve Anne too. She could talk to the doctor, or maybe to someone in Child Care. There's no point implicating each and every person who comes to mind. After all, you don't want to make any false accusations. Certainly not in a case like this."

The confrontation with Thorsten came back to her in a flash, and Julia cringed. Her grandmother was right – she didn't want to go down that road again.

"I'm going home," she decided. "And I'll call Mom to ask her to come back a bit early so we can talk to Anne together."

"Good luck," Gran said. "I'll call the two of you tonight."

Deep in thought, Julia cycled home. The sun was shining and the birds were singing, but it was as if a troubled shadow hovered over her. Thinking about Michael's visit tonight didn't even help – she was worried sick about Anne. She'd never been so scared in all of her life.

After putting her bike back in the shed, Julia crossed the street to visit the neighbors. Thorsten had suggested talking to his mother, so that's what she'd do first. It was possible Mrs. Ebner had noticed something peculiar about Anne's behavior too.

Sabine and her mother were sitting on the lawn playing a card game. Julia froze, a bud of panic blossoming in her chest. Where was her sister?

"Hey, Julia," Sabine greeted her. "Anne just left. She said she was going to her grandmother."

"To Gran?" Julia felt the blood drain from her face. If that were true, she would have bumped into Anne on her way back from Eichet... unless her sister had decided to cycle through the woods.

"See you later," she mumbled, running back to her own house to get out her bike again. At break-neck speed, Julia raced to the woods, gasping for breath by the time she reached the main forest trail running between the trees. From this point onward, she would have to slow down because of the bumpy road, but she tried to use it to her advantage by feverishly looking left and right in the hopes of spotting Anne somewhere.

When the path ended and the trees thinned out, Julia came to a complete stop and stared unseeingly at the blue sky peeking through the chestnut trees at the end of the trail. She felt sick to her stomach, dread sending a spike of adrenaline through her veins. The tension coursing through her body made her muscles feel weak.

Anne was nowhere to be found. She didn't believe for one second that her baby sister had decided to visit Gran today. She'd been wanting to go back to the forest since last night, and so she'd snuck off, disappearing deep into the woods.

Julia patted both her pants pockets looking for her cell phone until she remembered it was still at home. No phone calls to Anne or her grandmother, then. In despair, she slowly swiveled around, peering in every direction. She parked her bike against a tree and in a last-ditch effort to find Anne without help, Julia started to jog alongside the edge of the woods. Maybe she'd discover Anne wandering around somewhere if she headed north, where the forest turned darker and denser.

"This is crazy," she mumbled to herself after trotting along for five minutes without finding a trace of her sister. There was no point spending a fruitless afternoon darting around like an idiot.

Just as she decided to turn around and go back to her bike, Julia suddenly did spot someone walking between the trees further up north. The figure was still far away, but it was definitely some hiker trudging through the woods. He might have seen Anne somewhere. Julia closed her eyes and tried to slow down her breathing. She'd wait here and address the person when he emerged from the forest. When the walker drew nearer, she saw it was a boy not much older than she was.

Her heart stopped when he came even closer. The sunlight hit his long, blond hair. Two bright, blue eyes bore into hers. He emerged from the trees and Julia's hands started to tremble.

She was staring at the angelic face of Legolas with Thorsten's blue eyes.

It was the Prince of the Forest. The boy Anne had drawn in her sketches – the drawings Julia wasn't supposed to have seen.

10.

"*Grüss Gott*," the boy greeted her politely.

Julia swallowed. "Hi there." Her voice sounded shrill, but the boy didn't seem to notice. He passed her and walked on, veering off to the right to get to the road leading down to Eichet. Julia hesitated for a second, then started to follow him at a distance, sweat pooling in the palms of her hands. She hoped he wouldn't look back.

Anne had met this guy in the forest. This very guy. She was sure of it. And this was her chance to find out where he lived and tell him to leave Anne alone. What if *he* had given her drugs? What if he had abused her, even? Julia tried to blink back tears. With a knot in her stomach, she followed the guy until he entered a detached house in one of the richer neighborhoods of Eichet, a short distance away from the next block of houses on the quiet street.

Julia indecisively stopped behind a big tree next to the boy's residence, her eyes fixed on the front door. Now what? Was she absolutely sure this guy had done something wrong – or was she about to saddle another innocent person with a bunch of sinister motivations and make a fool of herself for the second time today?

Frowning deeply, Julia let out a sigh and turned around after memorizing the street name and the house number. She started to jog back to the place where she'd left her bike. Maybe she was kicking up a fuss over nothing. Maybe Anne would be back by the time she got home. And if not, she'd call her on her cell and tell her to come home immediately. She'd call her mom, too. Everything would be just fine.

When Julia turned into her street, Mrs. Ebner emerged from her house and crossed the street to stop her. "Julia," she said with a worried face. "What's wrong? Have you found Anne?"

"No, I haven't." Julia put her bike against the fence. "I'm going to call her now. And my mom as well."

"I'm sorry I let her go by herself. I feel so bad now. I didn't think there was any harm in letting Anne go to her grandmother, but then Sabine just told me..." Her voice trailed off.

"What?" Julia prompted the neighbor anxiously.

"Sabine says Anne is in the habit of going off on her own into the woods a lot lately. And she has no idea what Anne is doing there. Sometimes your sister would get a text message and she'd take off shortly afterwards, and she wouldn't tell Sabine who it was from, but she did mention she was going to 'work on her story'."

"Oh my God." Julia lowered herself onto the fence, her legs shaking. "And she only told you this *now*?"

"Yes, because Anne kept saying it was a secret. Sabine didn't want to betray her trust." Mrs. Ebner's face looked pale. "I think you should call the police. There's something fishy about the whole story, I'm telling you."

"I'm going to make a few phone calls." Julia went inside and ran up the stairs to get her cell phone and check it for messages. No missed calls or texts. She called Anne and heard it ring several times before switching to voicemail. "Anne, you have to come home right this instant," she said hoarsely. "And please call me back when you get this." She hung up and called her grandma.

"Hello?"

"Gran, it's Julia. Is Anne with you?"

"No, she isn't. Julia, what's going on? Did you talk to her?"

Julia took a deep breath. "No, I didn't get the chance. She wasn't here when I got home. I'm going to call Mom now, okay?" Her voice cracked.

"You do that. Let me know what happened, dear."

"I will, Gran."

Julia hung up and called her mom's cell. No reply. She didn't want to just leave a voicemail, so she called the landline. Fortunately, Uncle Helmut answered the phone after two rings.

"Hey. It's Julia. Is Mom still with you and Aunt Verena?"

"Yes, they're having coffee out on the patio. You want me to get her?"

"Please." While Julia waited for her mother to come to the phone, she got up and walked over to her sister's room. Haphazardly, she pulled open cabinets and drawers to look for Anne's sketchbooks and diary. Maybe she'd find some more clues in there.

"Hi, sweety. Have you talked to Thorsten?" her mom said, interrupting her search.

"I have, but he doesn't know anything. Mom… Anne is gone. She lied to the Ebners about wanting to visit Gran and she took off to go to the forest alone. I think…" Julia took a deep breath, a sob escaping her throat.

"Slow down," her mom called. "What happened? Why are you so upset?"

In fits and starts, Julia told her mom what Thorsten had said, what Gran had told her and the mysterious guy she'd bumped into when she was looking for Anne in the woods.

"Okay. I'm coming home right now," Ms. Gunther said, her voice trembling. "But first I'm calling the police. They might be there sooner than me, but you can go ahead and talk to them. Tell them the *exact* same story you've told me. I'll be there as soon as I can."

Julia clicked off. In the meantime, she'd managed to dig up a big pile of sketches Anne had made. She blindly stared at the other portraits her sister had done of the blond boy from the woods. There were three more besides the drawing she had already seen once, and the resemblance was striking. She had to give these to the cops as evidence.

Anne's desk drawer contained her diary. It was locked with a flimsy lock that didn't seem too hard to pick. Julia took the diary downstairs to get a small screwdriver from the toolbox. After three attempts, she managed to pry it open.

Julia sat down heavily at the kitchen table, the book in front of her.

When she opened the diary, Anne's childlike handwriting stared up at her from the pages. Julia wiped away a lonely tear, clenching her fists. The police just *had* to find her sister, and maybe she'd discover some clues in here to help them do that. Quickly, she flipped through the pages until something in the margin caught her eye. It was a whole string of hearts, connected by an elegant line that looked like a vine. The hearts were colored in with green felt pen. Julia's heart sped up as she started to read the decorated diary page.

"Me and Sabine started our work on the tree house, and when she went home I stayed behind to walk a bit deeper into the forest. And something happened there. It was like a dream! There was a beautiful boy there, sitting on a tree trunk. He started to talk to me and he

said he thought I looked beautiful too! He said I look like a princess. But I'm not supposed to tell anyone I saw him there. I think he might be the Prince of the Forest!! Is he actually real?"

"So today I asked him whether he was the prince of the woods, and he told me I had guessed right. I can't believe it! He says the portal to his palace is somewhere in this forest, and that is why I can't tell anyone about him or about our meetings. He's trying to hide the entrance to Fairyland so no one else can find it. Before I went home, he danced with me and he even kissed me, just like in the storybooks. I'm so in love!!!"

"He gave me some mushrooms today. He said that if I ate from them, I'd be able to see the fairies living on the other side of the portal for just a few seconds. It was so weird. First I saw all kinds of beautiful and wonderful things, but afterwards I had to throw up. I guess it's because I had to come back to the human world."

"I sat in his lap with his arms around me, and I ate another one of those fairy mushrooms. It felt like I was floating. He said he'd make me his princess when he returns to his palace. Every day he tells me I'm pretty!! He's my dream prince."

"He was angry with me. I showed him a drawing I did of his face, and he tore it up. And then he yelled at me, saying I should never tell anyone about him or the entrance to his realm because something terrible would happen if I did. I was planning to tell Julia about him, but now I'm scared. Why was he so angry? Isn't he in love with me anymore?"

Julia's stomach turned as she pushed the diary across the table and leaned back in her chair. This was so perverted and *wrong* on all levels that she couldn't stop trembling. So it really *was* that blond boy she'd met in the woods. That sick pedophile had touched Anne. He had held her in his arms, kissed her, fed her shrooms. He'd lied to her so he could turn into her fairytale prince. And she, Julia, had innocently told Anne this very morning that the prince couldn't hurt her and couldn't force her to keep seeing him if she didn't want to.

And suddenly, she remembered the phone call Anne had received while she was in the bathroom. Maybe it hadn't been one of her classmates at all. Maybe it had been that boy, telling her to come see him in the forest. So that's why Anne had seemed so anxious and insecure.

Julia startled when the doorbell rang. Fighting back her tears, she got up to let the cops in. She had to be coherent for their interrogation. The diary could be used as evidence, too, so it was a good thing she'd found it.

But it wasn't the police. When she opened the door, Thorsten was standing there. "H-hey," she stammered. "Weren't you supposed to work until three?"

He stepped inside. "I clocked out a bit early. I was worried about you." He cast her an inquisitive look. "And rightly so. You look terrible. Have you talked to Anne yet?"

Hearing her sister's name was too much. Julia burst out in tears. "No," she wailed. "Anne is gone. She's disappeared. And I'm so scared that this boy may have hurt her."

"Hold on. *What* boy?"

"The boy from the woods," Julia whispered. "The boy she drew. The boy she talks about in her diary." She headed for the kitchen on trembling legs and showed Thorsten the diary and the sketches, relating the story about bumping into the mysterious Legolas-lookalike in the forest, the drawings Anne had made, and the creepy stories she'd come home with.

"The police are on their way and I'm sure they'll take the guy in for questioning," Thorsten reassured her, a grim look on his face. "He'll think twice before bothering Anne again. I don't think he has hurt her – he wouldn't dare. He knows she made sketches of him, after all."

"I hope you're right," Julia replied dejectedly. She got out her cell – still no messages. "But, Thorsten – what if she *doesn't* come home? What am I gonna do?"

"Let's give it some time." Thorsten put his arms around her, rocking her back and forth gently when she started to cry again. "Just calm down."

A few minutes later, the front door swung open and Ms. Gunther stepped inside, three police officers following in her wake. She looked at her oldest daughter anxiously. "Anne is still gone?"

Julia blinked at her mom. It was time to tell her all the other things she'd discovered, but she didn't even know where to start. Luckily, Thorsten stepped in and showed the police the diary and the drawings, telling them everything Julia had told him. He also gave them the address of the mysterious boy in the sketchbook.

"We'll go there and check it out," the detective leading the team promised them. "I think I'll get out a search warrant immediately. If he's keeping that little girl in or around the house somewhere, we'll find her."

"Can we come?" Julia asked timidly.

The detective shook his head. "You don't want to, really. It won't be pretty. I'll be back here as soon as I can."

The police left and Ms. Gunther slumped down on the kitchen bench next to Julia and Thorsten. "I should have paid more attention to her," she mumbled vacantly. "I should have been home more. I shouldn't have let her wander around alone so much."

Julia's heart cracked when she heard her mom blaming herself. Admittedly, she'd thought the very same things herself just a few days ago, but it wasn't her mother's fault this had happened. Besides, what could she have done differently, anyway? She was a single mom with two daughters.

"Don't do this, Mom," she whispered, pulling her closer. "Don't be so hard on yourself. How were we supposed to know what was happening in that forest?"

"I'm sorry," her mom replied, a desperate sob in her voice.

Thorsten got up. "I'm gonna ask Sabine what she knows one more time," he said determinedly. "Maybe the right questions will jog her memory. My mother said she knew more about Anne's wanderings in the woods."

Julia looked up. "Are you coming back?" All of a sudden, she badly needed his support. He gave her the strength to believe in a happy ending.

He nodded. "I'll be back soon," he promised.

Ms. Gunther jumped to her feet and started to bustle around the kitchen, viciously scrubbing all the countertops with a sponge. "I can't sit around like this," she explained when Julia caught her eye. "I'll lose my mind if I start thinking too much."

Julia smiled wanly, left the kitchen and sat down on the bottom step of the stairs clutching her cell phone.

The first thing she did was call Axel to tell him about the events of the day.

"What?" he exclaimed disbelievingly. "I'll be there as soon as I can. We were on our way to Moritz's band practice anyway, so we're already on the bus."

"We?" Julia parroted.

"Yeah, Gaby and me. We'll be there before you know it, okay?"

When the doorbell rang, both Julia and her mother almost tripped on their way to the front door, but it wasn't the police. Thorsten was there, flanked by Sabine. The girl anxiously looked up at them all. "I didn't know she was doing dangerous things," their youngest neighbor said in a strangled voice. "She always looked so happy when she came back from the forest. And she said I shouldn't tell her secret to anyone."

Ms. Gunther put a consoling hand on Sabine's head. "You can't help it, sweetheart. Why don't you tell us now? Tell us all you know about Anne and where she always went."

"Well, she said that if I ever stumbled upon some kind of door in the woods, I shouldn't go through it, because it would upset the Prince of the Forest."

"A door?" Julia thought of the portal Anne had talked about in her diary.

"Yes, that's what she said. I thought it was weird. You find doors in houses, and there are no houses in the woods. I thought she was just telling me about stuff in her story. I knew she was busy writing and drawing things for it."

"Isn't it possible there's some abandoned cabin somewhere in the woods?" Thorsten suggested.

"No idea," Julia replied. "I've never encountered anything like that, but then again, I mostly stick to the trails when I go running or biking."

"Maybe we should go look for her?" Sabine looked around the circle of grown-ups, her lip trembling.

Thorsten nodded. "I think we will, but not with you tagging along. I'm not losing any more little girls to that forest today."

Sabine pleaded with her brother, but to no avail. She sulkily followed him out the door.

It didn't take long for Axel and Gaby to show up on their doorstep. Gaby ran up to her best friend and hugged her tightly as Julia wordlessly buried her face in Gaby's dark hair. "Oh my God, Gab, this whole day is like a nightmare," she sniffed, barely audible.

Axel hugged his aunt, and they all kept quiet for a few seconds. Then Julia pulled away from Gaby and took her and Axel to the kitchen to show them the sketches and the diary. Meanwhile, her mother made tea for everyone.

"That sick *fuck*," Axel spat, shoving the diary across the table when he was done reading. "You know what? I hope the police lock him up for the next thirty years. People like this shouldn't be allowed out ever again." He fell silent, his face white as a sheet. Gaby gently took his hand and pumped it encouragingly, which caused Axel to slump against her shoulder with a weak smile aimed in her direction.

Julia observed her two friends from across the table and felt the ghost of a smile cross her face. It looked as if yesterday's movie night had been good for Gaby and Axel.

When the doorbell rang yet again, it was Detective Spitzer, who had visited the boy's house in Eichet, followed by Thorsten. The elderly man entered the kitchen, his face grave.

"So?" Ms. Gunther looked up at him fretfully.

"We didn't find Anne." He grabbed a chair and sat down heavily. "We conducted a house search, but we couldn't find anything suspicious, or not much, anyway. We did find some magic mushrooms in the boy's bedroom. His name is Andreas Mittelmayer. We took him into custody for an interrogation at the station, so I'll keep you up to date and call you later in the day." The officer took a minute to drink from the mug of tea Julia handed him, and then continued in a quiet voice: "Having said that, we found some other items in the house that raised our suspicion. Different kinds of chloroform... but Mrs. Mittelmayer is a vet, so she needs narcotics for her job sometimes. Besides, you can't use chloroform to drug someone by surprise. That's an urban myth."

When Detective Spitzer had left, the five of them remained seated at the kitchen table as if stunned. Anne hadn't been in Andreas's house. So where *was* she? Was it possible she was still roaming the woods?

"Let's go look for her," Thorsten burst out. "For Anne, or for that mysterious door she was talking about... *anything*. We have to take action."

"I'm going to phone Grandma and Aunt Verena," Julia's mother announced. She grabbed Julia's hand in passing. "Don't stay out too long, okay? And please take your phone with you."

Julia nodded. She and Thorsten each got their own bikes, while Gaby and Axel borrowed Ms. Gunther's bike to ride it together. Gaby sat on the baggage rack and tightly held on to Axel, who was cycling.

Julia stopped pedaling her bike momentarily when she remembered her date with Michael. He would come to her place tonight. Wasn't it better to cancel their dinner together? Then again, she did want to see him. She wanted him to comfort her and hold her close, just like Thorsten had done earlier today. And for all she knew, they'd find Anne in the woods now, and this nightmare would be over before he even showed up.

When they got to the forest, they followed the main trail for a while until Thorsten got off his bicycle. "Let's leave the bikes here and walk." He pointed at a dark patch of trees blocking their sight. "Sabine told me where we can find the tree house they were working on, so we can use that spot as a meeting point and each go into one direction to do a search."

"Good idea," Axel agreed. "The place where Anne used to meet up with that creep can't be too far away from there."

A little while later they reached the hut and spread out. Thorsten picked the westbound direction, Julia went north, and Gaby and Axel went east. They'd been coming from the south, where all the hiker and bike trails were, so they didn't need to look there. Everybody was wearing a watch or carrying a phone so they could keep an eye on the time. The four of them had agreed they'd walk for a half hour and then turn around, so they'd be back at the tree house in one hour.

Julia was the first to get back to the meeting point after going north without finding anything. She'd picked up some pace and jogged the last bit, so she wasn't surprised to find no one else there yet. Wiping the sweat from her brow, she sat down on a tree stump and checked her cell. Maybe there was news from one of the other search teams.

She had two new messages. The first one was from Michael. 'will b there @ 4.30, martin's letting me off early :) c u soon!! x'

The second one was from Gaby. 'jules, i found a hairpin that looks like 1 of anne's. marked the spot & walking back now. have 2 call the cops!'

Julia's stomach lurched. So Anne really *had* ventured out deep into the woods. Thank God Gaby and Axel had found something. At least the police would have a better idea of where to look for her sister now.

'dear michael, all kinds of things going on here & none of them good... my little sister went missing. possibly abducted. please b here ASAP. I'll pick U up from the bus stop. x julia' she sent back quickly before calling Gaby.

Her friend picked up on the first ring. "Hey, Jules," she panted. "We'll be there in five. That hairpin... it's one of the pink Hello Kitty ones. Axel is sure it's from the set he gave her for Christmas."

"Good to hear you guys found something to track her," Julia said hoarsely. "I'll be waiting."

When she hung up, she saw Thorsten approaching in the distance. He was already shaking his head to indicate he hadn't found anything.

"Gaby and Axel found something," she called out to him.

He sped up and settled next to her on the tree stump. "Really? What did they find?"

"A hairpin from a set Anne wears a lot. I just don't remember if she was wearing hairpins this morning."

"Well, we should call the detective. Who knows, that Andreas guy might have confessed by now."

It wasn't long before Gaby and Axel got back to the tree hut too. Axel silently handed the hairpin to Julia.

She recognized it immediately. "Yes, that's hers. Oh God."

"We drew a map of how we walked to get to that place," Gaby said, waving a set of directions scribbled down on the back of a store receipt.

"Let's go home." Julia got up. "We should notify the police."

The four of them cycled back as fast as they could. Ms. Gunther was in the yard talking to Mrs. Ebner when they got back. Her face turned white as a sheet when Julia showed her the hairpin. "Oh, no," she whispered in shock. "What… where did you find that?"

"Deep in the forest," Axel replied. "But we didn't see any sign of Anne herself."

Julia's mother burst out in tears, looking completely deflated. All energy had left her.

"You should take her inside," Mrs. Ebner suggested to Julia and Axel. "Your grandmother is in the living room sitting by the phone in case the police call back."

Gaby and Thorsten followed the others inside. "Hey, Gran," Axel greeted the old woman dejectedly. "Why don't you stretch your legs and let Julia sit by the phone? She needs to call the police station."

Julia's hands were shaking as she dialed the number. "Hi, I'm calling about Anne Kandolf, the – missing girl," she stammered. "Can I speak to Detective Spitzer, please?"

As she was put on hold, her cell phone dinged. It was a text message from Michael. "Oh crap, he's already at the bus stop," she mumbled, showing Gaby the message. "Could you please go get him? He doesn't know exactly where I live, and I promised to meet him there."

"Consider it done." Her best friend smiled weakly and left the living room.

Just then, the Muzak on the other end of the line was interrupted when the detective answered the phone. "Spitzer," his voice boomed.

"Detective? It's Julia Kandolf. I just went into the woods with my friends and we found a hairpin belonging to Anne. We think she lost it when she met up there with Andreas Mittelmayer. I just don't remember if she was wearing it this morning. It's also possible she lost it a few days ago."

Detective Spitzer sighed. "Actually, I was about to call you and your mother. Things are not looking good. Andreas Mittelmayer hasn't told us a thing. He doggedly maintains he has never seen Anne in his life. We couldn't find a single trace of Anne's presence at his place. No one in the neighborhood remembers seeing the two of them together. Andreas's phone doesn't list her phone number, nor does it show any calls or text messages made or sent to Anne's cell phone, so there's no proof he's been in touch with her by phone either. And of course, your sister's phone is nowhere to be found, so we can't use that as evidence."

Julia swallowed hard. "So what are you saying?"

"I'm saying we have no right to detain him any longer. I can't keep someone in custody just because of a kid's diary and a few drawings." Detective Spitzer lowered his voice. "Look, I'll keep him here for the night. Officially I can only send out officers to look for a missing child after twenty-four hours, because most of the time, kids running away from home resurface before that time and our help isn't necessary anymore. I can't do anything for you at the moment, but that will be different tomorrow afternoon. Unfortunately, Andreas Mittelmayer will be released tomorrow morning first thing."

"You can't be serious!" Julia exclaimed. "He could harm her before you'd be able to find her!" Everybody in the living room was staring at her, their faces shocked.

"I understand your concern. Unfortunately, I can't change the law. In fact, I'm already bending the rules by keeping him locked up until tomorrow. I normally wouldn't even consider doing that, but since a young girl is concerned, I'm trying my best to help you out. And I'll be frank with you, I don't trust that boy, not for a second, but I can't base my decisions on a gut feeling. I have to abide by the law."

"Well, could you at least send one of your officers over to watch Andreas's house once he has been released?" Julia proposed desperately.

"I can't. Without proof, we have no reason to keep him under surveillance. But you are free to keep an eye on him yourself. I won't stop you from doing that."

Julia mumbled a thank-you to the detective, who promised to be in touch tomorrow afternoon, before slowly putting the receiver down.

Thorsten walked over to her and put a hand on her shoulder. "So, what did they say?"

Julia stoically reported to everyone what the police had said. Her mom and grandma turned even paler than they already were.

Axel clenched his fists. "Unbelievable. Well, nobody's gonna stop me from patrolling outside that sick pedophile's house day and night," he grumbled.

"Count me in," Thorsten said. "I can't believe they're letting him go."

"They have to," Ms. Gunther mumbled flatly. "You're innocent until proven otherwise. The police can't just go around and arrest everyone who's been accused of a crime." She blinked her eyes, forcefully pushed back her chair and marched into the kitchen.

Julia turned to her grandmother. "Has she called Dad yet?" she mouthed.

Gran shook her head. "Not yet. She wanted to wait for the police to get back to us. I can call him now if you like."

At that instant, the door opened and Gaby stepped inside with Michael in tow. "What happened?" she inquired worriedly, looking around the circle of ashen faces in the room.

Michael immediately rushed to Julia and embraced her warmly. "I'm so, so sorry," he mumbled. "Gaby told me everything."

"The police won't start looking until tomorrow," Julia sobbed, no longer able to hold back her tears now that Michael was here to comfort her. "They couldn't get a peep out of that guy. And he'll be a free man tomorrow morning."

Gaby's eyes widened. "They're waiting until *tomorrow*? What the hell? But they *know* Anne didn't run away from home."

"No, they don't," Axel replied. "She left of her own free will. She made up an excuse to go to the woods. Nobody forced her. I hate to admit it, but we're pretty much screwed."

"No, we're not," Thorsten said heatedly. "We can go back to the forest. We can look for Anne ourselves."

Michael looked up, fixing Thorsten with his gaze. "You think she's still there?"

"Well, where else could she be? When the police searched Andreas's house they couldn't find anything."

"So why didn't we see her wandering around when we combed the woods earlier?" Gaby threw back.

Thorsten fell silent. "She could be... lying somewhere," he finally said, a look of discomfort on his face.

Julia winced. "What do you mean?"

"Don't assume the worst. He could have sedated her and hidden her someplace."

"Behind a door," Gaby mumbled pensively. "Somewhere behind that door that we haven't found yet – that gateway she wrote about."

Michael resolutely got up and looked at Axel and Gaby. "Can you two bring me to the spot where you found the hairpin? If she's really around there, we'll find her."

They all looked at him in surprise. He sounded determined, so much so that he didn't seem to consider the possibility they wouldn't be successful. Julia frowned at him in puzzlement, but she didn't comment. It was wonderful of him to volunteer his help immediately, now that the police proved to be more or less useless until tomorrow.

When she got up, she noticed how weak her entire body still felt after her disheartening talk with Detective Spitzer. Michael grabbed her hand, squeezing it encouragingly. "I'll help you," he whispered. "Anne will turn up again."

Ten minutes later, a group of seven people had assembled to venture out into the woods once more. Julia's mother, Thorsten's mother and Michael were now a part of their search team too. Julia's grandmother would stay at home and wait for Anne there, just in case she resurfaced after all.

"Let's go," Axel said, heading the troupe with Gaby at his side. Julia followed them, flanked by her mom. Behind her, she could hear Thorsten and Michael talking to each other.

"Which direction did you go in when you went out to look for her earlier?" Michael wanted to know.

"Axel and Gaby went east," Thorsten replied. "And they went pretty far into the woods. They got to the part without any clear hiking trails, according to Julia."

"That's right." Michael paused. "People generally don't go there."

Julia pricked up her ears. Just how much time had Michael spent in these woods, exactly? He sounded like he knew every last little detail about the forest. She couldn't help but think of the person he'd been before, in school and during classes - not like your average member of Team Treehugger. So how did he know all these things? Something didn't add up.

She turned her head to look at him. Michael was still talking to Thorsten, but somehow he had felt her stare. He looked back at her, smiling reassuringly. His sweet, genuine smile gave her strength, and for just one moment, Julia could forget about all the questions running through her mind. Michael was here, by her side, to take care of her and help her. He was in love with her. What could possibly be wrong with this picture? She was just worrying too much.

She looked straight ahead again. Her mother put a hand on her back, rubbing her shoulder. "He seems like a nice guy," she said with a tiny smile. "I'm sorry I can't be happier for you right now."

Julia bit her lip. "Oh, Mom." She held on to her mother's arm and decided not to say anything else.

After a forty-minute walk, they got to the place where the hairpin was found. Gaby and Axel looked around indecisively. "So… this is the spot," Axel stated, throwing Michael a questioning look. He was the one who'd asked to be taken here, after all.

Michael nodded. He took a few slow paces forward, lightly caressing Julia's arm in passing. His next few steps were to the left, away from the search party, and he came to a standstill next to a young oak tree. And then he closed his eyes.

Nobody spoke when he squatted down on the ground to put his hands on the soil directly around the tree. A shiver ran through her body when Julia observed what he was doing. It reminded her of the way she'd often sat underneath *her* oak – as if she was somehow connecting with the roots under the earth. As if she could feel what the tree was feeling. Michael was doing the exact same thing right now: that much was evident. He was talking to the forest.

Abruptly, Michael jumped to his feet. "Over here," he said softly, stalking off into the woods without hesitation, the rest following in his wake.

Julia caught up with him. "How do you know…" she stuttered. "Do you know if…"

"She's still alive," he said, slipping his hand into hers like he'd done it a thousand times before. "Don't worry."

Despite his words, Julia couldn't help her mounting anxiety as they walked on, getting deeper and deeper into the forest. When Michael finally came to a stop, they were standing in a small clearing next to a patch of fir trees and the foundations of an old, demolished forest cabin.

"Look at that," Thorsten exclaimed in surprise. "So there really *was* a house here once." He cast a look around. "But no sign of a door."

"She's really close," Michael said softly, looking up at the sky and cocking his head as if listening intently. "She's underground."

Julia's mother sucked in a breath. "What? But you said she was still alive!"

He nodded. "She is. She's not dead."

"A hole, or a ditch," Gaby mumbled absently, nudging Axel. "Do you see any signs of digging somewhere?"

Axel, Gaby, Thorsten and Mrs. Ebner started to circle the remains of the house, looking for tracks or traces of digging. Julia didn't leave her mom's side –

Ms. Gunther looked shell-shocked, tears running down her cheeks despite Michael's reassurance.

She watched the rest of the group walking around. Michael hadn't joined them; he was leaning against one of the fir trees and seemed miles away. Julia stared at him and suddenly it hit her how *different* he was from the rest of them in this moment. He reminded her of a clairvoyant she had once seen on TV, a man who was in the habit of helping the police track down missing persons. Why was Michael so sure they would find Anne here? It *had* to have something to do with his accident and the blow to the head he had suffered. It must have given him some kind of second sight.

As she watched him, he was moving away from the tree, his steps weary like he was some sort of somnambulist. Michael made his way to an area to the left of the fir trees – a patch of soil covered in thorny shrubs. Julia followed him with her eyes, her heart skipping a beat when his foot pounded the earth below and didn't make the sound she'd expected. It sounded hollow, as if a cavity was hiding under the bushes.

The others had also picked up on what Michael was doing, Axel and Thorsten rushing toward him. "What the hell was that sound?" Axel cried out, squatting down to take a closer look.

"This is not solid earth," Thorsten murmured. "There's wood underneath. Or at least that's what it sounds like." He dug around in the shrubbery, cursing when thorns cut into the skin of his hands. One of the branches got stuck in his jacket sleeve, and when he stepped back, he suddenly seemed to pull up the entire bush, root and all, tearing it out of the earth.

"No *way*," Gaby exclaimed. "Those bushes are *fake*. They were put here by somebody recently."

"The earth around them is tamped," Axel nodded.

Julia raced down to the spot where Michael had made his discovery, her mother and Mrs. Ebner following suit. Meanwhile, the boys were busy clearing away the other prickly bushes. It didn't take long before they had unearthed a kind of large hatch made out of dark, wooden planks.

A silence descended among them, Julia fixing her eyes on the hatch while fighting back tears. Had Andreas made this to hide her sister? How could Anne possibly be buried underneath these planks and still be alive?

"We have to lift it," Axel said tensely, looking around. "Could we use a sturdy branch as a lever, you think?"

Julia peered around and located a firm, thin branch lying under one of the fir trees. She dragged it back to the hatch. Gaby brought another similarly-shaped branch, and together, they wiggled them under the corners of the hatch. Michael and Axel used their weight to lean on the branches and force the shutter up, while Thorsten tried to lift it more by slipping both hands under the planks once there was a tiny crack.

When the dark wooden hatch finally came up, all the packed dirt on top of it fell away with a rustling sound, the last few thorny branches dropping aside.

Julia's jaw dropped when she set eyes on the flight of steep stairs hidden underneath the hatch. The stone steps led to a narrow, underground door.

11.

"So there really *was* a door in the middle of the forest," Gaby mumbled absent-mindedly. She'd moved up to her best friend to put an arm around her shoulders.

Axel took a tentative step down the stairs, eyeing the bolt on the entrance. "You think that door can be opened?" he wondered aloud.

"Hold it," Thorsten said. "Shouldn't we call the police? We might mess up clues if we break and enter ourselves. You know… fingerprints or something like that."

Everybody seemed to wait for each other. "Let me," Ms. Gunther then spoke. Seemingly calm, she wrapped her silk scarf around her right hand and walked down to carefully slide the bolt open. She paused before pushing down the rusty door handle, biting her lip when the door swung outward with an ominously creaking sound.

Julia rushed down the stairs at once. "Anne?" she called out, stepping into the dark room behind the old cellar door after her mother. She couldn't see a thing. Behind them, Axel shuffled down the steps holding a small flashlight he always carried on his key ring.

"Oh my God," Ms. Gunther gasped.

In the dim light of Axel's flashlight, they saw Anne lying on the floor. She gave no sign of life. Her hands and feet were bound with rope. Julia stifled a scream, numbly stepping aside when Gaby and Axel rushed forward to cut the ropes with Gaby's pocket knife.

And then, she felt a gentle hand on her shoulder. "Everything will be all right," Michael whispered in her ear. "She's just unconscious."

A sob rose in her throat. Julia turned around and pressed her face against Michael's chest. He kissed her cheeks and held her tight until she stopped shaking. When she looked up, her eyes fell on Thorsten and his mother, still standing at the top of the stairs anxiously clutching each other's hands. "She's okay," she managed to utter. "She's still alive."

In the meantime, Axel had lifted his little cousin, cradling her in his arms as he went upstairs. Anne's face looked white as death, but her breathing sounded regular. "You were right. She was sedated," he told Thorsten. "This is not normal sleep."

"How long do you think she's been lying here like this?" Gaby asked, a hint of panic in her voice. "Chloroform can't keep people under for this long, can it?"

"It can if he used a lot," Thorsten said. "But a high dosage means Anne could slip into a coma. We have to call an ambulance right now." He whipped out his cell phone and called 112.

Julia was intensely grateful for Thorsten's level-headedness and resolve. The others, herself included, all seemed too shocked to do much. Her gaze landed on Michael, still standing next to her on the stairs. She had no idea how on earth he had managed to find her sister, but she'd be forever indebted to him. With a deep sigh, she moved closer and flung her arms around him again. "Thank you," she whispered. "You saved her life."

"They're on their way," Thorsten said as he put away his phone. "We're gonna have to carry her to the forest edge."

"No problem. Axel and I can take turns carrying her," Michael offered.

"I'll walk the first bit," Axel nodded.

Ms. Gunther caught up with Michael when the group started moving to get to the edge of the woods. "How did you *know*?" she asked quietly, her voice awestruck, her eyes full of wonder.

Julia's ears perked up – her mother was asking Michael the exact same question she'd been dying to ask.

Michael shook his head, keeping quiet for a long time. "Instinct," he replied at last. "I... I can't explain it. I'm sorry."

Julia squeezed his hand. "It's okay. Really. We're just so happy."

As they approached the edge of the forest, the blue flashing ambulance lights could be seen through the trees. Two paramedics lifted Anne from Michael's arms and carefully put her on a stretcher inside the ambulance, hooking the little girl up to a monitor instantly.

Julia's mom turned around and addressed her oldest daughter. "I'm going with them. Can you go home and tell Gran the news? As soon as I know more, I'll call you."

A taciturn crew watched from the bus stop as the ambulance drove away. Although they were all happy Anne was found, it wasn't at all certain she was out of danger. Thorsten had been right about the chloroform sedation.

"We'll be home," Mrs. Ebner said when they all got back to their street. "If there's news from the hospital, please let us know."

Julia hugged both neighbors tightly. "Thanks for all your help," she mumbled when she hugged Thorsten.

"You've been a good friend today. I'm so sorry I didn't trust you before."

He smiled. "That's all right. No worries." He let go of her and mumbled: "By the way, Michael is a really nice guy. It's kind of annoying, but I can't seem to hate him."

She smiled back. "It's sweet of you to say that."

"Oh, well, that's me," he winked. "Sweet as sugar, and nothing but praise for my competitors. I just *really* don't understand how he managed to find Anne so easily."

"Yeah, same here," Julia mumbled. She stared at Thorsten as he went inside before turning around, deep in thought. Her friends had already gone to the living room, and when she entered, she found Axel and her grandmother huddled together on the couch, her gran crying tears of relief. "Thank God she's alive," she said in a trembling voice. Julia sat down to hug the old woman as well.

Once everyone had grabbed tea and cookies from the kitchen, Gaby tapped Julia on the shoulder. "Is it okay if I call Tamara? She joined Florian to go see Moritz's band practice, but she was worried sick when I told her what was going on. I haven't talked to her since I got here."

"Yeah, of course. They can even drop by if they want."

"And is it okay if I order pizzas for everyone?" Michael asked. "I don't know about the rest of you, but I'm famished. And I don't think anybody here feels like cooking at the moment."

"Great plan." Julia smiled at him.

While Gaby and Michael were each making their phone calls, Julia got up to help her grandmother make another big pot of tea in the kitchen.

"He's a special boy, your Michael," Gran pointed out while washing some cups in the sink. "That bright look in his eyes when he looks at people – it's like he sees more than the rest of us do."

Julia turned around, thoughtlessly plunking down some teabags on the table. "You think he's got the same talent as you? You know, like a second sight or a very sharp intuition?"

Gran nodded. "It seems likely. How else could he have done what he did today?"

"I don't know. Dumb luck?"

"Come on, my Julia. You don't really believe that."

"No, not really." Julia lifted the kettle from the cooker. "He just... *knows* things. Especially about me. What kind of music I like. What I like doing in my spare time. He even knows the songs I wrote. You know, stuff I never even told him about."

"And it makes you feel uneasy?"

"No! Well, maybe sometimes. I mean, I want to know how he does it, but at the same time, I don't give a damn. He is *so* in love with me. What the heck does it matter that he has a way of knowing things he shouldn't?"

Grandma slowly nodded. "Well, if you want to understand him, why don't you ask him?"

Julia blushed. "Because I don't want to scare him off. Maybe I'm afraid he'll wake up one day and be like the old Michael again... the Michael who never had eyes for me."

"My dear child, of course not. That's nonsense. Whyever would that happen?"

"Gee, I don't know. What made him realize he was in love with me after all? I could just as easily ask him *that*."

"Well, whatever you decide, it can't hurt to ask him what you want to know. If I were you, I'd get it out of the way if it bothers you."

Of course her grandmother was entirely right. Most of the time, Julia managed to forget how strange the whole situation with Michael actually was, but sooner or later she'd come back to the same questions running though her head – questions she'd never get the answer to if she kept her mouth shut.

When the pizza delivery guy arrived with their food, Florian, Moritz and Tamara spilled into the hallway after him, pulling Julia into a big group hug.

"Thanks for coming," Julia said softly amidst the friendly huddle. "We're still waiting for news from the hospital."

"I ordered some extra portions just in case," Michael commented, winking at Florian when he looked up to zoom in on the pizzas.

Moritz elbowed his boyfriend in the ribs. "You're burning holes in those boxes, you glutton. Is food all you can think about?"

Florian chuckled. "Sorry," he lamely apologized to Julia.

"No problem," she shrugged. "Like Michael said, there's enough for everyone. Let's go to the living room."

Tamara was the first one to enter, her gaze landing on Gaby sitting on the couch holding hands with Axel. She opened her mouth to say something, then thought better of it when her sister shot her a warning glare. Smirking from ear to ear, Tamara flopped down on the couch right next to the new couple and poured herself some soda.

Julia sat down on the other couch, scooting closer to Michael when he handed her a plate with a big pizza slice on it. "I know you're not very hungry, but you should eat something," he said. "You'll feel better."

She nodded wordlessly, dutifully munching on the salami-topped slice. When her phone suddenly rang, she put down her pizza and snatched her cell off the table. It was her mom. Her hands shaking with nerves, Julia answered the call. "Hey, it's me."

"Hello, honey!" Ms. Gunther replied cheerfully. "Anne is awake. She's still very weak, but she can talk and the doctor said she's out of danger. She'll recover just fine. Detective Spitzer just left – he recorded her testimony. She'll be able to testify against Andreas Mittelmayer."

"Really? That's great!" Julia exclaimed, meeting her friends' eyes with relief. "So they'll keep him behind bars? Will you two be home by tonight?"

"No, that's too soon. The doctor wants to keep Anne under observation for the night. I can sleep in the sick ward in the bed next to her, so I'll spend the night here too."

"Great! That's good, that you're allowed to stay close to her. I'll come to the hospital first thing in the morning – I'll call in to work."

"Looking forward to it, sweety. Can I talk to Gran for a bit?"

Julia handed the phone to her grandmother with a smile on her face, then told her friends everything her mom had said.

"So she's awake!" Axel said. "Good news. That means her abductor can't lie his way out of this anymore."

Tamara shivered. "I can't bear to think of what would have happened if you guys hadn't found her on time." She gingerly looked at Julia. "Did he... was she... did he *touch* her while she was sedated?"

"I don't know." Julia tried to stop herself from picturing it. "I'll hear all about it in the hospital tomorrow. The main thing is that she's safe now and she's awake. We'll cross the next bridge when we come to it."

"Can we visit Anne in the hospital?" Florian asked.

"You can tomorrow, but I don't think she'll stay there for long. They just wanted to keep her for the night, just in case."

Julia exhaled deeply before sitting back down next to Michael to eat the rest of her pizza, her appetite finally returning.

Michael slipped an arm around her shoulders. "You should probably walk over to the neighbors and tell Thorsten and his mother the good news too," he said.

Julia nodded, feeling her cheeks flush slightly. Why did *Michael* of all people have to be so considerate toward the boy next door? Thorsten and Michael seemed to genuinely like each other. Suppose they became friends – *that* would be awkward. Not to mention problematic.

She picked up the phone lying on the table. "I'll send him a text," she mumbled. "I don't feel like going out anymore."

After dinner, her grandmother went back to Eichet. Tomorrow, she would join Julia for a hospital visit, hopefully taking Anne and Ms. Gunther back home by noon. Gran had arranged to borrow her neighbor's car to transport everyone.

"How about it, Gaby-Baby?" Tamara said to her sister while they were piling up empty plates. "Shall we head home too? I can't *wait* to hear about the recent developments in your love life,"

Gaby instantly turned red. "Don't be stupid."

Her sister chuckled. "Oh, come on. I was forced to listen to you trying to inconspicuously bring up Axel in every single conversation we had all week. Well, guess what – now you can be *conspicuous* about him! Isn't it just wonderful?"

Axel popped up behind them. "Am I hearing this right? You've been gabbing on about me to your sister?" he teased Gaby.

"Well, yeah," Gaby replied clumsily, blushing even redder. "You think that's lame?"

"No," he said, cracking a shy smile. "I think it's kind of cute."

Gaby groaned. "I'm not *cute*, okay?" she said defiantly, trying her best at a dark face.

Axel pulled her into his arms. "No, of course you're not. Sorry." Then he kissed her, cutting off whatever Gaby was going to say next. She fell silent and leaned into him.

Julia couldn't help but grin like an idiot at the scene unfolding in front of her. Her best friend had finally succumbed to True Love – she'd never seen Gaby this lovey-dovey with anyone.

"Do you all need a ride?" Moritz inquired, his face doubtful. "I don't know if that's gonna fit."

"She'll be sitting on Axel's lap." Tamara jabbed a thumb at her sister.

Moritz started to laugh. "Okay. That's solved, then." He turned to Julia. "Hey, it's a shame I dropped by under circumstances like these, but thanks for the hospitality."

One by one, her friends left the house until Julia found herself standing in the hallway with just Michael for company. All of a sudden, she didn't know what attitude to adopt. It hadn't been part of any plan to be alone with him in a deserted house at night – the only time that happened before had been back at his place, that one evening.

Abruptly, she took a step away from him. "Would you like another drink?" she blurted out. "Or were you about to go home, too?"

Classic – she'd made it sound as if she couldn't wait for him to leave. Julia cringed inwardly.

Michael caught her gaze. "You're nervous," he established calmly. "You want me to leave?"

Gran was right: he *really* saw more than most people. "N-no, not exactly," she stuttered. "Of course you don't have to go."

He stepped closer, pulling her into his chest. "So you want me to stay?" he asked softly.

She bit her lip. "Not exactly," she whispered once more. "Or, maybe... gosh, I don't know."

He cracked a smile and kissed her forehead. "Why don't you just tell me what you're thinking?" he said seriously. "Be honest with me. Please, Julia – it bothers me when you're afraid to be yourself around me."

"I'm not *afraid*," she protested. "I just... I don't want it... to go like the first time we were alone together." Her face flushed red when she heard herself utter the words.

A hurt look crossed Michael's face. "You think I just want to stick around to have sex with you?"

Julia stiffened, shrugging noncommittally. "No. Of course not. But... well. It's possible, right? I just don't know. Sorry." All her thoughts jumbled together and she looked up at him, her eyes stinging with sudden tears. Crap. That was the last thing she needed right now – another bout of tears.

Shaking his head in disbelief, Michael hugged her tight. In his arms she couldn't stop herself from sobbing again. At the same time, she calmed down in his embrace. "Please don't worry so much," he softly mumbled into her hair. "The only reason I want to stay here is because I don't want to leave you all by yourself after a horrible day like this. That's all. You can trust me." His last few words sounded almost desperate. It was obvious how much she'd upset him.

"I know," Julia replied hoarsely, stroking his cheek. "I do. I do trust you – I know I can. It's just so *weird*, this whole thing."

"Weird?" he repeated.

Her heart sped up. "Yeah. You being so different, I mean. The way you look at me so differently after the accident." At last – she'd said what was bothering her. She was curious to hear his reaction.

Michael nodded pensively, staring off into the distance as if looking for the right words to say. "I understand you," he said at last. "Julia… I'm not the same person anymore."

She pulled him into the living room, sitting him down on the couch before taking a seat next to him. "So why not?" she persisted.

He cleared his throat. "When I woke up in the woods, I saw you. Everything around me felt so *intense*. I've never experienced the world as passionately as I do now. Colors, scents, music. Everything's different. I can do more. I can see more. I *sense* more."

Julia silently absorbed his words. Michael's story reminded her of an old movie she'd seen a few years ago, featuring John Travolta. He'd been hit by lightning or blasted by a UFO – she couldn't remember what it was exactly – and this had caused him to develop special abilities. Could it be something similar had happened to Michael? Was that the reason his personality had changed so much?

"You were reborn," she whispered.

"Something like that." He took her hands in his. "I know I hurt you before, but I won't do that again. You couldn't trust him, but you *can* trust me."

He kissed her. Julia crawled into his embrace, felt the heat of his hands on her body, sensed the love he felt for her throughout her body. It felt completely natural to seek shelter with him, as if he'd been her refuge for years. When he lifted her in his arms and carried her up the stairs toward the bedrooms, her stomach fluttered nervously, though.

Once they got to the landing, he pulled his mouth away from hers, looking left and right into the corridor. "So, uhm… where's your room, actually?" he inquired with a sheepish grin, sounding so genuinely innocent it made Julia crack up with laughter. She felt the anxiety drain from her body.

"Why don't you put me down, and I'll show you," she suggested with a smile.

Her bedroom door was open. Michael hesitantly followed her in, gazing around in awe as if he had entered a majestic cathedral. His eyes drifted past the posters of natural parks and waterfalls on the wall, the multi-colored fairy lights she'd strung onto the wall and the ceiling in the left corner, her shelves crammed full of books, and the keyboard next to her desk before finally landing on her. "Yes, this is your room," he simply said. With a smile he sat down in the lazy chair in the right corner. "No TV?"

Julia chuckled. "No. You think that chair should come with a TV set?"

"No, not really. It's kind of a book-reader's chair, don't you think?"

"Anne actually has my TV in her room. I never watched it a lot anyway. And she wants to watch her DVDs every morning, so…"

Julia walked over to her bookcase to take out Gran's storybook about the Prince of the Forest. Sadly, all it made her feel now was that her dreams had shattered beyond repair. This book had done too much damage – without it, Anne might have never fallen for Andreas Mittelmayer's stupid stories about magical realms and secret doors. Abruptly, she felt sick with guilt – she should have read Anne stories from the *Stop Child Molestation Handbook*, not these useless fairytales.

"What's that?" Michael asked, getting out of his chair and walking over to her.

Julia put the book back with a deep sigh. "Nothing."

He rubbed her arm. "Is that the fairytale Anne started to believe in?"

She blushed with shame. "Repeated to her over and over by her big sister, who should have known better," she replied bitterly.

"Don't blame yourself."

"But I *am* to blame."

"You're being unfair to yourself," Michael insisted. "She's got a vivid imagination, just like you. You couldn't have known this would happen."

"True, but maybe I should have just kept dreaming on my own, instead of infecting my sister with all my fantasies."

He remained quiet for a moment. "Do you still like to dream?" he asked her curiously.

Julia sat down on her bed. "Yes, of course I do. I mean, I'm trying to be a responsible grown-up, but I kind of suck at it. The other night, I even dreamed about the forest being magical. In my dream, the trees were talking to me. They were looking for you."

Michael stared at her. "They were? Why?"

"No idea. My phone rang and it woke me up." Julia observed him closely. He somehow seemed shocked she'd dreamed about him. Was that so strange?

"Do you ever dream about *me*?" she wanted to know.

He sat down next to her. "Yes. A lot," he admitted, his cheeks light-pink. "I wrote you that poem because of a dream I had about you."

Julia's heart was hammering against her ribs when she bent over to grab her scrapbook from underneath the bed. "Look, I stuck it in here," she said softly, her hands clammy when she opened the book. She had *never* shown this book to anyone, not even to Gaby. Michael took it from her. He stared at his poem in her book, then flipped a few pages back and smiled. He was so clearly admiring her handiwork that just for a moment, she felt like a true princess of the forest, sitting next to her royal suitor.

"This is what I pictured your dreams to be like," he gently mumbled. "This is beautiful, Julia. I hope you never stop dreaming."

She scooted closer to him, touched by his words. "Thanks. You're so sweet to me." She closed her eyes and stifled a yawn.

He kissed her on the cheek. "You want to go to sleep now?"

Julia looked up at the clock above her door. Half past nine – it wasn't anywhere near her normal bedtime, but it was probably a good idea to get some extra sleep. "Yes, maybe I should," she replied.

"You got some blankets for me? I'll sleep on the couch downstairs."

"No, don't." Julia grabbed his hand. Only now did she realize how badly she didn't want to be alone. "You can sleep here."

Michael looked at the single bed, blinking his eyes nervously. "With you? Well, I don't know… I, uhm…"

"We have a spare mattress," she interrupted his rambling. "I can put it in my room."

"Ah." He raked a hand through his hair. "Okay. I guess we can do that." He shot her an apologetic look, blushing a little. "Sorry. I promised to be a gentleman, but I'd be having a *really* hard time with that if we slept in the same bed."

Julia's face reddened too. "You would, huh?"

"Uhm, *yes*. Obviously." He shrugged and looked away. "Okay, so – let me get that spare mattress. Where do you guys store it?"

Julia bit her lip to stop herself from laughing out loud. She'd embarrassed Michael – never in a million years would she have thought that were possible. "In the hall closet," she replied, getting up to help him carry the mattress to her room.

A few minutes later, they were each in their separate beds in her room, illuminated only by the fairy lights in the far corner. In the soft, dreamy light, Michael looked at her, curled up in his makeshift bed. "Good night," he said with a smile. "You're safe with me. If you have any nightmares, you can wake me up, okay?"

"I will." Julia pulled up the blankets all the way to her chin. "I'll be fine, though. I feel calm now. Thanks to you."

"I feel good when I'm with you." Michael got up to switch off the light in the corner. It wasn't quite dark outside yet. In the half-light of dusk, Julia observed him walking back to his bed to crawl under the covers. "My heart longed to be with you," he whispered softly. "And now I've found you."

Julia sighed in satisfaction, closing her eyes. Michael's words seemed familiar. Had he told her this before? She couldn't remember, but it wasn't important right now. Slowly, she felt herself drifting off into a deep, dreamless sleep.

The next morning, Julia's grandmother turned up at nine o'clock sharp. Ignaz, her neighbor, loudly honked several times to alert Julia to their arrival.

"Is that idiot trying to get the whole street to come with us to the hospital?" Julia grumbled. Quickly, she handed Michael a mug of hot coffee and ran to the door. "I'm not done having breakfast yet," she shouted at Gran, who was just getting out of the car. "Why don't you come inside for a few minutes?"

Ignaz and Gran followed Julia to the kitchen. They both gazed questioningly at Michael, who turned slightly red under her grandmother's scrutinizing look.

"Good morning," he mumbled. "I'm sorry we're running late. I just couldn't seem to wake up. Julia knocked on the guest room door like, three times, but I slept right through it."

Gran cocked an eyebrow and refrained from commenting. Julia tried her very best not to giggle. Poor Michael – he was trying so hard not to embarrass her in front of her grandmother, who clearly didn't buy his story. "More like four times," she supplied, nodding vigorously before nudging her gran in the side when the old woman started to grin mischievously.

"I wouldn't mind some coffee, actually," Ignaz piped up, glancing at the coffee pot on the kitchen top.

In the end, they left for the hospital at ten past nine, dropping Michael off at the bus stop before turning onto the main road leading downtown.

Ignaz let them off at the front entrance before turning into the car park. Julia entered the hospital together with her gran, a smell of antiseptic and bleach hitting her full force. She hated this odor, associating it with illness, pain and death – the death of her grandfather. She hadn't been back ever since he'd died in this hospital, and she hoped this would be the last time.

Ms. Gunther was waiting for them at the reception desk. The dark rings under her eyes made her skin look even paler than it was, but her smile brightened her whole face. "I'm so happy you're both here," she enthused. "Anne has been asking for you all morning. She had a good night's sleep."

"You didn't, I take it?" Gran rubbed her daughter's pale cheeks. "You look crumpled."

"I couldn't sleep." Ms. Gunther shook her head as though she was trying to rid herself of nightmarish images. "I kept thinking about what might have happened to Anne, over and over again. How this Andreas must have touched her – defiled her."

"He was a creep," Julia said flatly. "He was stunningly beautiful, but he had this *dead* look in his eyes. It was as if something inside of him had withered away."

The three of them walked over to the bank of elevators. "Last night, when Anne was asleep, I went over to the police station," Julia's mother told them quietly. "I wanted to look him in the eye; the boy who'd dared to touch and abduct my beautiful child. But once I got closer to that prison cell, I couldn't go in. I was allowed, but something stopped me. He didn't see me, but I did get a look at him."

"Why did he do it?" Gran asked just as quietly. "Did he say anything about his reasons in the confession?"

Ms. Gunther sighed. "Detective Spitzer told me he talked to Andreas's mother. He didn't exactly grow up in a stable family environment before they moved to Salzburg. She was married to a man who didn't just beat her up on a regular basis but also turned out to have abused her daughter. She only found out after the abuse had stopped, but it was enough for her to file for divorce. That's why she moved here."

"And nobody thought of sending Andreas to a shrink to cope with the entire trauma from his childhood?" Julia asked in astonishment.

"No, apparently not. His mother did send her daughter to Child Care Services and had her apply for counseling. Now that Andreas is in jail, it seems likely the boy was as much a victim of abuse as his sister was."

"That might explain his need to escape to a fantasy world filled with portals to magical realms," Gran said. "Or why he has such a distorted image of sexuality."

It was strange, but all of a sudden, Julia could almost feel sorry for the guy who'd abused and tricked her sister. He must have escaped into a dream world to cope with his life, just as she had done so often – the only difference being *she* had never harmed anyone in doing so. In all likelihood, he didn't even know right from wrong.

"So, is he gonna get professional help now?" she asked timidly. "Or will they just sentence him to years in prison without any counseling?"

"Look, that's not for you to worry about," her mother replied in a soothing voice. "Let the police handle it, honey."

Julia still felt overwhelmed by her mother's story by the time they entered Anne's room. She had a room of her own, and her little sister looked so fragile and vulnerable in the big hospital bed that Julia couldn't stop herself from storming forward and pulling her into a warm embrace. "I'm so grateful you're still alive," she whispered.

Anne pressed her tiny body against Julia's, a stifled sob escaping from her throat. They wordlessly clung to each other for a moment that seemed to last forever.

"I was protected," Anne then said almost inaudibly.

"Protected? By whom?" Julia blinked at Anne in bewilderment.

Anne smiled. "When I was asleep, I could hear voices. I think they were coming from the woods. They told me help was on the way. They said you would find me. That's why I wasn't scared."

Julia cast a glance over her shoulder, but her mom and grandma were still in conversation. They hadn't heard Anne's story. "Did you hear Michael's voice as well?" she inquired curiously.

Her sister shook her head. "Well, I don't know what Michael sounds like, exactly, but it couldn't have been him. It was a different kind of voice. I think it belonged to someone who lived in the forest for centuries. Someone old, but his voice sounded young. It was the strangest thing."

Julia frowned. It seemed as if Anne still believed in her fairytales about the Prince of the Forest, and it had to stop. It was dangerous to hold on to silly fantasies any longer.

"The Prince of the Forest doesn't exist, okay?" she snapped. "It's just make-believe, Anne."

Anne's eyes welled up with tears. And then she smiled, looking old and wise and ageless. "I know that boy wasn't him. I know that now. But I *was* protected by something in the woods, Jules. I felt love all around me."

Julia decided to give up. Anne sounded like she'd had a near-death experience, including all the requisite sensations of unbounded love and voices from beyond. The only thing missing was a light at the end of a tunnel. But maybe it was a good thing Anne had experienced the ordeal like this. She had almost died in that horrible hole in the ground. In the elevator, her mom had told them about Andreas's heavy sedatives almost killing Anne. Thank God there hadn't been any signs of sexual abuse – thanks to Julia, Andreas had been arrested before he'd had the chance.

It was time to try and get things out of her head. Her hand tenderly caressing Anne's forehead, Julia whispered: "I'm happy someone protected you, darling. And now you're safe with us."

Gran joined her by the hospital bed to give her youngest granddaughter a cuddle. "Are you allowed to go home today?" she asked.

"Late afternoon," Anne nodded. "They wanted to keep me here for a few more hours to see how I'm doing, that doctor said."

"That's very good news, sweetheart."

As Julia absently listened to her mother, sister and grandmother chatting to each other, she typed out a text message about how Anne was doing and sent it to all her friends, including Thorsten. He'd helped her and supported her so well before the others had arrived at her house; she couldn't have managed without him. Michael would probably read the message during his coffee break; he was working this morning. She'd asked him to tell their boss why she wasn't there today. Martin would have to schedule her on one of her free days to catch up on working hours later.

'so good 2 hear she's doin well!! CU at flo's l8r? he invited us 4 a terrace get-together! xx' Gaby texted back after a few minutes.

'sure! what time?' she replied.

It didn't take long for other messages to start pouring in. Everybody said yes to meeting up on Florian's roof terrace at four o'clock. It was time to catch up with her best friend! Gaby and Axel were suddenly an item, and Julia hadn't even been able to talk about it with her.

She smiled. Now that Anne turned out to be okay, her summer was looking bright. She had a wonderful boyfriend, Gaby had hooked up with her cousin, she had a cool job, and they'd all be off to visit England next month. 'hey, u gotta tell me ALL abt Axel ;)' she typed out to Gaby.

'sleepover tonight? everybody's gonna be there today eavesdroppin & stuff... or has michael taken my place?? :p'

Crap. Gran knew Michael had spent the night at her house. Her mother would *not* be amused if she found out. If only Gran would shut up about it. Nervously, her gaze darted between her mother and her grandmother. She wished she was telepathically gifted so she could beg her grandmother to not tell her mom.

"Do you think Ignaz could drop me off at the bookstore later?" she asked. "I want to talk to Michael and apologize to Martin for bailing on him today."

Gran smiled warmly at her. "Of course. You must be eager to tell him how everything went. I wonder what he told his parents when he got home last night. That must have been quite a story, don't you think?"

Julia blinked at Gran owlishly. Maybe telepathy really *did* exist... or maybe Gran was just being her wise, old self again, trying to avoid causing trouble when there was no need for it. "Thanks," she mumbled humbly.

Anne had to rest again, so the visitors were ushered out by a nurse. They left the hospital and found Ignaz in the parking lot. He dropped Julia off at the edge of the Old Town and promised to return to the hospital later to drive Anne home together with her mother.

Julia whistled a happy tune as she strolled toward the bookstore. Maybe it was a good idea to work for a few hours today before visiting Florian. She felt upbeat and energetic. Anne would be home by tonight, Gaby would stay over and they'd catch up on everything and nothing.

All had ended well thanks to Michael. Julia thought back to her grandmother's words: Michael saw more than the rest of them did. Had he told his parents? Or his other friends? She didn't think so. He had changed, and she was the only one who knew just how much. There was no real explanation for it, but it didn't matter. It was as it was. And everything about the way things were made life great.

12.

"**I**'m going!" Julia yelled in the direction of the kitchen. She was in the hallway, hopping around on one foot, trying to tie the shoelaces on one shoe and balancing a stuffed overnight bag from her shoulder.

"See you tomorrow!" Anne and her mother hollered back.

Julia would have loved to have breakfast with them, but she'd overslept and now she had to hurry like crazy to make it to work in time. Two minutes ago she'd stormed into the kitchen to grab a banana and indignantly ask her mother why she hadn't woken her up.

"Because you have to set your own alarm?" her mother had replied with a smirk. "You're eighteen, you know. In other words, a responsible adult. Do you want me to wake you up for college after summer's over and check your homework as well?"

"I *did* set my alarm," Julia grumbled. Her mom's sarcasm was too much for her this early in the morning.

Her shoelaces were tied. She rushed through the yard and turned right to get to the road leading to the bus stop. Sadly, her sprints weren't what they used to be. She'd gradually gotten out of shape ever since things between her and Michael had become serious. Time was scarce – she now worked four days a week, and in her spare time she mostly hung around with Michael. A few days ago, Gaby complained to her, demanding a framed picture of Julia so she'd 'remember what her best friend looked like'. Fortunately, they were going to London soon, so that would be the perfect opportunity to spend time with her friend. In the meantime, Michael had also bought himself a ticket to join them. They'd agreed that the boys would get their own dorm in the youth hostel and the girls would get another. Tamara was now the only one in the group without a partner, and she'd whined about their expedition turning into a 'couple's trip with one sad single tagging along'.

"Don't fret," Gaby had replied with a naughty grin. "We'll find you a sexy Englishman, and we won't even mind if you take him up to our room."

Julia tore around the corner and caught sight of the bus just closing its doors. "Wait!" she screamed, even though the bus driver couldn't possibly hear her. Arms milling, she sped up even more.

Unexpectedly, the front door swung open again and Thorsten's head popped out to grin at her.

"In a hurry?" he chuckled. "I told the bus driver to wait for the cute blonde trying to stop his bus with her bare hands."

Gasping for breath, Julia got on the bus and nodded at the driver gratefully, then followed Thorsten to sit down somewhere in the middle.

"Where are you off to this early?" she asked. "Don't you need to catch the other bus to Eichet?"

"No, I'm not working today. It's time to take care of some uni stuff. Getting all the appropriate documents stamped and such. You know the drill."

Julia nodded in comprehension. Thorsten would start his sophomore year at Salzburg University after summer, so that meant a lot of red tape. Thankfully, her mom had helped her with her own application, even if she was supposed to be a 'responsible adult' by now.

"And where are you going with a heavy bag like that?" Thorsten inquired, eyeing Julia's bulging baggage. "Are you always dragging that much stuff to work?"

Julia shook her head. "This is my overnight bag. Because I'm staying at Michael's house tonight after work. You know." She flushed a little as she said the words. It was the first time she was going to spend the night at his place since their first date. Actually, she was kind of nervous. Of course he had a ginormous house with at least four guest rooms, but he *also* had a king-size bed in his own room.

Thorsten caught her blushing. "Ah. Okay," he nodded, pausing for a few seconds. "Well, you've been together for a month now, right? Spending the night is part of all that jazz. You know." He playfully nudged her in the side, which made her turn even redder. Thorsten was probably wondering why this seemed like such a big deal to her – he was two years her senior *and* he'd been a freshman at Graz Uni last year.

"Yeah, you think?" she mumbled.

He smiled. "Nah, I'm just yanking your chain. You should take as much time as you need for these things. Don't feel rushed or anything."

Julia nodded, falling silent when a group of young children with colorful backpacks got on the bus, a mom ushering them inside like a mother hen. It looked like a birthday party.

Anne had celebrated her birthday a few days ago. The day had gone reasonably well, even though Anne had been quieter and more reserved than usual around her friends. The gruesome event she experienced had had an indelible impact on her. Ms. Gunther had decided to book sessions with a child psychiatrist twice a week, to minimize the risk of Anne sustaining trauma from unresolved issues later on.

"Are you still happy with him?" Thorsten suddenly asked out of nowhere. He tried to sound laid-back, but failed.

Julia turned toward him, blinking at her neighbor in surprise. "Why, yes. I am. Very happy," she stuttered. "I know people still don't understand how it all worked out for us, but..."

Thorsten had heard stories about Michael from her cousin. Axel still had to get used to the idea that she and Michael were so close. A few days ago, they'd all convened in Julia's yard to celebrate Anne's birthday in the evening, and Julia had accidentally stumbled into a conversation between Thorsten and Axel. Her neighbor had asked her cousin some things about her history with Michael – and undoubtedly Axel had related to Thorsten how her boyfriend had cold-heartedly dumped her first before suddenly changing his mind. Axel didn't hate Michael, but he wasn't fawning all over him either. "If someone hurts my family, it will take that person a while to regain my trust," he'd confessed to Julia once. "But hey, as long as he makes you happy, you won't hear me complain."

Thorsten heaved an unhappy sigh. "I don't have to understand," he mumbled softly. "I can see the way he looks at you, and that's what's important. The past is dead. And he's a really nice guy." He cleared his throat. "I must be a bit jealous. Still."

Julia tried not to gape at him. "Oh."

Her gaze drifted to the world outside. Thorsten's words confused her. She couldn't understand why he still had these feelings for her when she was very clearly off the market. Plus, he looked like every college girl's wet dream, so he'd have a girlfriend in no time after summer. And yet, he didn't seem to be able to forget about her. It almost made her feel guilty – after all, there had been a time when they had definitely clicked, and she'd welcomed it for a while before Michael had gotten back in the picture again.

She started when he put his hand on her arm. "Hey, you," he said gently. "I don't want to make things difficult. It's just that you stirred something in me that I've never felt before. That's why I'm having kind of a hard time forgetting about you. Oh yeah, and the fact that you live across the street doesn't really help, either."

His dry tone made Julia smile, but his words took her by surprise at the same time. They were such sweet words, sounding so genuine and straightforward. For just a split second, thinking back to the whole saga of getting Michael's attention smarted a little bit: he'd needed more than just a few days to realize she had stirred something in *him*. But no, she shouldn't think like that. He had turned into a completely different person after his accident in the woods, and she'd already forgiven him for his appalling behavior before that a long time ago.

"Thanks," she said in a slightly strangled voice, smiling warmly at Thorsten. "And my apologies. I'll move out as soon as possible."

Thorsten started to chuckle. "Oh, come on. That won't be necessary." He cocked his head. "Or were you planning on renting a room in the city anyway, once you start college?"

She shrugged. "Not really. I live close by. And I like it at home. It's cozy. And cheap, of course."

"Well, I see no other solution but for *me* to move out," he replied. "I mean, I'm filthy rich. And my parents are an absolute horror, so…"

Julia rolled her eyes. "Sarcasm bites. You and my mom should start a club together. She's really good at that, too."

Thorsten raised an eyebrow. "How is being in a club with your mom going to help me to run into you less frequently?"

"True that." Julia blushed. "Not such a brilliant idea after all."

"Hey, don't you need to get off here?" he suddenly said in alarm.

Julia sprang up when she saw he was right. They'd pulled up next to her stop. "Hey, thanks! I wasn't paying attention." She hauled her bag over one shoulder and waved at Thorsten before getting out and setting a course for the bookstore. It was going to be a hot day; already the sun was burning down relentlessly, and it wasn't even nine in the morning yet. Julia could feel the sweat gather on the skin under her bag strap. She hoped Martin would drag out the kitchen table onto the patio again today, so they could have lunch outside. Inside, it was sheer horror on the second floor at this temperature.

"*Servus*," she greeted Marco and Silke, who were waiting on the steps in front of the store. "Shop's not open yet?"

Silke shook her head. "Martin got here a minute ago, but he's escorting Michael back to the bus stop. He was feeling really sick."

"No way! Really?" Julia immediately dug up her phone to see whether Michael had called her. Not yet. She would send him a text straight away. 'silke just told me ure sick? I'll B w/ u asap, ok? xx'

"Hey, you look all pale," Marco said worriedly. "You want to leave a bit early today? After lunch? I can fill in for you, if you want."

"You could? That would be fantastic." Julia shot him a grateful look. Marco was a life-saver: she'd leave straight after lunch and go to Michael's house to nurse him back to health. His parents weren't home, because his mom was on vacation and his dad was on one of his business trips.

When Martin opened the store just after nine, Marco asked straight away if he could take Julia's shift. Martin didn't mind. "I'm sure he'll appreciate your visit," he told Julia. "He was feeling really nauseous. Must have eaten something wrong."

The morning seemed to crawl by, now that Julia was mostly waiting for lunchtime. When the store closed at noon, she once again thanked Marco wholeheartedly before running out the door. Once outside, she decided to walk to Michael's house on the Giselakai – it was even hotter now, and a ride on the bus would be uncomfortable. Besides, she needed the exercise. If she picked her route carefully, she could stay in the shade almost all the way. Large platans and chestnuts lined either side of the pedestrian lane flanking the river, so the only sunny part of her walk would be the bridge she needed to cross to get to the other side of the Salzach.

Thankfully, a soft wind was blowing. Julia hitched her bag on one shoulder, brushed the hair from her face and put it up in a ponytail. Everything around her looked peaceful. Little boats were floating down the river, but no larger ships could be seen. The water level was extremely low due to the July drought. The weather had been hot and sunny throughout Europe this summer, and it wasn't over yet. Julia smiled when she thought of London – they'd be able to ride double-decker buses to tour the city, do touristy stuff and take pictures of all the monuments before retiring in Hyde Park during the evenings.

It took her twenty minutes to get to Michael's place. When he opened the front door, Julia gaped at his pallid face. "Oh my God. You really look like shit," she exclaimed.

"Always nice to hear," Michael responded with a faint grin. "Please come in."

"You got food poisoning?"

"No idea." Michael took her to the living room and flopped down on the couch with a sigh. "I don't feel like eating anything, that's for sure. I just feel like catching some fresh air."

Julia took a seat next to him. "So you want to go out?"

He nodded. "Once I feel slightly better, I actually want to drive to the forest behind your house. Just strolling underneath the trees, in the cool shade."

"Sounds good to me." Julia poured them both a glass of water from the pitcher on the table. She hadn't been to the forest herself for quite a while. Ever since Anne's abduction, she had tried to avoid the woods. Whenever she felt like going for a run, she chose the paved road to Eichet. A little while back she'd decided to use the forest trail for a workout session, but memories of all that had happened there had come flooding back to her – Michael's accident, her oak tree getting sick and shedding leaves, the secret meetings between Anne and that creep Andreas. She'd never thought she'd come to think of the woods as a dark and sinister place. Maybe it was a good idea to go there together with Michael and try to recapture the sense of security she'd always had among the ancient trees.

After teatime, Michael was doing well enough to leave the house again. Together, they got into Michael's mom's car and drove to Birkensiedlung.

Michael parked the car on the same spot that the ambulance had used when the paramedics had come to take Anne to the hospital. Julia slipped her hand into

Michael's and breathed deeply in and out. The fresh air was doing her good. Overhead, the leaves in the canopy whispered in the soft breeze, and suddenly, she remembered what it had been like to be in the woods before the dark events of the past few weeks had changed her perception of them. This place had stayed the same – it was she who had changed from the inside out. And that was a pity. After all, Michael had told her to keep dreaming. He didn't need her to change or turn into a down-to-earth, responsible grown-up anytime soon.

"Come on, let's go," he softly said, walking along the forest trail and taking a right turn after a few minutes. He left the path and took her straight to the clearing where her oak was silently waiting for them – at the site of his accident.

They tacitly stood and stared at the oak. More leaves had turned yellow since the last time Julia visited her tree. When would the forest wardens come and chop it down? They usually cut down ailing trees in the fall, to keep the woods healthy. This year, their job would be scheduled around the time she'd start college.

Julia swallowed thickly. The thought of no longer having a sanctuary to find refuge whenever times were tough made her throat constrict painfully. But then Michael squeezed her hand, as if he could feel her sadness, and she looked aside with a smile. She *would* have a sanctuary. She could take refuge in his presence. He would be there for her, and all would be well.

He turned to her and smiled back at her. Somehow, he always managed to do that when she looked at him from the side. It was no longer a source of astonishment for her that he seemed to sense her gaze on him. Ever since he had told her of his experience of life upon waking up after his accident, she assumed he was just more sensitive than most people. That's how he must have managed to find Anne. The police had been back on his doorstep several times after locking away Andreas Mittelmayer, even though Andreas had confessed to the charges. The fact remained that Michael had inexplicably known where her sister had been hidden away, but Detective Spitzer put an end to the interrogations by writing something in the police report about profilers, mediums and people with a sixth sense helping the police force sometimes.

Michael's voice snapped her out of her trance. "You want to sit down for a while?" he asked, pointing at the tree. Julia nodded. He was probably tired after walking all the way out here, so she sat down next to him, her back pressed against the sturdy tree trunk just like old times. Michael slipped his hand into hers, and a deep feeling of peacefulness spread through her body.

"It's so beautiful here," he mumbled beside her. "So quiet. So different than the city. And yet, I love city life. It's big and fantastic, full of people and life and love. Everything moves."

His voice had taken on a tone that suggested he wasn't really talking to her. He was thinking out loud, and Julia glanced aside to see the expression on his face.

"You love being in the city, right?" she asked.

He nodded pensively. "I can always feel you amidst all the people in it," he replied. "It's as if you're radiant with love for me."

In the quiet afternoon, Julia slipped her arms around his waist and kissed him on the cheek. "That's so sweet," she whispered. "Thank you."

Sitting underneath the trees and enjoying the cool shade made Michael gradually feel better. When they finally left the woods again, it was almost six.

"We're going to fix dinner," Michael announced as he pulled up in front of the house.

"And after dinner, let's watch a movie?" Julia suggested.

"Let's do that. Why don't you pick something you like?" Michael motioned her toward the shelves lining an entire wall in the living room. Julia had never seen this many DVDs together in her entire life, not even at the video store.

"I'll have a look in a minute," she said. "Shouldn't I be helping you in the kitchen?"

"No, you shouldn't. Why don't you play something on the piano? That's gonna inspire my cooking for sure."

He made his way to the kitchen, leaving Julia next to the grand piano in the living room. She sat down and lightly ran her fingers over the keys. Even though she was in a good mood, she started to play a mournful tune, to her own surprise. It was something that just came out of nowhere and felt as if she was leaving something precious behind in the song she was playing, although she didn't know what it was.

As she finished, Michael walked up to her. He caressed her shoulder. "That was beautiful," he said in awe. "You composed that?"

Julia smiled. "Yes. Just now, in fact. It's like someone whispered it to me... as though I've stolen this song from the trees in the woods."

He thought it over. "You could have. Maybe you're more open to some influences than others. That would explain why you liked to write your poetry in the forest as well."

He slid down next to her on the piano bench, snaking an arm around her waist.

"Don't you need to supervise your pots and pans?" Julia giggled when he started kissing her all over her face and neck. "Isn't our dinner going to burn?"

He shook his head. "The lasagna is in the oven, so that will take care of itself." He kissed her once more, searching her lips with his mouth. Her heart sped up when his hand ran up and down her back, making her shirt ride up a bit. Out of breath, she let him pull her up and walk her over to his DVD collection. They finally settled on 'Legend', one of Tom Cruise's earliest works. Julia had seen the movie dozens of times, but Michael hadn't.

"This is the first movie I bought on DVD," she told him enthusiastically, balancing two plates of lasagna and climbing the stairs. Julia had suggested they watch a movie in his room, because she secretly didn't like the living room that much – it was too big for her taste. Michael's bedroom was much cozier.

Michael was carrying her overnight bag. He threw it down next to the bed when they entered. "Geez, woman," he teased her. "What's in this bag? Bricks?"

"No, books, actually." Julia sat cross-legged and zipped open her bag. "They're for you – to borrow."

One by one, she handed them over to him, and he accepted them almost reverently, running his hand down the spines of her favorite books. Zweig. Brecht. Kafka.

"If you like them, I bet you can buy your own copies at the bookstore at a discount," she added with a playful smile.

Michael flopped down on his bed and put the pile of books on his nightstand. "You think Martin will give us the discount twice if we order them together?" He kissed her cheek when she scrambled up to join him on the bed. "Thank you. I'm going to pick one to read tomorrow. Now let's eat."

After polishing off their plates of lasagna, they both lay down on the bed facing the screen in the corner. Michael switched on the player. In the meantime, the sky outside had turned almost dark, so they'd drawn the curtains. It felt cozy and safe in his room. Julia scooted closer to Michael and closed her eyes, relishing the intimacy she felt being near to him. It felt so different from the first time she'd been in this room, lying on his bed, making out. That moment seemed ages ago.

She only noticed she'd fallen asleep during the movie when Michael woke her up by softly stroking her forehead and kissing her lips. "Hey, Sleeping Beauty," he chuckled when she opened her eyes. "I thought you said this was your favorite movie!"

Julia lifted her head and saw the credits roll. "Oh, too bad. I just missed the ending," she yawned, then turned over to him and kissed him back. His hand massaged her shoulders and neck, then slipped down her back to her tailbone. She moved in closer, letting his warmth soothe her. His breathing turned heavy when he kissed her more deeply and held her in his arms without breaking away. Usually when they kissed, they were somewhere outside or at her place. Now, they were in his house, and they were all alone. There was no need to let go.

She groaned in protest when Michael pulled away eventually, pushing her back and looking at her earnestly. "Julia," he said in a ragged voice.

Breathlessly, she gazed up at him. "Yes?"

"Should I..." His eyes darted to the door and back to her. "Shall I make you a bed in the guest room?"

She slowly exhaled and cupped his cheek with her hand. "No," she replied firmly.

A light grew in his eyes, but he still looked at her attentively. "Are you sure?" he whispered close to her mouth.

"Yes. Very sure." She blushed, but her voice didn't waver. This was what she wanted. *He* was what she wanted – and this time for real.

He pulled her into him and rubbed his cheek against hers, then mumbled in her ear. "I love you."

It was the first time he'd said those words. Julia's entire body was aglow with love and passion and emotion. "I love you too," she whispered back. "You keep me safe."

After that, she said no more. Nothing more needed to be said that night.

13.

"**O**h my *word*, look at that view!" Florian exclaimed excitedly, pointing down from their capsule. Far below, the Thames wound its way through the city like a glistening ribbon of blue, Big Ben and the Houses of Parliament flanking the river like miniature buildings.

"Yup. Great," Tamara deadpanned. She'd only found out she was afraid of heights when they'd already boarded the Ferris wheel, so she was sitting on the bench in the middle of the capsule holding Gaby's hand in utter terror.

"It really is great," Axel chimed in. He was standing next to Florian, filming the view with his camera. "Okay, so they charge you an arm and a leg to get on the London Eye, but it's worth every dime."

Julia was on the opposite side of the bubble, listening to Michael pointing out all kinds of sights to her. He'd been to London several times already, so he knew where to find the most famous sites from up here.

"Smile, you lovebirds," Florian called out to them at that instant. They looked sideways and he snapped a picture of them with his phone.

"What kind of birds?" Julia called back with a devious grin.

"Pigeons, of course," Florian replied with a wink. "Lots of those around here, right?"

Michael shot him a sour look. "Ha, ha. Very funny." Yesterday, he'd been fined by a bobby for feeding the pigeons on Trafalgar Square. "How was I supposed to know we're not allowed to feed some birds?

They're not exactly carrying banners saying 'We Pigeons Are London's Worst Pest', are they?"

Julia flung her arms around him. "Well, I thought it was adorable you wanted to feed the pigeons," she smiled. "You looked so cute with your hands full of breadcrumbs and this flock of eager birds surrounding you."

He chuckled. "Yeah, if only the police thought the same."

"What? You being cute?" Axel piped up.

Michael and Julia both burst out laughing. This was their third day in London and they were having a good time so far. Last night they'd attended Moritz's concert. Today, they were planning on having a picnic in Hyde Park in the afternoon. The girls had hit Tesco's this morning to do grocery shopping and brought the stuff up to their room. "I can only hope the mice won't touch it," Gaby had remarked sarcastically, since the youth hostel wasn't the cleanest place they had ever come across.

"Are we there yet?" Tamara asked plaintively, getting up on shaky legs to risk a glance outside the window. "Oh, good. Almost. I can't wait to get out of this thing."

After a few more minutes, the whole group exited the bubble and popped into the gift shop opposite the Eye. Gaby, Julia, and Tamara walked in first, their arms linked, and the boys followed behind. At the beginning of the trip, they'd all solemnly sworn not to turn this into a couples' trip, and so far, they had all been good. Julia hadn't even spent that much time with Michael – he was mostly hanging with the guys and he slept in a different room. Gaby and Axel were on their best behavior too.

Axel was chatting animatedly to Michael as they entered the store. He seemed to finally have gotten over the fact that Michael initially hadn't treated his cousin so respectably. Julia looked at the two of them with a smile. Axel *should* be happy for her, because this entire summer had been one long, jubilant string of happy occasions, just as she'd once imagined it in her dreams. At the end of the summer, Michael would move to Graz, though. She dreaded that moment – she was going to miss him so much.

"Hey, man, are you okay?" she suddenly heard Axel calling out behind her. Julia turned around and saw Michael sitting down on a folding chair next to the entrance. Florian was standing next to him, fanning him with a newspaper and offering him a bottle of water.

She quickly made her way over to him. "Is the heat bothering you?" she asked, touching his forehead. It felt cold as ice, despite the hot temperatures today.

Michael shook his head. "I'm just dizzy," he mumbled. "Just let me sit down here for a bit."

"You think it might be his ride on the Ferris wheel?" Tamara wondered aloud.

"Possibly," Julia replied absently. She crouched down and stayed next to Michael until the others had paid for their souvenirs at the checkout. His spells of dizziness were starting to worry her. He looked just as pale as when he'd left work one week ago when he was feeling sick. What was the matter with him?

"I'm taking Michael back to the hotel," she said decidedly once they'd left the gift shop. "Let's meet up in Hyde Park late afternoon, on the green near the Peter Pan statue."

"Are you sure?" Gaby asked. "You don't want us to come with you?"

"What, and ruin your last afternoon in London? No way."

Tomorrow morning they'd fly back to Salzburg, and Julia knew Gaby was dying to go to a few Goth shops in Soho they'd passed yesterday.

"Okay, whatever you say." Axel slapped Michael on the back. "Take it easy, man. We'll see you guys later."

Julia's fingers tightened around Michael's hand as they started to make their way back to the tube station. She hoped there'd also be buses outside the station – taking Michael home in a hot and busy underground train didn't seem like the best plan right now. Apparently, he was thinking the same thing, because he pointed at a cab waiting at the taxi stand near the station. "Come on, let's take a taxi home," he said tiredly.

"Are you out of your mind?" Julia gaped at him. "That's going to cost a ton! Do you know how *far* it is to the youth hostel?"

He shot her a feeble grin. "Oh well. Aren't you happy you have a rich boyfriend now?"

Julia shrugged and didn't respond. Michael was right – he could easily afford it. It just made her insecure whenever he threw around money like that. He wasn't trying to show off consciously, but she was simply used to a very different lifestyle.

She exhaled deeply when they crawled into the back seat of the cab. "Hyde Park Hostel, please," she said in her best British accent. The driver nodded, turned on the meter and drove off. After a thirty-minute ride to the hotel, Michael paid the driver a shocking amount of money, but Julia was actually relieved they got there so fast. Michael still looked very pale. He probably wanted to lie down in his room.

"Shall we go upstairs?" she proposed as the taxi disappeared around the corner.

He shook his head. "I want to go to the park. Sit under the trees. It'll do me good."

That's what he had done last time too. It had worked really well last week, so why not? "Okay. I'll just quickly run upstairs to get some drinks and my book," she said. "I'll be right back."

As she made her way up the stairs huffing and puffing – the cheap hostel didn't have a functioning elevator, and of course their rooms had to be on the fourth floor – she thought about which book to bring. She and Michael had been reading poems from her Daniil Charms collection just before they boarded the plane a few days ago, so she'd bring that.

"All righty, let's go," she tried as cheerfully as she could when she stepped outside. Michael still looked as white as a sheet, but he probably wouldn't feel better if she kept fussing over him all the time. It was a better idea to 'send him some sun', as he sometimes called it. Whenever she shared her stories with him and couldn't stop talking and beaming at him, he called her his sun, just like he'd done in his poem to her. She *knew* it was cheesy, but she didn't care – she was still way too much in love to consider *anything* related to her and Michael too sappy.

As they picked their way down the path leading into the park, up to the green where they'd agreed to meet with the others, Julia whistled a happy tune. After a few minutes, Michael veered off the path, pulling her along to a large, gnarly chestnut tree in the middle of the green. "Shall we sit down here? In the shade?"

The two of them picked a shady spot. Michael observed Julia with a smile as she rummaged around in her bag to get cans of soda and bags of potato chips. "You're gonna read to me?" he asked eagerly when she pulled out the Charms poetry book next.

She nodded. "That's the plan! Why don't you lie down with your eyes closed and a drink within reach?"

Obediently, he grabbed a can and settled against the trunk of the chestnut, his eyes shut. Julia leafed through the pocket book. It had once belonged to her grandfather, who had always been fascinated by Russian literature, leaving her his collection of translated poetry when he died. She'd read this book countless times, but this was the first time she was sharing it with someone dear to her.

She softly read out some of her favorites. 'A Romance', 'Petrov and Kamarov', 'A Song'. Every once in a while, she peeked at Michael to check whether he was still awake. Every time she did, she saw a faint smile playing around his lips. He was still sitting with his eyes closed, but the color had returned to his face.

Presently she turned the last page and read out the very last poem in the book.

"A man left his house
with a club and a sack;
set off
down the road
and never looked back.

He walked ever onward,
he walked ever straight.
Never slept,
never drank,
never drank, slept, or ate.

At dusk, he entered a forest
as dark as the night.
And since

that time
he has vanished from sight.

But if you ever happen
to come across this man…
then please
let us know,
as fast as you can.'

With a sigh, Julia closed the book. But when she looked up, she started. The smile had disappeared from Michael's face. He looked at her so mournfully, so solemnly, that she couldn't help but come over and sit down in front of him. "What's wrong?" she mumbled, caressing his face.

He extended his arms toward her and she disappeared in the circle of his arms. "I don't want to leave," he replied almost inaudibly.

She didn't understand. "Don't want to leave where? London?"

He shook his head, remaining quiet. Julia bit her lip and gazed into his eyes. He must have been thinking about Graz too – how they'd be apart in a few more weeks. With a heavy sigh, she put her head on his shoulder. "Everything will be okay," she mumbled, pressing her hand to his chest. "I love you."

Slowly, she could feel his body relax against hers. "I love you too," he said. "I don't know why I'm upset. Never mind me."

In the hours that followed, Michael gradually recovered from the strange weakness troubling him that morning. By the time the rest of their party arrived at the park, Julia and Michael were playing a game of badminton using a set of rackets they'd borrowed from a family sitting a little ways away from them.

"Look at you! Shopped till you dropped?" Julia asked with a glance at the bulging plastic bags Gaby was carrying.

Her best friend nodded. "I practically ransacked the store. And spent all my money, by the way. I don't have any pounds left to buy snacks on the plane tomorrow."

"She bought a really cool shirt," Axel supplied, winking at Julia. "Why don't you show it to Julia?"

Gaby flushed, pulling a shirt from one of the bags with a nervous giggle. It was a tank top featuring skulls, safety pins and the line 'I Love My Boyfriend To Death'. "Wow, talk about romantic," Julia appraised her friend's purchase with a grin.

"Ooh, squirrels!" Tamara pointed at a pair of gray squirrels running along the branches of the chestnut. "I'm so gonna feed them."

"No, you are so *not*," Michael said.

"I'm not? Why not? Will I get a fine like you?"

"No, but you'll be harassed by a whole bunch of obnoxious squirrels. They're *everywhere*. If you feed one, they'll get all their buddies and run off with our food."

Moritz sniggered maliciously. "Robbed by rodents," he intoned. "You think the police will believe us if we report it to them?"

The group sat down laughing and chatting but Axel peered at the horizon and frowningly pointed out a few dark storm clouds gathering in the west. "Guys, that doesn't look good. I think we're gonna be caught in a thunderstorm."

Florian grabbed his arm and pulled him down. "Just sit down, thou Prophet of Doom. We'll be fine."

Twenty minutes later, as a lightning flash zigzagged through the gloomy skies and the first drops of rain started to fall, Axel shot his friend a stoic look. "Prophet of Doom, huh?" he said calmly.

"Get lost," Florian snapped back. They rushed to fold the picnic blankets and gather the food as the rain really started to pelt down. Julia broke into a run as they exited the part of the green shielded by trees and made it back to the hotel first. Good to know she wasn't completely out of shape.

"Hyde Park Picnic Plan: fail," Gaby muttered, stepping into the lobby with mascara all over her face and strands of black hair stuck to her cheeks. "Shall we just sit down in the lounge and eat our food there?"

The lounge was the common room with computers, the bar and a giant flatscreen for the guests to entertain themselves. Julia and her friends claimed the three sagging sofas in the corner. Once everyone had changed, they unpacked the food and set the table for dinner. Florian was checking the weather forecast on his phone. "Oh, great," he moped. "It's sunny and hot in Salzburg, you guys. And here we are, in some fine, English weather."

"Well, maybe we should have our final picnic outside at my place tomorrow," Julia replied. "So we can celebrate the final day of our trip with a bit of sunshine."

"That sounds great," Moritz said. "My flight gets me back in Salzburg tomorrow afternoon, so I can join you all in the evening."

Julia sat back, mentally drawing up a list of stuff she'd have to get from the supermarket after getting back home. "Remind me to go to the store tomorrow," she told Michael, who just handed her a pack of sushi.

He smiled. "Don't stress it. Don't think of Salzburg yet – we're here now."

"You're right." She smiled back, scooting closer to him. He'd said he didn't want to leave. She wanted to be in the here and the now as well, enjoying her last evening in London with Michael and all of her friends. Once she was back home, she'd have to take care of more stuff than just groceries… the orientation period of the University of Salzburg would soon start. It would be the beginning of a new stage of life for all of them. Michael would move to another city, coming back home at the end of each semester only. Their lives would change, but she didn't want to think about that. Today was what mattered right now.

14.

The next day, Julia had gone straight to work to set up the picnic at her place. They'd had a calm flight without delays, and before saying goodbye to everybody at the airport, Julia had collected everybody's contribution for tonight's food.

Deep in thought, she got off her bike and walked it to the gate when a cheerful voice suddenly woke her up.

"Well, well... what's that for?"

Julia looked up from the heavy bags she was just unloading from the handlebars, staring straight into Thorsten's blue eyes. Her neighbor shot an inquisitive look at the grocery bags full of baguettes and snacks.

"Oh, it's for our post-vacation picnic," she explained. "Why don't you join us? We have enough food to feed the entire neighborhood."

"I believe you," he chuckled, cracking a grin when Julia tried to pick up all three bags by herself. "Here, let me help you."

She and Thorsten carried everything to the table outside, where Michael was busying himself making a big bowl of fruit salad. "Hey, thanks for helping Julia, man," he said when he saw Thorsten carrying two bags. "My stubborn girlfriend insisted she could take care of the groceries all by herself."

She'd wanted to do it herself because Michael still wasn't feeling too well after his bout of dizziness in London yesterday. He'd offered to help, but she'd declined because she knew he still felt sick. Making a fruit salad was the least strenuous activity of the day, so she'd asked him to do that and nothing more.

"No problem," Thorsten replied. "I carry around crates of insanely heavy groceries in the supermarket every day. Julia's mom is a real dictator of a boss."

"I heard that," Ms. Gunther sweetly sang as she stepped into the yard. "I'm cutting your bonus, young man."

Just as Julia and her mother were done putting all the food on the table, Axel, Gaby and Tamara pulled up to the house in Tamara's car. "London Calling," Tamara called to them from the driver's seat before parking next to the gate. She got out holding a six-pack of duty-free Guinness beer bought at the airport that very morning. Axel and Gaby followed her, carrying bags filled with salt and vinegar chips.

"*More* food?" Thorsten cried out in mock alarm. "Wow, you guys must be happy I swooped in to help you eat all that."

"I'm always happy to have you around," Julia told him with a warm smile. Thorsten glanced sideways, looking like he was about to blush. "Hey, shall I get my guitar?" he suddenly said, sprinting off before she could even say yes.

Julia blinked and turned to Michael standing a few steps away from her, giving her a thoughtful look. Suddenly, she felt like an idiot for saying things like that to Thorsten. She really hadn't meant for it to sound flirtatious – she'd meant every word – but it had an effect on her neighbor that Michael couldn't have missed if he'd been miles away. She hoped he wouldn't be jealous, because there was nothing to be envious about.

She gingerly strolled over to him and leaned in to kiss him on the lips. "I love you," she whispered against his mouth.

"I love you too," he mumbled back, staring into her eyes with so much love and tenderness that she wondered if she'd imagined his look of envy before.

When Florian and Moritz completed the party showing up with a large bowl of homemade potato salad, Thorsten showed up again too. After dinner, he played them some well-known songs on his guitar that everybody could sing along to.

"Okay, now play us something soulful," Tamara requested after they'd all blared the ending of 'Hey Jude' at the top of their lungs.

Thorsten looked down at his instrument, tuning the highest strings a little, before launching into the song he'd written himself. He looked up at Julia searchingly. She felt her cheeks flush red, shaking her head almost imperceptibly, but Michael had already nudged her and made her get up from his lap.

"Sing," he simply said, looking at her expectantly.

Her heart hammered in her throat when Julia sat down next to Thorsten. Damn, she was even more nervous than the time she had to play her own song In front of all her classmates at the graduation ceremony. Why was this so difficult for her? This was her old, familiar group of friends.

Her eyes darted from Michael to Thorsten and back, and it suddenly dawned on her why this was majorly awkward. This was the first time she would sing this song with the two of them together. It was Thorsten's song, but they were Michael's lyrics. It was like two worlds colliding, nothing being able to stop their fatal collision course.

"*Mein Ruf ist dünn und leicht,*" she sang in a bright and gentle voice. "*My call, quiet and eerie.*" The wind rustled the trees around the house as her voice gained strength and seemed to mesmerize her audience. She sang and poured all of herself into the music. When the song was over, everybody sat and gazed at her in admiration.

Thorsten turned to her and put his hand on her arm. "Thank you," he quietly said. "That was beautiful."

She turned red. Last time, he'd thanked her differently. She stared at him with an unspoken question in her eyes. *Can we ever be just friends?*

His blue eyes seemed to send her a message back. *I will always look at you in my own, special way.*

Gaby broke the silence by erupting in applause, and the rest followed suit. "Wow, that was amazing!" she said. "Did you write that together?"

Thorsten shrugged shyly. "Kind of." As everybody started to fire off questions at him about his music, Julia quickly got up and went inside to get a glass of water from the kitchen. When she left the kitchen to go back outside, Gaby was waiting for her in the hallway.

"Jules," she said. "I don't think inviting Thorsten was the best idea you've had today."

Julia blinked at her. "Why?"

"Oh, because it's painfully obvious he's still in love with you. And because you are a bit too friendly with him. And Michael can clearly see that."

"Oh." Julia cringed. "No. You think? But I didn't mean it like that, Gab. You understand that, right?"

Gaby shrugged reluctantly. "Yeah, kind of. But the question is, do *they*?"

"I... I don't know," Julia said miserably. So she *hadn't* imagined Michael's envy after all. This whole situation sucked. She had to talk to him tonight. Gaby was right – she was being stupid. "I'll explain it to him. I promise."

"We're going to play a game of poker," Florian announced to Julia and Gaby when they came back to the table. "You girls are in, right?"

"Only if I can be on Axel's team," Gaby demanded.

"Naturally, Your Gloomness. Nobody would dare to keep you apart," Florian replied meekly. Axel slapped his friend on the head, then pulled Gaby onto his lap.

They played for hours. When it got so dark they could no longer properly see the playing cards by the light of the outdoor lanterns, they decided to call it a night and clean up. Julia recruited Gaby and Tamara to bring all the dirty plates to the kitchen, while she gathered all the empty deposit bottles into a plastic bag to dump in the shed. Her mom could take them to work and return them at the supermarket.

She halted when she heard two people talking behind the shed – Michael and Thorsten. Were they talking privately? Nervously, she edged forward and tried to catch what they were saying. She couldn't quite make out Michael's voice, but he sounded resolute, whereas Thorsten seemed upset.

"I'm not asking you without reason," she heard Michael tell her neighbor.

Thorsten exhaled in frustration. "I'm sorry, but seriously? How can you ask that of me? Surely you can see..." His voice wavered. "You *know* how I feel about her."

"And that's why I'm asking you."

"Excuse me? Look, I know you don't have to take my feelings into consideration, but..."

"I hope I've made myself clear," Michael interrupted him mid-sentence. When he whipped around and turned the corner, Julia tripped backward and tried to slink away unnoticed, but it was too late. He bumped straight into her.

"Oh, hi," she babbled nervously, casting around for an excuse to be here. "I, uhm... had to put these bottles in the shed, so..."

His gaze shifted from the bag stuffed with soda bottles to her face screaming guilt. "You saw me talking to Thorsten?" he asked calmly.

She turned red. "Okay, yes. But I didn't mean to eavesdrop."

"That's all right. I had to talk to him to ask him something having to do with you."

Yes, that had been abundantly clear. Michael had told Thorsten in no uncertain terms to stay away from her. That's why her neighbor had sounded so distraught. Michael was jealous, and frankly, he had every reason to be.

"I'm so sorry," she whispered. "I shouldn't have… you know…"

"I'm not blaming you for anything," he mumbled.

And then he kissed her. His lips softly explored hers, his hands running up and down her back. The world around them seemed to hold its breath. The wind had died down and the full moon had risen. Overhead, the stars twinkled in the nightly blue of the sky, dappled in red streaks of sunlight at the horizon, where the sun had set. Julia felt his breath on her cheek when he slowly pulled away from their kiss. "I love you with all my heart," he said.

"And I love you." Julia smiled. "Why so serious tonight?"

"Well, I just am. I want you to know I mean every word I'm saying."

They leisurely strolled back to the table holding hands. Their friends were having a last cup of coffee.

Thorsten was nowhere to be seen, and Julia knew exactly why. Maybe she should drop by his place tomorrow, just to clear the air.

"We're leaving in a few minutes," Tamara said. "Some of us have to work tomorrow."

Gaby scrunched up her face. "Why-oh-why did I have to sign a two-month contract at the stables? I've been to London now. I don't really need the money anymore."

"Why don't you save up for your next break?" Axel suggested. "Maybe we can go somewhere together."

Gaby's face lit up. "Definitely! Okay, fine. I'll muck those damn stables for a few more weeks." She shot Axel a passionate and longing gaze. Julia couldn't help looking aside and shooting Michael the same kind of look. In response, he bent over and kissed her softly.

When the coffee was gone, all the guests left. Michael was the last one to leave. Julia waved goodbye to him at the gate when he drove off in his mom's car honking the horn at her.

She could still feel his lips on her mouth as she climbed the stairs. Humming a tune, she switched on the light in her room and half-heartedly hit a few notes on the keyboard in the corner. The tune she was humming was the song she'd composed just before the London trip – the mournful song she had played on Michael's piano after their afternoon in the forest. The song she had aptly named *Farewell*, because it felt as though she was leaving something behind in the melody of that tune.

Julia sat down and started to play it again, the sounds drifting outside through the open window, up into the sky where the pale moon shone, down to the edge of the forest where she had said goodbye to things this summer and learned new lessons. She was on the threshold of a new chapter, and it was time to turn the page in her hand.

At that moment, her mother coughed quietly, standing in Julia's doorframe. "What a wonderful song, darling," she observed. "Is it something new?"

Julia looked at her mother thoughtfully, then shook her head. "No, I don't think so. It feels old. I call it *Farewell*."

Ms. Gunther nodded. "I think I understand what you mean."

Julia smiled. "Good night, Mom." She got up, switched off her keyboard and prepared for bed. As she drew the curtains and closed her bedroom door, she heard her mother softly singing her song in the hallway. With a satisfied sigh, she crawled under her comforter and read in her scrapbook until her eyelids started to feel heavy. That's when she turned off the light and invited the dreams in.

15.

A voice woke her from her dream.

Julia sat up in bed with a start. For a second, she thought Anne had called her name, but that couldn't be – she was staying with their dad in Innsbruck for the week. She looked around her room bathed in cold moonlight. Didn't she close the curtains before? Or had she forgotten?

And then, she heard it again. A clear voice sounding like bells, seemingly coming out of nowhere. "Come out to the woods."

A shiver ran down her spine, but it was because of the chilly wind blowing in through the window – the voice didn't frighten her. It sounded warm and friendly. Julia rubbed her face. Her forehead was slick with sweat. No wonder she had goosebumps all over her body in the wind touching her skin. She got up and walked over to the window to lean outside. There was no one down there who could have called her.

Without thinking too long about it, she got dressed and snuck quietly downstairs so she wouldn't wake her mom. Julia stepped outside into the yard. The moonlight turned everything to silver, lending the world a fairylike atmosphere. She glanced down the road running past her house, momentarily shrugged, then started to walk in the direction of the forest. Who knows, maybe she had become as sensitive to the woods as Michael had. Maybe the woodland sprites had called her out to dance.

Julia smiled. Good to know she hadn't turned into a boring, responsible adult just yet. Who in his right and rational mind would take a stroll to the woods in the middle of the night because a mysterious voice had summoned them? Actually, this was kind of exciting – something that could have happened in one of her fairytale books.

Once she got to the forest trail, her feet automatically took her in the direction of her old meditation spot. Her oak stood silently erect amidst the other trees, partly shrouded in shadows. However, the moonlight clearly illuminated a familiar figure standing next to the oak tree. He looked like he'd been waiting for her.

"Michael?" she asked in surprise. "What are *you* doing here?"

He took a step toward her and softly kissed her cheek. "I want to talk to you."

"Uhm… here?" She raised an eyebrow.

He nodded solemnly. "Yes, here. This is where it all started." He took her by the hand and slowly stepped back until they were standing directly under the oak, their faces lit by moonlight seeping through the foliage. Julia held her breath. Michael's eyes had never looked as vividly green and intensely sad as they did now. His whole face looked different, but she couldn't quite put her finger on the reason why.

"You heard my voice?" he asked.

"It was you?" She blinked at him. "How could I possibly have heard your voice in my head?"

"Because our connection runs very deep," he replied. "Because I've been hearing your voice in *my* head for years."

She shook her head in confusion. "You lost me, sorry."

His gaze fell down, to his hand touching the tree trunk. "You used to come here to draw, to write, to sing, read or dream. This was your realm. You felt safe here. And I kept you safe – I was the angel that went with you."

A strange sensation ran through Julia. This was it – Michael was going to tell her more about his sudden attraction to her after the accident. But why wasn't he making any sense? What had he said exactly... he'd offered her safety under this tree?

"So... uhm... you used to come here too?" she ventured.

He stared into her eyes, even more forlornly than before. "I used to *be* here."

Her eyes grew wide with astonishment. She gingerly looked up at the branches of the oak. *Her* oak.

"What do you mean?" she whispered.

"I guess you could call me a prince of the forest," he softly replied. "A *real* prince. An oak tree – an ancient being with a forest life of many centuries, living in connection with all the other creatures of the forest, rooted in soil."

Her mouth turned dry. "A tree," she said in a monotone.

"A tree," he nodded.

This was unreal. It was crazy. She had never heard a more bizarre story in her life, and yet, Julia knew he wasn't lying. She could sense it.

"What... how..." she stuttered, then stopped. She didn't know *what* to ask.

Michael gently caressed her face. "You have always sensed that trees have a certain life force," he continued his remarkable tale. "You felt they could feel. That *you* could feel them. And you can. Trees are souls – very quiet, peaceful souls that peek up from the soil like sprigs, grow into green twigs and then, even bigger. Their life seems eternal. And a tree soul is never alone –

it is always connected with the other souls around it. And when a tree has lived out many hundreds of years and its time is almost up, it falls into a slumber. It sleeps, losing its individual awareness, merging with the consciousness of the woods once more, to be reborn as a young shoot."

Michael leaned against the oak, running a hand through his hair. His voice dropped. "But sometimes, it's different. Sometimes, a tree connects with a human being at the end of its life. A human who often visits the tree, for example. And this connection jolts it awake, so to speak. This means the tree soul won't dissolve into the forest consciousness – it pulls loose and is reborn as a human, usually as a child or other family member of the person who released it from its tree existence. This is how our souls evolve, from species to species. Sometimes from tree to animal, sometimes to human."

"And you... you had a connection like that with me," Julia said in a wavering voice, staring at Michael wide-eyed. Except it *wasn't* Michael. And in a way, she had always known.

The boy in front of her nodded. "Yes, I did. But my bond with you was different from what the other trees had always taught me. I didn't *want* to be born as your child or grandchild. I wanted to be with you... as an equal." He smiled shyly. "It was only when I ended up in this body that I realized I was in love with you. As a tree, I didn't have enough understanding of what it was I was feeling, but as a boy, I did."

"This body." She touched his shoulder with some trepidation, then his head, his cheek. "What did you do to it? Did you steal this from Michael?"

He shook his head. "No, of course not. He came tearing through the woods on his motorcycle and his wheel caught on a protruding root by the side of the road. The road was slippery with rain, and his bike overturned, throwing him off. His head hit a stone, and he was gone." He put a hand on hers reassuringly. "He died on impact. He didn't suffer."

Julia couldn't help but well up at his words.

"I saw his soul floating away, reuniting with the source. He looked... peaceful. It was then that I made the swift decision to leap from my old body to this new one. On Midsummer Night, when the force of lightning connects the powers of heaven and earth, above and below – that's when this becomes possible."

Her knees buckled. Michael supported her as she sagged down against the oak. "This is impossible," she mumbled. "This *can't* be real."

"And yet, you know it is," he calmly said. "I think you've always felt it, but you couldn't explain it."

She shot him a suspicious look. "Hmm. Can you read my thoughts?"

He smiled, looking roguish all of a sudden. "Sometimes. As a tree I could always hear your thoughts, but now it happens in flashes."

"So did you pick... *him*... on purpose?"

"No, because I had nothing to do with his accident. I didn't even know who he was until I entered his body and my... or actually, *his*... memories returned. It's a striking coincidence I ended up in the body of the boy you were in love with yourself. Or maybe not – I don't really know if there is such a thing as coincidence. It's a typically human word. In the forest, all are connected and everything happens for a reason."

Julia's head spun. Now she finally understood why he seemed to just *know* so many things, and how he'd been able to find Anne. How he had known about her taste in books and her love for music, and how he had recognized her own song. He was her oak – a soul supporting and consoling her whenever times were tough. And in return, she had touched *him*, woken him up from slumber, offering him a chance at a new and different life.

"Why are you telling me all this now?" she asked in a choked voice. "Why didn't you tell me sooner?"

His ensuing silence frightened her. He exhaled, then said: "Because I thought I wouldn't need to."

Her heart turned cold. "But now you do?"

"Yes. Now I do." He looked at her, a lone tear rolling down his cheek. "Because you see, I can't stay."

She gaped at him uncomprehendingly. Actually, she didn't *want* to comprehend.

"This is not how it's supposed to go," he continued reluctantly. "I no longer feel at home in this body. I get sick more and more often. The forest is calling me, forcing me to die the natural way. To come back later. To really be reborn as a human. That's the way it has always been, and that is the way it must be now."

Slowly but surely, his words sank in.

"No." Julia grabbed his hand, looking at him helplessly, flinging her arms around his body, *not* his body. If only she could do more. If only she could embrace his soul, hold on to him until they would both rise above and come back to this world much later. "You can't do this. Don't go. Please, please don't leave me."

"I have to," he mumbled into her hair, a stifled sob in his voice. "I have to leave. And now you know why."

He stepped out of her embrace and looked at her in silence. Then, he cupped her face in his hands and kissed her. He kissed her softly, his lips landing everywhere on her nose, her cheeks, her mouth, her eyelids when she closed them and started to cry.

"I love you more than I have ever loved anyone in this world," he whispered.

They stood there for a long time, under the moonlight, their gaze locked on each other, their fingers intertwined. And Julia couldn't believe this would be the last time. It wasn't fair. It was too soon.

She wiped the tears from her eyes with a trembling hand. "How long?" she wanted to know.

"I don't know. I can feel my strength decline." His thumb caressed her other hand resting in his. Once again, she pressed herself against him with a soft cry.

"Do you have a name?" she asked. "I want to know your real name."

He shook his head. "It's not a name like humans have. I don't know if you'll be able to understand if I open your mind to hear it."

"Please try," she urged him. "Please. I want to know who I am in love with."

She remained in the circle of his arms, feeling him pressing his forehead against hers. For just a second, it was like something squeezed the insides of her skull, and then the doors of her mind flew wide open. She closed her eyes and gasped as she heard an indescribably beautiful sound. It was the whisper of the wind playing in the trees of the woods, a tinkling of little bells, the turning of the earth as it spun silently in space, the rustling of flowers budding in a rush as if caught on fast-motion camera. It was the life force coursing through everything, compressed into a single syllable.

He let go of her and lifted her face. "That's my name," he mumbled. "But to you, I will always be Michael."

"It sounded splendid," she whispered in awe. "You are splendid. I love you so much."

Once more, he kissed her – the ghost of the oak who had fallen in love with her, the boy from the woods who had reached out to her as Michael. She clung to him tightly. She didn't want to let go.

But then a tremor shook the forest floor. Julia looked around in panic. What was this… an earthquake? What was happening?

She cried out in fear when she was swept off her feet and tumbled backward, Michael's hands slipping from hers. Her back hit the floor, her hands grasping desperately at the carpet under her fingers.

Julia blinked her eyes and froze.

She wasn't in the forest at all. She was sitting on the floor of her bedroom wearing sweaty pajamas. Outside, the sun was shining, but her curtains were still closed. Her comforter had slipped off the bed with her.

In a daze, she rubbed her face. Unbelievable. "A dream," she muttered hoarsely, just to hear her own voice and make sure she was awake this time. "I dreamed it all."

Julia got up on wobbly legs. It hadn't really happened . She hadn't gone into the forest and she hadn't talked to Michael, but it had all felt so real that she was still in a complete stupor. She stumbled into the hallway to use the bathroom and freshen up. Absently, she got dressed in a summer dress and her ballerina flats.

Her cell showed the time: nine-thirty. Good. That meant Michael was probably awake as well by now. With a frown, she scrolled through her list of contacts and called his number. Apparently, his phone was switched off, because it went straight to voicemail. Oh well – she'd just show up unannounced. He wouldn't mind. He was only doing the afternoon shift today, and she really needed to see him right now. She had to get that awful dream out of her system ASAP, and holding him in her arms and telling him about her strange dream would definitely help a lot. And yet, her plan felt wrong. Everything about this morning felt wrong.

"I'm going to see Michael!" she hollered through the kitchen window when she saw her mom sitting in the back yard with a cup of coffee and toast.

"Have fun," her mom called back. "What time will you be back? Your father is coming here this afternoon to return Anne."

"I'll be home for lunch," Julia promised, her voice quavering with false cheer. Whistling shrilly, she left the house and quickly walked to the bus stop. Pretending to be more upbeat than she really was would help chase away the shadows of her nightmare before arriving at Michael's house. In order to distract herself from her dark thoughts, Julia pulled out her player and flipped through the playlist until she got to her favorite Chopin tracks.

After a twenty-minute ride, she got off at the corner of Michael's street. As Julia put away her MP3 player, she started to walk faster to get to his house as soon as she could. An inexplicable feeling of dread was mounting in the pit of her stomach, and she wanted to get rid of right *now*.

And then her heart stopped. The blue flashing lights of an ambulance reflected off the front of his big, luxurious mansion. A group of people were huddled together on the drive.

"Julia." She felt a hand on her shoulder. Axel stood next to her.

"What's going on?" she asked anxiously.

Axel's face was ashen. "I got here five minutes ago. We were supposed to swap some London photos. His mother..." His voice cracked. "She was standing on the drive in front of his house, crying, clutching her cell. 'Not again', she kept saying."

Julia swallowed. "Not again *what*?"

"Jules... he's gone," Axel whispered. "He's dead. He died in his sleep."

It was as if someone hit her on the temple with a heavy club, sucking away all the light and love from her body and soul. Julia couldn't breathe. The next thing she knew, she was on the cold tiles of the drive, staring up at the blue sky above. The back of her head hurt terribly. People were gathered around her, and someone was holding her hand. How had she ended up here?

"Where's Axel?" she croaked.

The person holding her hand squeezed her fingers. "I'm right here. You fainted, okay? Just stay put, someone's getting you some water."

She wanted to lie down forever. In fact, she never wanted to get up again. Just like *he* was never going to get up again. Michael was gone – he had been taken away from her. Only now did it fully sink in.

"How can he be *dead*?" she squeaked despondently, turning her head to look at her cousin.

Axel looked at her with doleful eyes. "I heard those paramedics tell his parents that he had brain damage. They asked his mom and dad whether he'd suffered from strange behavioral changes lately. Apparently he suffered a cerebral hemorrhage."

Julia was lost for words, her brain whirring, thoughts racing through her mind about last night's dream and what it could mean. She'd talked to him, and he had told her he had to leave, and why. Was it all true? Was that how he had chosen to tell her the truth?

She would never find out now – there was no way to ask him anymore. He would never again hold her in his arms like he had done after yesterday's picnic, under a starry sky. He would never kiss her in the moonlight of her dreams anymore.

Desperate, howling sobs started to climb up through her body, escaping from her throat. Julia managed to sit up and swatted away the glass of water someone was holding in front of her.

"Please take me home," she begged Axel. He nodded and quietly helped her getting to her feet. Julia looked around, her gaze landing on Michael's parents, their faces drained of color. They looked broken and lost, standing next to the ambulance containing the body of their only son. She looked up at Axel and he supported her as she stumbled toward them.

"He's dead," Michael's mother said blankly, her red-rimmed eyes full of sorrow. She extended her arms and pulled Julia in a tight embrace that took her breath away. Michael's father stroked her shoulder. Julia couldn't look at the gurney inside the ambulance – it was just a body, a lifeless shell. Nothing to say goodbye to. He was somewhere else, she was sure of that.

"He loved you," Michael's father told her quietly, handing her the photo frame from Michael's nightstand with a trembling hand. The picture of the two of them hugging had always been next to his bed. "Here, you should have this."

His parents kept talking to her, but the words slipped past her. Julia hoped Axel was paying attention, because she wouldn't be able to remember what Mr. and Mrs. Kolbe told her – about the funeral, whether she wanted to play something on the piano during the ceremony, because Michael had loved to hear her play.

"I will call you later," she managed to choke out. "I'm going home now. Sorry."

Axel took her to his car parked on the curb. Silently, he drove to Birkensiedlung, Julia sitting next to him like a statue.

"I called Gaby, by the way," he finally broke the silence. "She'll come to your place as soon as possible."

"Thanks." She stared out the window unseeingly, only coming back to the waking world when Axel turned into her street. She had to do so many things. Everyone had to know – she should call her other friends, as well as tell her mom, her grandmother, and Anne…

"Why don't you sit outside?" Axel suggested when he saw her clutching her phone in despair as she got out of the car. "I'll take care of things. Talk to your mom. Make some phone calls."

With a shaky breath, Julia sat down in the lawn chair her mom had used to relax in with a cup of coffee this very morning. She closed her eyes and heard Axel crunch past her on the gravel drive. Through the open window of the living room, she caught fragments of phone conversations that she couldn't quite follow.

"Hey… what the hell happened to you?" A familiar voice caused her to open her eyes. She blinked up at Thorsten's anxious face. As he squatted down next to her chair, he took her hands in his. "I saw Axel taking you home in his car. You sick or something?"

Julia shook her head. "He died," she said, her voice sounding way too loud in her own ears. The more she said the words, the truer they'd become. If she remained still, maybe he would come back. Maybe her silence would undo his death. But she knew she couldn't keep quiet. She *wanted* to talk about him – tell everybody why he had stolen her heart. Say his name.

"Michael," she added, when Thorsten gazed at her uncomprehendingly.

"*Michael?*" His voice shot up. "What the…. what are you talking about? You can't be serious. Did he have an accident, or…?"

"No." Her throat felt raw. "They said he had brain damage. He died last night. Instantly. He didn't suffer." Michael's words in her dream.

Thorsten was lost for words. "Jesus," he finally stammered, sinking down on the lawn with crossed legs. "How is this... did he know? Was he aware that he was terminal?"

"He never mentioned it to me." But she knew better – he *had* mentioned it. In Hyde Park, two days ago, he had told her he didn't want to leave. He didn't want to disappear into the dark woods, like the man in Daniil Charms's poem.

"I can't believe this," Thorsten said, obviously shaken. "You know, he actually talked to me last night, and..."

Julia sighed. "Yes, I know," she interjected. "And I'm sorry. He was just jealous, that's why he wanted you to stay away from me."

Thorsten frowned, shaking his head. "No, he didn't."

Julia blinked in confusion, mentally going over the conversation she'd listened in on, hiding behind the shed last night. "I don't get it. So what *did* he tell you?"

Thorsten cleared his throat. "He asked me," he replied wearily, "to take... care of you once he was gone."

"Take *care* of me?" Julia swallowed.

"Yes. And I told him he was a blind idiot for asking me, of all people, to watch over you like an older brother. I mean, it's pretty obvious that I like you as more than just a little-sister-slash-girl-next-door."

Only now did the meaning of the words she'd overheard start to make sense. Michael hadn't asked Thorsten to stay away from her - he'd asked Thorsten to *be there* for her once he was gone. Fresh tears welled up in her eyes.

"I had no idea," Thorsten mumbled vacantly. "I thought he was talking about him leaving for Graz. But he... he must have been talking about *this*. He knew – just like he always knew stuff."

Julia closed her eyes. In her mind, she could hear the wind sing, the flowers grow, the earth turn around its axis. He couldn't be gone. She couldn't deal with this.

"I have to be in the woods," she suddenly said, getting up in a rush.

"Jules, don't go. Just stay put." Thorsten tried to grab her hands, but she took a step backward.

"I'm going. Tell Axel where I went. I just need to be alone for a while."

"Fine, but I'm joining you," Thorsten replied determinedly.

The flicker of a smile passed over her face, despite the situation. "I won't be alone then, will I?"

He raked a hand through his hair. "Too bad. I'm not letting you go all by yourself. Not like this."

She hesitated, then nodded. She stalked off to the bike shed while Thorsten went inside to tell Axel where they were going. Not much later, she was on her way to the forest cycling like crazy, Thorsten sitting behind her on the baggage rack, his arms around her waist. Julia was completely out of breath when she reached the main trail, but she didn't slow down, almost tripping over her own legs in her rush to get to the spot where she and Michael had met up in her dream.

She stopped dead in her tracks when she saw the oak. The place had looked like before in her dreams, but the reality was different. Her oak tree had lost almost all of its leaves. Its life force was gone – the boy from the woods had taken the gloss and brilliance from this holy place, and he was nowhere to be found. What was it she had come to find here?

"Do you want to sit down, maybe?" Thorsten asked her, panting from exhaustion himself. She'd been running through the forest without as much as glancing back.

Julia turned around, shrugging desolately. "I don't know," she said in a voice drained of all emotion.

He strode up to her. "Come on," he said, putting an arm around her slumping shoulders comfortingly. "You didn't bike and run all the way to this place to just leave now. Anne told me you went to a special place in the forest sometimes – a meditation spot to gather inspiration. That's this spot, right?"

"Yes." She slowly nodded. "It was, once."

He gently guided her to the shady spot under the oak. Julia lowered herself onto the ground, leaning back against the trunk. Thorsten sat down beside her, still holding her hand. She nervously breathed in and out.

"Take your time," he encouraged her with a smile.

Julia slowly removed her hand from his grasp, pulling up her knees and hugging her legs. She looked skywards.

Far above her head, tiny white clouds floated by in the blue sky, oblivious of the drama playing out in her life on this sunny day. Soundlessly and uncaringly, they drifted past her, past the oak, past Salzburg into the big, wide world. The few leaves still clinging to the tree branches softly rustled in the breeze dancing through the woods.

A tear ran down her face when she thought of that one afternoon she and Michael had been here when he felt sick. He'd come here to gather strength. If her dream was really true, she could now understand why. But how *could* it be true? He had simply suffered brain injury due to the accident, and the effects had finally caught up with him. That was the only reasonable explanation for his strange behavioral changes and his sudden death.

"I'll stay close," Thorsten mumbled, getting up to give her some more space. Julia watched him go, a warm feeling stirring in her heart. He wasn't going to abandon her. Michael had asked him to take care of her, and he would.

Her thoughts drifted back to last night's dream. Michael had told her what was going on and why he had to leave. He had always insisted she should keep dreaming, because it was such an important part of who she was. But whether the dream was real or not, it wouldn't bring him back.

"Return to me," she whispered in a choked voice. "Please, come back. Give me a sign."

The forest kept quiet. A stray oak leaf fluttered down, landing on her knee. Julia looked up and stopped trying to blink away her tears. She couldn't do this. It was too much.

At that instant, her cell vibrated in her pocket. Oh crap, it was probably Gaby asking where she was. Her best friend had come all the way to her house to console her, and she wasn't even there. Julia stretched out her legs and pulled her phone from her pants pocket to read the text message.

'I new message. Michael.'

Speechlessly she gaped at the display. *What?*

Her trembling hand put the phone down in the grass. Julia exhaled deeply, rubbed her eyes, then cast a sidelong glance at her cell still blinking with the same notification. She hadn't imagined it. It really *was* from him.

There had to be an explanation for it. Maybe he'd sent out this message hours ago, only for it to be picked up by her phone now. Mobile networks weren't always one hundred percent reliable. And yet – she had asked for a sign, and here it was.

Her fingers quivered as she picked up her phone to read the message.

'sweet Julia, i will miss you. i will never forget you. whenever you hear the trees rustle with music singing in the woods, then stop and think of me. but don't wait for me. i am free now. and you have a head filled with dreams and a long life filled with love ahead of you. let the sun shine. X, forever your michael.'

She read the message over and over. He could have sent her this before his death, if he'd felt himself slipping away in the middle of the night, knowing he didn't have much time left. The message could have been stuck up there, between satellites, landing in her phone hours after the text was sent. But those last few words... he had said the same thing in her dream last night – that to *her*, he would always be Michael. Or was she just clutching at straws?

Julia put away her phone and looked around searchingly. She held her breath. For just a moment, it felt as though he would be right behind her, like he'd been watching her all this time. He would smilingly step out of the trees to pull her into a warm embrace. She pricked up her ears. Didn't she hear footsteps approaching? Who was going there, in the forest of her dreams?

A soft rustling filled her ears. The whisper of the wind, the voices of the trees, the spinning movement of the Earth turning and turning endlessly in the immeasurable vastness of space. The music in everything.

And then, Thorsten emerged from the treeline, heading back to her with a sweet smile on his lips. He carefully pulled her up, hugged her tiny frame, and stroked her hair. She felt his warm body against hers. "Come," he whispered. "I'll take you home. Everyone will be there to comfort you. There's no need to be alone."

Julia started back to the main trail, taking one step at a time, clinging to him for support. Her hand felt safe in his. Overhead, the birds sang, making the entire forest alive with music.

"I know," she replied softly, yet purposefully. "I'm not alone."

Acknowledgements

Writing my first book (Shadow of Time) involved a lot of research, because the story was set in Navajo Nation, a place I had never visited myself. The Boy From The Woods was far easier in that respect, because I lived in Austria myself. I was there in 1998-1999 as part of an exchange. My German was crap, I had never lived anywhere but home with my parents, and I had no idea how the country worked. In other words, I had the time of my life! It was fun getting to know all kinds of things that were different about Austria, such as the fact that Austrian stores always close for lunch (not so much when you thought you'd be doing some lunch-time shopping, though!) and that people always greet each other by saying 'God greets you' (*Grüss Gott*) or 'I am your servant' (*Servus*). I really enjoyed incorporating those elements into the storyline while writing this book.

And now, it's time to thank a lot of people. First of all, my sister Marije for reading the first draft of this story and crying at the end. She even called me a bitch, if I recall correctly (maybe you did, too, because of the way things ended). I realize I may have upset some people, but I really couldn't have ended this story any other way. This was the way it was supposed to end.

Second of all, my Dutch editor Marije Kok and my American editor Alexis Arendt for thoroughly going through the Dutch and English manuscripts. Thank you so much for your hard work and dedication!

I would also like to thank my father for freely translating my German poem to English, Daniil Charms for writing such incredible poetry (the poem used in the book was freely translated from the Russian original by me and partly adapted from the translation by Matvei Yankelevich), and the Ebner family in Birkensiedlung, Salzburg for renting out a room to me back in 1998-99 when I studied there. I used to live on the same street as Julia and Thorsten ☺

Last but not least, a big thank-you to all the bloggers who reviewed my book and helped me by promoting my work – I couldn't do this without you!

As for the music in this book: if you want to listen to the songs Julia and Thorsten wrote, you can go here:

http://youtu.be/-t3z17iqm1k
http://youtu.be/C7XipXNwdUs
http://youtu.be/EnqviSljxLY

Until next time!

Best wishes,
Jen Minkman.

http://www.jenminkman.nl

Twitter: @JenMinkman

Facebook:

http://www.facebook.com/JenMinkmanYAParanormal

e-mail: jenminkman@hotmail.com